A SCHEDULE OF DRUGS IN THE VALLEY OF DEATH

SARAH REITH

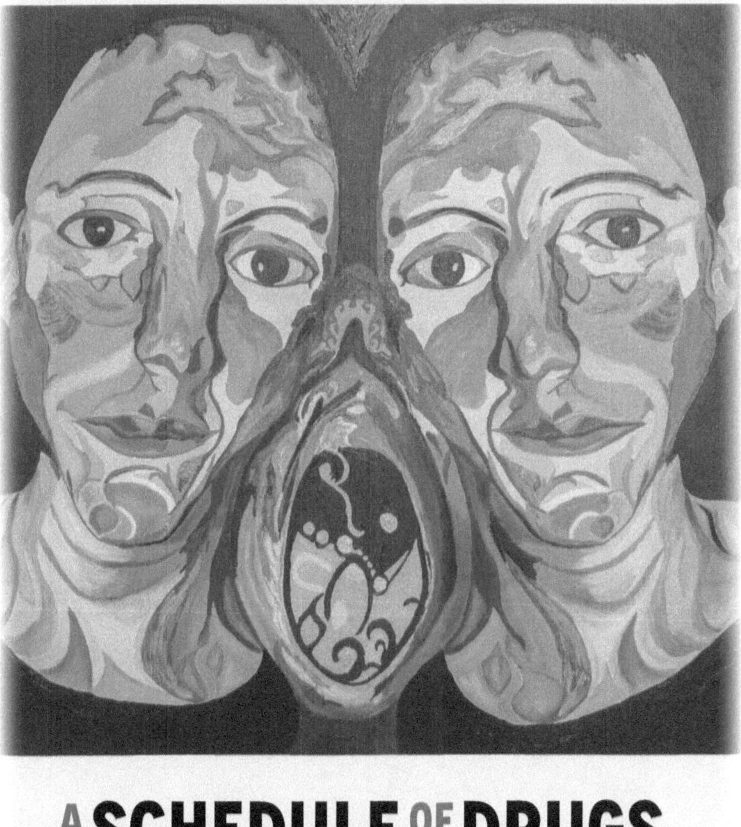

![cover illustration]

A SCHEDULE OF DRUGS IN THE VALLEY OF DEATH

BInk *Bink Books*
Bedazzled Ink Publishing Company • Fairfield, California

978-1-945805-62-2 paperback

Cover Art
by
Sarah Reith

Cover Design
by

Bink Books
a division of
Bedazzled Ink Publishing Company
Fairfield, California
http://www.bedazzledink.com

For my grandmother, Suzanne Reith,
who left me the riches of her wit, her letters, and her love of books.

ACKNOWLEDGMENTS

I took so many shiny things and tucked them into my nest. I don't know who I'd be without Foxglove, and Lisa, and everyone who came through in those days when we all needed a place to heal our wings.

Elizabeth Raybee shared her workshop full of broken things, and showed me how to make a beautiful whole with jagged edges, missing pieces, and a deft hand with a hammer.

Cynda Valle taught me faces, and colors.

Michael Charnes showed me that life can be a poem, with lots of false starts and rough drafts. Thanks to Amethyst and Rosie, for some of the best lines.

Noel and Carol Hale gave me a safe place to land, whenever I fell. Danny Sheehan put things back together, every time.

The Black Oak writers, Kristana Arp, Kate Gaston, and Roberta Werdinger, are daring and strategic. I'm lucky to have them.

Sadie and Harriet always make sure I get my walks, and Stuart Campbell is the nest I keep my heart in.

PART ONE

PORTRAITS OF ANCESTORS

MY NAME IS Isobel Reinhardt, and I am living more dangerously than I ever have before. I am a portrait painter, which may not seem especially daring, since it means I spend my days listening to podcasts, dipping my brushes in water-based oils, and cleaning them in non-toxic odorless mineral spirits. I no longer listen for the footsteps of angry men with guns. I can trust my colleagues not to place me in harm's way—unless you count the occasional comment from those who have accorded themselves the privilege of judging other people's work. But painting human faces is riskier than anything, because it takes a jeweler's precision and a constant awareness of the savagery of human beings.

Since we as a species have always had the regrettable tendency to bash each other's brains in, we have also developed a hair-trigger response to the slightest sign of a possible threat in other people's faces—especially those that are just the tiniest bit different from our own. For this reason, people have powerful reactions to portraits, even if they are fully aware that an oil painting is not about to raise a rock and cave in their skulls. But I know for a fact that if I paint a nostril half a millimeter too small or too wide, I am guaranteed to set off a family feud that lasts for generations. I could give a lip a certain curl and provide a man's descendants with an ancestor who sneers.

It's generally best to avoid smiles.

Smiles, like butterflies and sharks, do not do well in captivity, which is the whole point of painting. Painters exist to capture a moment, an expression, a condition of the light. We are here, with our solvents and our pigments, to capture the look on your face and pin it to the wall. To make it stop moving, so we can look at it forever. And if there is one thing no one wants to look at forever, it is a fleeting moment of joy. Eternal joy is a dreadful thing to catch sight of in the corner of your eye as you are walking down a hallway lined with portraits of your ancestors.

People want a painting that hints at crimes and madness, but preserves the nobility of line they know their forebears possessed. Therefore, if a customer's grandmother ran for her life in the middle of the night, you can paint her toiling along a lonely road, but not scrambling over a wall with her panties showing and dirt in her teeth. If a client's mother was notorious, paint her as an Italian courtesan, of the honest, poetic variety. And if her father was a wire-walker and a convict and a connoisseur of obscure enjoyments, well. It's as good a place to start as any.

PATERNAL ANCESTORS

MY FATHER GUSTAVE named me Isobel for a fine, if slightly abstract, ancestral reason: he thought Isobel Reinhardt was linguistically perfect, considering that we are native speakers of a Germanic language with a largely Latin vocabulary. If Gustave Reinhardt had been a medieval Italian poet, he would have written love poems full of puzzles and acrostics and heretical commentary on obscure theological texts. I am sure the twentieth century was a terrible disappointment for him.

However, I am not at all sure why the name Isobel represented all things Latin to my Spanish-speaking gringo father. I'm a little more solid on the significance of Reinhardt, because onomastics, or the study of proper names, is an actual discipline with books and papers and Wikipedia entries, rather than a whimsical decision on the part of someone I haven't seen for more than half my life.

I happen to know that Reinhardt, in German, is full of pre-Christian warrior qualities. It is a name defined in terms like *brave counsel, sound decision, manly virtue,* and, suddenly, *fox.*

Wait a minute: how did a fox wind up in this thicket of square jaws and grim determination? His presence is a violation of parallelism. His call is a wild scream that sounds like puppies being disemboweled by a night heron. He is cunning and lovely and entirely unsympathetic, as we can see by how eagerly his hunters pursue him.

On May 15, 1992, *The Washington Post* reported that Gustave Reinhardt of San Francisco, California, had been indicted by a grand jury. He was wanted for questioning. And he was "at large." That is a matter of public record. There is also a public record stating that my father was a "drug kingpin," with "lieutenants in the field." (*The Baltimore Sun*, an inferior paper, demoted him to "Middle Man," and reported that he was "lurking.") It was boilerplate, but it made me feel like I came from somewhere, like there was a place for me in the succession of some enchanted kingdom ruled by outlaw royalty. I was fourteen years old. I was heavy and slow, like the lumbering young of quick-moving prey, in a year when the hunters are fierce.

The truth is, I liked those Penny Dreadful articles. As long as they lasted—which wasn't long at all—they brought some flair to the hardship of losing my dad. There was a lighthearted quality to their casual viciousness, like hidden limericks in a document full of tax codes and severities. I read them again and again, soothing my sorrow with their badly-drawn caricature.

And that's the thing about missing parents. They give their children a reason to grieve, as if reason were a bulwark against all the pointless sorrow in the world. In this way, the absentee father provides his heirs with something to hold onto. At last, you who are gone. Let us be thankful, let us say grace, for all the missing fathers.

My dreams about my father are as dark and deep as organ meat. The colors are muted, like illustrations from a favorite children's book, crumpled and smeared and left outside in the sun. There is to them an emotional texture of forgotten birds' nests and the basements of abandoned ruins. The limited palette makes them feel like woodcuts, illustrating a fable about being lost in an ancient city, in a magic field, in a clearing peopled by fairies at certain phases of the moon.

Gustave Reinhardt was so many things, in the short time that I knew him. He was a wire-walker in a gold lamé jumpsuit. He was a Hari Krishna in a saffron robe, a cardsharp in a cheap black suit. Finally, he was a fugitive with a profusion of facial hair; and then he was gone. Just gone. He is, now, a swashbuckling ancestor, like the preacher who built a canoe and traveled alone through some rivery region, trying to convert the heathen. He, too, left a family behind.

Before he was a fugitive, my father served several short sentences for various infractions. You could say he lost his enthusiasm for the incarcerated lifestyle. He spent years of his youth requesting permission to read certain books; receiving pawed-over packages; trading stamps and cigarettes for girlie magazines. More than anything else, he cleaned his cell. He even invented a special way of scrubbing the floor that maintained the suppleness of his *dan tien*, so essential to a wire walker's balance. In his experience, tidiness was the direct result of brutal control.

Just not his. I think he was humiliated by how zealously he cleaned his cage, because in freedom, he cultivated a slovenliness that had a vengeful quality to it. He was like a man deprived of meat for years, gorging on bacon and beef until his sweat smells like dead bodies, all the time. "I want my home to look like I walked in with everything I own in my arms," he would say, "and then I just spun around with my eyes closed and let it fly all over the place." The way he said it, he made it sound like a wise old proverb.

But this is only possible if you have a place of your own, and belongings to clutter it with. It's the easiest thing in the world to be neat if all you have are a few second-rate goods from the prison commissary. Being a slob was an expression of freedom, but it could only be practiced with proper equipment, which my father sought out like a man who believes the Platonic ideal can be paid for in cash.

He bought strange machines made with little-known alloys. He bought a whistle synthesizer. He bought recordings of classical music at prices only the listeners of classical music expect to pay. He wore long-sleeved cotton T-shirts because he could not endure the sun on his skin, or the way synthetic fabrics rearranged the hairs on his arms. He wore them until they were frayed at the cuffs and stained at the pits, and he wore them to specialty stores where people could only bear to be dressed by their tailors in Tuscany. He would demonstrate his knowledge of the specialty product with such tremendous expertise that people assumed he was a genius—and then he paid with a wad of hundred dollar bills that made them think he might also be an eccentric millionaire. He may have been. He didn't keep very good records. His quarters were cluttered with objects he paid for with money he earned, doing exactly what he felt like doing.

There was something majestic to the disorder that reigned wherever he lived, like the most advanced principles of science that can only be explained through chaos theory. There was no one else like him.

My father, I used to say. My dad. I think now, with some disgust, how obvious it must have been that I was in love with him. I have so little gentleness for all my younger selves, my poor, eager younger selves who were so doggishly in love.

That said, any story about him should be about love. But I find myself looking for some deeper meaning in the words and actions of an elusive genius, trapped by stupid passion like anybody else. It is impossible to believe the humiliating fact that brilliance, like beauty, signifies nothing.

When I realized my knowledge about him was as puny as the hole he left in my life was vast, I called my grandmother, who had been born Lisette Saulé. She, too, had a string of unrelated anecdotes about a man who was clearly a stranger to both of us.

She began at the beginning. When my father was in daycare, she told me, a young woman who was studying child development wrote her thesis on little Gus. He was such a remarkable child. An outlier, as they would call him today. She remembered that he was very obedient, which rings true because she is not a woman who considers it high praise to describe someone as eager to obey.

The little Gus I knew left a suitcase full of psilocybin mushrooms next to a security guard in an airport—on purpose—while he went to the bathroom. He ambled out, nodded amiably to the officer, and strolled off with several life sentences' worth of smuggled contraband.

"Do you know why I nodded?" he asked me, as if this single act were the only questionable element in the entire story. Of course I knew why. I was also old enough to understand that there is no one in the world more pedantic than a man who considers himself a criminal mastermind. If I wanted to avoid a lecture, I would have to come up with something that sounded insightful. I would have this feeling often in college, as I struggled to convey the impression that I had understood some complicated worldview, some work of genius beyond my comprehension.

"Because if you made a big deal out of thanking him," I sighed, "he would notice you and remember you."

"*But* if I just walked off without acknowledging him," he added, "he would think I was afraid of him and want to know why." Chances are, he did this instinctively, and analyzed it afterward, so he could admire his strategic brilliance as well as his daring.

"I *know*," I whined, fidgeting. He would have reprimanded me if I had said *Duh*, because *duh* is not a proper part of speech, and only dullards allow improper utterances to escape their lips. In some ways, little Gus was still the obedient son of a woman as scrupulous in her grammatical correctness as she was in her convictions.

Miss Lisette Saulé left the Catholic Church, after what sounded like a bracing, cerebral, excessively unconsummated affair with a priest. She was beautiful, like a dark-haired Faye Dunaway, with broad graceful bones in the plains of her face. In 1940s America, this daughter of French Catholic immigrants was unaffectedly bewildered by the ability of intelligent adults to go on believing in God. "I don't know why he was always looking for spiritual explanations," she said of my father. Maybe "always" is overstating the case a little, but no mother is likely to forget about it soon, when her son spends a season canvassing the airport with the Hari Krishnas.

It's true that Gustave Reinhardt was not a proper atheist; which is to say, he didn't make his way to unbelief through finely argued logic, as his literary mother did. Many years before she was married, Lisette Saulé had tea, two times a week, with a handsome priest who was always pressing her to have just one more nibble of his housekeeper's excellent scones. He marveled at the elegance of her arguments against the existence of God and promised that when he finally won her over, he'd arrange for her to speak at Catholic retreats to those whose faith was wavering.

Instead of rejecting the barbarity of dogma in a civilized setting, my father took peyote. He saw the Virgin Mary weeping, in a desert that cried out for prophets and visions of saints.

He asked her what she wanted, and she raised her tearstained face to him.

"Follow my son," she replied. My father reported this encounter with the kind of scorn he levelled at children who use made-up words like *duh*.

"Get outta my trip!" he told her angrily.

It is always permissible to use contracted adverbial prepositions when communicating with drug-induced hallucinations. One does it for effect, particularly if one is a showman with an unerring sense for the importance of breaking the rules appropriately.

The rules were subtle and intricate, involving parts from several decks, like Gustave's favorite card game, Pan. We read Coleridge, but we were not under any circumstances to discuss this. It wasn't shameful, exactly: more like a minority religious practice in a regime known for sudden repressive crackdowns.

"Have you read *Rime of the Ancient Mariner*?" I asked a friend excitedly; and my father, ordinarily so sympathetic to pedantic urges, took me aside to lecture me about the importance of not being a snob. It was like he knew there was something about our lives that should be kept secret; but he couldn't quite work out what it was.

He took me to R-rated movies, during the last few years before every school kid in the country was yawning with boredom as the victims of bizarre murders littered every movie screen. I think this was his idea of a continuing education program on the inexplicable values of the puzzling culture we found ourselves stranded in. A typical post-viewing session went something like this:

"Daddy," I began, as we sat cross-legged on the floor, unwrapping burritos at ten o'clock at night. We were bachelors at Daddy's house, and I loved it. "I don't understand the joke that one guy told. Where he goes, geez, you got a big pussy, geez, you got a big pussy; and then something about an echo?"

My father chewed calmly, then swallowed.

"A lot of people think a woman's vagina loses its elasticity if she's promiscuous," he explained, with a very slight smile of even slighter pity for such ignorance. "So the joke is that this guy's girlfriend has a lot of sex partners, and he's such a loser, he can't find a woman who will have a monogamous relationship with him. It's very self-deprecating." He killed that joke decisively, but I will remember it forever.

He was always careful not to condescend to me or make unnecessary mysteries of things. But I always suspected that he was disappointed at my failure to demonstrate any sign of being a prodigy. I still can't tell you, off the top of my head, how to convert a fraction to a decimal, in spite of how often it's been explained to me. I had a tutor one time—yes, and I had ballet lessons, too, if you really must know—who made paper cylinders and cubes with graceful, intelligent hands in an effort to explain geometry. I preserved my immunity to this instruction fiercely. I think I believed it would rearrange the way I was trying to organize my brain at the time, but now it seems I was just a spoiled child with no inkling of what I was about to lose.

My grandmother told me that my father's IQ was in the high 150s, which is genius level, but only professor genius, not Nobel prize-winning genius. Of course, it doesn't take brains to be a criminal. It takes brains to be a fugitive for twenty-five years.

And fugitives run in my family. There is a maddening historical determinism to this, as if free will and logic were among the cumbersome heirlooms left behind in yet another wild midnight flight. I don't know when it worked its way into the gene pool, but even when we're not actively committing crimes—and every family has its slackers—we Reinhardts are a flight risk.

We lose ourselves the way jewelry gets lost at the border; how crops are lost in a drought; and even how a train of thought goes missing in an argument that's lost. We get lost trying to find answers, the way I did when I traveled to the land of the original Reinhardts and found nothing at all but a grave.

IF YOU SAY you are lost in German, without specifying whether you got that way while walking, driving, or riding an elephant, the default assumption is that you are lost on your spiritual path. Try this: walk up to a complete stranger in Frankfurt and announce that you are lost. He will look right through you, like someone who knows better than to get caught up in bad performance art or low-brow social experiments. Besides, they have laws against that kind of thing in Germany. You can't be ontological in public—not in a country with a medieval crimes museum, several perfectly preserved Stasi prisons, and a booming tourist trade in death camps.

Incidentally, the German word for "lost" is "verloren," which sounds a lot like "forlorn."

I found the grave of a man named Walter Reinhardt, the year I was lost in Germany. He was a soldier's homecoming gift, born in 1918, and he died three years before I was born. His gravestone was a little crooked, which made it seem like Walter Reinhardt was leaning back to distance himself from all those other dead people, noisy and boisterous in their large family plots. His grave was laced with extravagant ivy, which provoked a couple of distinctly American associations for me: the Ivy League and kudzu. Was this dead lonely Reinhardt a rarefied scholar, or helplessly lost in non-native plant life?

The year I was in Germany, a non-native plant in spite of my name, was the year of broken shoes. Every pair I had when I arrived broke its back on the cold round cobblestones of the ancient city. Every pair I bought when I was there lolled apart by the end of a week, like my shoes were making fun of how I talked—not at all like a proper German Reinhardt. And for a long time afterward, my shoes simply vanished from around my feet, like they were made of tissue paper and my feet were made of snow.

I was not particularly good at being in Germany. I was also not good at being a wife or a college student or, come to think of it, anything—not since I was a scrappy sunburned kid who was really good at climbing trees.

And then, when I was ready to get lost, I came home.

MATERNAL ANCESTORS

WHEN I WAS ten years old, I was very good at keeping secrets. My mother (who had no way of knowing anything about our family history) claimed we were descended from Kaiser Wilhelm's bodyguards, who took elaborate oaths of secrecy. We knew how to protect our own. We could withstand interrogations, pleading, threats, and trickery.

It was important to know about this atavistic ferocity, at the progressive alternative public school she sent me to. We celebrated Kwanzaa at the elementary school named for a pioneer in children's education. We called our teachers by their first names. We shared a campus with a Japanese bilingual school where the boys kept their backpacks on as they played in the yard, and we only ever heard them speaking Japanese.

But I remember a joke that didn't match the innovative use of art in math class, or the rousing workers' ballads or the woven scarves the teachers wore. It was all in the setup, as any good comedian or trained interrogator will tell you. It went like this: a swarm of avid little boys would descend on a victim, their eyes alight with maniac glee.

"Does your mother *work?*" the leader would sneer. His name was Chad Brenner, and he was the fastest runner in school.

"Well, *duh,*" I'd begin, impersonating my idea of a kid whose mother had a legitimate job. Children are the worst criminal accessories ever. All that stuff about quarterly expenses and the clauses of the Mann Act was fine for Mother's legal and financial teams. But that "duh" was barely out of my mouth before Chad Brenner's chorus was howling, "Which corner?" and whooping like they'd pulled off a coup. No ten-year-old has ever been as conscious of letting down the Kaiser's bodyguards as I was, every time they played that joke on me.

Little boys have always lacked historical perspective. In California in 1987, everybody's mother was on her way to work. Mothers were bursting out of commuter trains. They were doing lunch, rather than dishes. They were power-dressed in pencil skirts and puffy sleeves that made the most aerobicized young matron look like a cross-dressing linebacker.

My mother, who knew a thing or two about the importance of costume and power play, informed me that my classmates were training to be shame-filled johns. "They're only ten," she explained. "The girls they'll pay for sympathy haven't even been born yet."

My mother understood the ratio of sympathy to semen with a machinist's precision. If Caitlin Swift ever worked in an office, it would be a corner office, with windows and a view. You understand now that my mother was, in fact a whore; that I failed to protect her secret, though I wasn't even the tiniest bit tortured.

Caitlin did not regard this as a shameful secret: just a dangerous one. After all, she was a damned good whore. She also claimed to be a feminist. In San Francisco, all throughout the 80s and into the 90s, she belonged to one of the nation's first sex workers' collectives. She could quote case law, chapter and verse, pertaining to whoredom and whores. "Did you know that sex workers are forbidden to gather," she cited. The only part of that sentence indicating that it might have been a question was the placement of the verb.

To round out her education, my mother went to lots of workshops on intimacy and communication, which are (not always, but often) expensive euphemisms for sex work. From a series of ferocious, kittenish women, she learned that a statement can be softened by phrasing it as a question. Enthralled by this new idea, she clamped on her figurative hard hat, drew on her metaphorical gloves, and fell to work, making herself less intimidating by bringing a breathy curiosity into her speech.

It didn't work. My mother was so quick in her certainty that she could barely sketch the outline of a query before she moved to fill in the facts. "It's considered a form of treason," she announced, less than a full moment after asking rhetorically what I knew about why sex workers are forbidden to gather.

It was not my job to answer questions, anyway. It was my job to listen attentively when my mother needed what she called "a sounding board." I learned a lot about how to make an accusation with a question, and how to wonder about things silently; but very little about asking for answers.

Meanwhile, my mother was busy attending workshops on the intricacies of running a sex workers' collective in the Internet age, and generating intimacy with kinky strangers. It was hugely entertaining and time consuming. It threatened the stability of the free world, which, she pointed out, was not free at all, but based on the unpaid labor of women. She fell just short of accusing the world's wives and daughters of being industry scabs, choosing to focus instead on how tirelessly she and her cohort worked to disrupt the unnatural order of things. As a traitor, she wasn't just some high-end whore. She was Mata Hari of the culture wars, with her eye on the masculine hegemony.

I was not at all qualified to absorb the things she was prepared to teach me. I was repressed and unattractive and knew already that I would never inspire the kind of fascination that is worthy of betrayal. But there is a strong tradition of ignoring precedent in my family. My mother's mother was a beekeeper, and her father owned oil wells in Saudi Arabia. Caitlin joined him one summer in high school, and never forgot it. She wore a veil, this woman of the night, this Constitution-toting member of the ACLU.

For as long as I can remember, my mother has carried a large leather wallet with images of Indian elephants and gesturing monkeys on it. She says she needs something big enough to carry her passport and her copy of the US Constitution. "That way," she explains, "if I get stopped by some cop who wants to search my car . . ." Here, she waves the document, as if she has only just this moment been moved to do so. She is a consummate performer, and her gestures are exactly the same, every single time.

If an officer of the law ever announces his intention to search her car, she has her strategy all planned out: she will pop open her glove box and produce her license, proof of insurance, and a copy of her ACLU-provided US Constitution. "Oh, *look!*" she'll exclaim. "Isn't it *nice*, how they just send these things out to all their faithful members. I have more of these than I know what to do with. Now, where would I find the Fourth Amendment?" I should note that my mother is white, female, looks about seventy-five years younger than the sixty-four she is, and speaks perfect Standard English. She might be taken aside for a discreet talking-to if she speeds down Market Street throwing explosives while announcing through a bullhorn that she is a member of a feminist sex workers' collective.

I think every day that passes without a chance to outwit her adversaries is a disappointment for my mother, who travels with toolboxes full of sex toys and unusual prosthetics. Her luggage contains costumes that are almost architectural, designed for the dual purposes of intimate athletic performance and easy cleaning. She can stow all of it into her silver CR-V at a moment's notice. She resembles a soccer mom, until she starts talking.

For Caitlin Swift, conversation is an exercise in throwing hand grenades. "You would be amazed at how many men love to be fucked in the ass!" she exclaims, as if she is charmed to note some subtle and endearing tendency. "*Straight* men!" It is a motto she says so often it's taken on the quality of homily. I half-expect to see it stitched onto a sampler and hung up by the door someday. Once, when we passed a vintage clothing store called Up Your Alley, she murmured gravely, "They really don't know what they're talking about, do they, sweetheart?"

It's important to remember that she didn't become a prostitute until she was well into her thirties. It's not her first language, but she speaks it fluently, with an outsider's thrill of discovery. To me, it was all too obvious that she was fascinated with the lingo, rattling off the names of things she would and would not do. I thought she sounded overly thematic, like an aging secretary who has overcome her inhibitions about looking ridiculous and wears a silly hat to work on Saint Patrick's Day. She was entirely too enthusiastic, too eager to show what she knew. It's the perfect combination of traits for a customer service professional, and Caitlin thrived in the industry.

She was always very good at becoming an integral part of any situation, while simultaneously distinguishing herself within it. She was the only mother at the New Feminist Childcare Co-Op with a glossy red pedicure peeking out of her Birkenstocks. She wore mascara with her granny glasses. She was smart and fun and serious, and men had a way of sitting at her feet in adoration as she lectured them on Joseph Campbell and the Great Goddess Har, Patron Saint of

Sacred Harlots. "I love your mother's mind," they told me, with every appearance of sincerity. She was a smart girl with Abbie Hoffman hair, and every man who fell in love with her believed he was the only one who noticed how goddamned sexy she was.

For my mother, prostitution was an ongoing graduate seminar in pre-Judaic religious studies, with the goddess Ishtar and her Wondrous Vulva stationed at the temple door. She was impossibly sincere. And she walked it like she talked it, with six-inch platform shoes and ritual paint on her face. "You have to have a certain—how do you say," she said playfully, *"je ne sais quoi."* Her fake French accent was a sexy purr. "To call yourself Lilith. In *this* field." Her working name was Lilith. She was victor of the field.

While her story has elements of tragedy, she did not become a practitioner of the world's oldest profession for any of the usual tragic reasons. She was never abused or addicted to drugs. She didn't even have an eating disorder. Caitlin Swift went to a private school where she learned dressage. She played drums in an all-girl punk band. She sat in the front row of her college physics class when she was sixteen years old, wearing tie-dye and a miniskirt, and answered every question right without ever raising her hand. Then, abruptly, she fell in love with a man who rode a unicycle on a slack wire while juggling fiery clubs. Gustave Reinhardt was a smart girl's bad boy, spouting esoteric theory and treating oppressive conventions as if they didn't even exist. Every time he launched himself across that wire, he told a story about danger and adventure and the bravery to wonder which was which, on any given day.

And then he fell. He landed in a wheelchair, which the surgeon at SF General Hospital told him he'd better get used to. He would be there, the doctor said, for the rest of his life. He was twenty-eight years old.

Actually, my father jumped. At the end of every act, he jumped from the wire for dramatic effect, glittering and leaping in the costume my mother made him. This defiant submission to gravity was the perfect finale for an act of such exquisite control; but one day, he landed wrong. That's all. He landed wrong, and my parents headed up to Mendocino County, where my mother grew pot and my father learned to walk again. A cherry tree bloomed in a richness of light as thick as loam. Caitlin labored like a pioneer, chopping wood and hauling water and tending the chickens and the garden that fed her little family. She was powerful and all-giving and inexhaustible.

As soon as he could, my father was out of that bed and in between the sheets and legs of another woman. Alizarin was younger than he was, younger than my mother, with a fine full figure and long curly hair. One night, at a children's slumber party, Alizarin stood naked at the top of the stairs and ordered all the little girls to stop giggling immediately. She was backlit by the lamp from her bedroom so she looked like a nude Madonna, all full of semen and secrets and wrath. Her daughter's name was Jezebel, and Jezzie was a crybaby.

"I wanted to find out what was going on with your father," my mother explained, when she'd cleaned up her face and straightened her hair. There was nothing rarefied about her good looks now. She had a product and a mission in mind. This is how my mother the scholar, the would-be priestess of a long-dead cult, became a prostitute in the spirit of research. She was sure that she would solve the mystery of men's desires by approaching them where they grazed in the wild. She'd compile data on their secret fetishes, their weaknesses and appetites. She collected endless unrelated anecdotes, never came up with a unifying principle, and eventually became a phlebotomist. "Still sucking!" she remarked triumphantly, as if we had all agreed that it is a triumph to render one's life in a punchline. Because there are years of my childhood that we did not spend together, these stories are difficult to verify. What I am almost sure of is this:

My mother was not a streetwalker. She never worked for a pimp. She was not "full service," which means she performed various non-coital services for men who paid her upwards of six hundred dollars an hour to babysit their fetishes. Out of this, she sent generous remittances to my grandmother, who took care of me in the wary, fatalistic way that people do when they're not sure why they keep feeding a stray cat.

My mother's mother, Francine Swift, tended to her bees. That is literally the only thing I ever saw her do. I am not entirely sure the bees served any financial purpose. I think Francine regarded money as unladylike; so much so that speaking of it would be crude, like addressing the matter that appears by some obscene miracle in the commode. Of course, I have no idea how she felt about anything, because speech, to my grandmother, was just one more noxious sound produced by the body, and therefore best avoided or politely ignored.

Francine Swift woke up every morning at four a.m., crept around on long-toed stockinged feet, and retired at six-fifteen p.m. Between these hours, she tended to her bees. She murmured to them in a gentle buzz that might have been a particularly noisy form of telepathy. She drove them around to various farms on the outskirts of central California, bumping along back roads with a sense of direction as sure as that of a worker bee coming home to her hive. I assumed for a long time that she was sneaking the bees into these orchards, tucking them away at the edges of forests and fields. I thought of the bees as tiny victims of persecution and my grandmother as their champion, poaching nectar on behalf of all these miniature, tragically toiling fugitives.

Caitlin, who never took the time to stare at bees, had plenty of stories about them, too. On a good day, the queen bee was a successful dominatrix, ruling the hive with her sexual prowess. More often, all the bees were tragic drudges, even the queen, who gathered all the genetic material she needed in a single maiden flight and spent the rest of her life churning out eggs in the dark. To Caitlin, the hive was an irresistible symbol of the totalitarian state. She was obscurely offended by how unthinkingly the sexless workers spent their lives creating a concoction of unbearable sweetness, simultaneously doting upon and enslaving a single corpulent female, engorged with more eggs than she could ever lay. The brutality of it horrified and fascinated her.

But I have seen her moved to the extreme of putting on her sunglasses by the poignance of a queen's one flight into the sunshine, where the males all take their turns at fertilizing her. To my mother, this was a wild festival of love, never to be repeated. She saw a dreadful sacrifice in singular events that cannot be improved upon; where fates are sealed in an hour and no one ever strikes out their own; never doubles back to re-examine possibilities; is burdened forever by choices they made and things that happened to them.

Francine was a little less staggered by the metaphorical possibilities of insects. She made her living by their expertise; because of course the farmers paid her to pollinate their crops. Of course she had a barn full of shining equipment; and of course she haggled fiercely with the merchants who carried her products, her soaps and her candles and her slabs of waxy honeycomb, dripping with the life's work of half a well-fed hive.

She saw nothing mysterious about the creatures that absorbed her so entirely—though she never did find out why that one colony abandoned a perfectly good hive in the spring of '79, or where they went when they did. She accepted the bees on their own terms, and didn't take their sudden passions as a personal affront. She took refuge from pathetic fallacy in stern reality, accepting, even, the fact of descendants whose behavior she declined to explain.

Reality, in my grandmother's childhood home, was as stern as the preacher who took his own eldest stepdaughter as his second bride in Christ; who reduced her mother to the status of a cast-off concubine and did not ever spare the rod to spoil the children who never did grow up quite right.

I never met my great-grandparents. I don't even know their names. But I have an impression of a sturdy two-story farmhouse with cedar trunks full of handmade quilts. I have a memory that is not a memory of a clean-swept yard, dotted with fine red hens. It is very much like my grandmother's house, transplanted to a big flat state with a wide-open sky. I would like to see it someday, with its wrap-around porch and its hayloft and the attic with that one small window where so many silent horrors were endured.

The day she turned sixteen, my grandmother made an unauthorized sortie on the family's strictly inventoried pantry. She removed a day-old loaf of dark bread, a large wedge of hard cheese, and a sizable chunk of cured ham. With these provisions, she made her way to Texas—though she never said how far she went, or where the road began.

She called home once. She was in a hospital after a car accident, with injuries the doctor told her might be fatal. "You'd better call your mother," he told her. "Before we go into surgery." I linger on that scene sometimes, where an old-fashioned surgeon, perhaps a veteran of the European killing fields, looked at my wounded young grandmother and recognized her need to hear the truth. I think something came alive in her then. Something was seen and spoken to, with the respect that it deserved.

She obeyed. Or maybe someone did it for her. Maybe a very young nursing student stood twisting the cord of a heavy rotary phone in her fingers. Maybe she was about to hang up when an old woman finally picked up the receiver in a farmhouse gone silent and empty. Maybe a stranger heard a stranger's voice say coldly, I do not have a daughter by that name; and then the decisive clunk of a receiver, falling back into its cradle.

In her childhood home, Francine earned double rations of contempt. She was an undutiful daughter and a disobedient wife. She stole her mother's bread. She drove an automobile, in the days before the mandate that all windshields be made of laminated glass. For the rest of her life after the accident, gleaming slivers of windshield worked their way out of her scalp, spawning like bloody stillborn fangs onto her pillow at night.

Eventually, she married an aspiring oil tycoon and began to place cucumber slices over her eyes so she wouldn't lose her looks. When her husband died, she bought a piece of property on the outermost edge of Monterey County, at the foot of a red-rocked mountain bristling with yucca and blanketed with sage. At night, coyotes howled meaningfully into the bowl of the star-studded sky.

On one of her very few visits to Francine's farm, my mother decided to read *Titus Andronicus* with me. It was very important for us to be better than all the sentimental little girls who were reading *Wind in the Willows* and *Anne of Green Gables*—though Caitlin never did explain what the consequences would be, if we failed. We cannot possibly have watched Anthony Hopkins as Titus when I was seven years old, because Julie Taymor's film version of the play did not even exist until I was a grown woman. Still, it is Hopkins' Titus I see, snapping his daughter's neck, when I remember my mother saying, "I'm enough of a Darwinist that that makes sense to me."

What did she mean by that? Did my mother really believe that honor killings are a form of natural selection? Never mind the lapse in feminist theory. How closely had she read her Darwin? Surely no scholar, amateur though she was, would blurt that out by way of discussing bedtime stories with a child.

Maybe her mind was coarsened by then: by Marek, who never tired of a very proper teahouse ceremony wherein Caitlin known as Isis, dressed like a drawing by Toulouse-Lautrec, reached into her innumerable ruffles and expertly aimed a stream of urine into Marek's waiting cup; by Georges, who masturbated fiercely as my mother called Inanna, wearing rubber gloves and nurse's whites, prepared catheters for him while talking dirty in Latin; by all those countless men and all the countless ways they demanded she fuck them in the ass.

Even worse—and I hold my breath every time I think of it, like that woman I knew who was so afraid of spinal meningitis that she held her breath whenever she passed a trash can, is this: my mother believed her own mother should have been destroyed, like a nightingale too wounded to sing. Following this logic, she herself never should have been born, and I, Isobel Reinhardt, am the undesirable consequence of someone neglecting a duty to murder a child.

That—and now I exhale, because it is a tremendous relief when the worst thing happens—is what she meant when she read about a tragic hero murdering his ravished, mutilated daughter; when she put her finger on the line so she'd remember her place; thought about it for a moment; and said, yeah. That makes sense to me.

My mother the feminist. My mother the whore.

"IZZIE. I AM so sorry." She sighed tragically. My mother was the first person I called when I came back to San Francisco from Germany in the summer of 2008. Already, it was not going well. "I wish I had known about this before—well, sweetie. I've made *plans*." She lowered her voice, as if she were sharing a secret I'd begged her to tell. "I have *Company*." My mother's orthography is so flawless I can actually tell by the tone of her voice when she has made an unconventional decision to capitalize a noun.

"Mom."

I rested my forehead on the cool cinderblock wall beside the payphone. It was soothing, until I noticed a glistening spray of wet blood on the vomit-colored paint. It looked like a junkie had used an open vein to make a graffiti piece on the nature of longing and fulfillment.

"You did know," I began reasonably.

I have an illogical belief in the power of reason, especially when it comes to my mother. I have a conversion of the heathens fantasy that at some point, I will say something so reasonable that she will cry out, "Of course! That makes perfect sense! From now on, I'm going to interact with you in a way that indicates my undying respect for your intellect and maturity." I continue to believe in the inevitability of this scenario, in spite of the fact that I have duplicated exactly the opposite result, more times than I can count.

"You knew," I went on, "because I told you."

"Oh, honey." My mother barely sighed this time. She could have been yawning. "You know I don't keep track of those things."

I pounced. "So you didn't have the information, or you had it and it wasn't important enough to keep track of?" This is what happens to people who raise their children to believe they are more intelligent than everyone else. "Are you just high?"

"That is not a relevant question, *Isobel*," she replied, italicizing my name to signal the impropriety of the inquiry. I hated how casually she claimed the right to behave like an upstanding citizen, now, after years of X-rated anecdotes and revolting observations. As if I went around making gratuitous drug references in spite of how well I'd been raised.

"You're right," I conceded. "I am way out of line. I should have known that whatever you dragged in off cougr.com would be a lot more rewarding than being supportive of your boring daughter. I'm just crawling home from the greatest humiliation of my life."

"You don't even know what humiliation is," she promised. "Humiliation is powerful medicine."

"Which we know by how much money rich perverts pay for it," I agreed.

"Will you let me have the floor for longer than a soundbite, Isobel." My mother hates my name. To be precise, she hates the fact that my father named me. She likes to imply that she was so in love with him that she never dared to contradict him. It makes my flaky, philandering dad sound so much more thrilling than he was, so forceful and sure of himself; so much like he gave a shit. You'd think I'd be used to my mother's sexual revelations, but this nostalgia for my father's potency still makes me squirm. It's an irritating tragic chorus that always opens with several repetitions of my first name, unabbreviated and without diminutives. But this time she had something different for me.

"The reason people pay to be humiliated," she began, enunciating as clearly as if she were reading a statement to the American Psychiatric Association, "is that humiliation is a powerful tool to gain access to what is inside them."

Like the giant dildos you bury in their colons, I managed not to add. I may have a latent sense of propriety, after all.

"I'm just saying that some of the people I've met in my life—" My mother, the foul-mouthed oracle, has a wide-ranging spectrum of euphemisms so banal they don't even register as such.

For example, "people I've met" can be directly translated as, "people who have paid me thousands of dollars to do things they would pay thousands more dollars not to have anyone find out about." This makes it difficult to tell a simple anecdote about something cute the dog did.

"Some of the people I've met in my life are very powerful, very creative individuals," she continued meaningfully, "specifically because they have been able to use their suffering as tools to get where they need to be in life."

It sounded like something a trust-fund coprophiliac would say as he reclined on Egyptian cotton sheets, an artisanal vintage mellowing in a cut-glass crystal vessel, his eyes overflowing with feeling as he bared his soul to the discreet and understanding beauty at his side.

"You should write a self-help book, Mother," I told her. "You could call it *Fuck Your Way to the Top.* Seriously. Think about it." I hung up the phone.

THERE IS A level of proficiency in a foreign language where it can be said that you know just enough to get yourself hurt. Thus, if you weep at Gretchen's final speech to Faust or plunge into a pit of black despair following some Herr Professor's undisguised contempt, you should consider yourself rewarded for all the sunny afternoons you've spent toiling through grammar books. What else did you expect from a language with sixteen ways of saying "the?" Once you are capable of absorbing the nuances of cruelty in a new language, you have achieved a measure of something that is often called success, by those who use humiliation as a tool to get where they need to be in life.

In the German higher education system, success or failure depends upon a final oral exam. Which I failed, my premise being fatally flawed. I had thought, after muffling my life in wifery for three and a half years, to make a brilliant career as a German-speaking academic. Why not attend an elite European university and read Nietzsche in the original, present a talk on Nietzschean metaphysics, and be hailed as an original thinker? It was a singularly unphilosophical line of inquiry.

After my humiliation, which I had enough linguistic aptitude to appreciate in most of its subtlety, I did what any self-respecting solitary Nietzschean with a will to power would do: I called my mother. Crying.

"Oh, sweetie," she said. "Why don't you stay with your dear old mom in the city for a while."

So I gave her my flight information and limped home with one red suitcase full of second-hand clothes and little yellow German volumes I fully intended to read. Now, in addition to being a failure, I was the forgotten daughter of aging whore.

I called Alizarin.

PART TWO

A SCHEDULE OF DRUGS

DIGITALIS

I AM NOTHING like my mother. But both of us are like that silent woman who walked all the way to Texas, eighty years ago or more. We have been experts at walking away for all our generations now. We are very good at giving up hope. And Mendocino County is where we go to give up. It's where we go to consort with our demons, which is quite a bit different from facing them down.

WHEN I FLED to Mendocino, after skulking away from Germany, I rented a room in a mansion with a beautiful widow named Reina Serrano. I felt like a character in a Hawthorne novel, though I couldn't remember which one. The widow had big friendly teeth and enormous fake breasts and great, long, liquid eyes, all of which gave her a tragic, laughing air.

Reina picked me up hitchhiking at the airport in San Francisco, which was probably not the most ill-considered thing either one of us had ever done. We drove north from "The City" (as Caitlin calls it, since there is no city but San Francisco and Margo St. James is Her Prophet), enumerating the shortcomings of men all the way home. A five-gallon bucket of paint sloshed along in the back like it was chiming in on the conversation. I found out later Reina had a rental cottage she repainted so often the back seat of her car had a permanent bucket-shaped dent in it.

As we climbed north along the 101, she told me her husband was addicted to porn. "He would rather watch it online than have . . . real intimacy," she told a stranger in the darkness of a speeding sedan. I'd been a foreigner so many months, I'd gotten used to secrets in the dark; to how generic people are in the most private parts of their lives.

For example: there is a hulking stone church in Germany that's been dark since the end of the Enlightenment. It's a place people go to be at one with the Almighty while snapping selfies with religious art, some of which is conceptual and modern. To the right of the altar, there is a large screen which I think is supposed to symbolize the inside of a confessional. People file up to the altar, light a candle, and write a secret on a small piece of paper. The screen is eight feet tall and twenty feet long, and is covered with scraps of secrets and shame. I know, from being in the dark and far away, that there is a woman with a spiky cursive hand and a child with an unknown father; that someone with a doctor's scrawl never loved his mother; and that a hundred and twenty miles north of San Francisco, there is a man who would rather watch porn than get laid.

"What a fucking douchebag," I said, by way of analysis. I had no way of knowing. Still, by the time we reached our destination, we had agreed that I would rent one of two empty bedrooms in the second-story southwest corner of her Dutch Colonial Revival home. We sealed the deal by pressing hands, her right and my left, both a little greenish in the console lights. We were keeping an eye out for deer and highway patrol, so it was like we made a major life decision during the boring part of a suspenseful movie.

The house had a gambrel roof that made it look like it was wearing a Mennonite bonnet. There were cobblestones on the outside walls, and alcoves shaded with wisteria and sprawling oaks and white-barked plane trees with prickly red seed pods. It was the kind of place that only exists in fairytales and novels, where houses have names and no one has to explain their income bracket. It had a circular drive. It had a wrought-iron fence and a gate with heavy hardware that clanked.

Why shouldn't I live in a mansion for a while? Virtuous peasants in fairytales did it all the time. In Germany, I had lived at the foot of a hill with a castle on top. I had traveled to ancestral lands in search of learning, and learned only that I was a fool. I had married for love, and been lonelier than I had ever known. I'd been setting goals and laying plans, as if my life were a series of intelligible events. Now I understood that life would be a magpie's nest, littered with sparkling things. It would be a fascinating miscellany, like the flea market in Berlin, art made of trash, or Chewing Gum Alley in San Luis Obispo. If I based my life on a model like that, I would find it full of fascinating junk: the accidental haikus of partial shopping lists and the occasional careless treasure. It would be a new beginning, made of scraps and cast-off things.

I dragged my bright red suitcase into the marble foyer of a labor of love.

Reina began to show me the light switches. She dimmed the uppers and brightened the lowers and lit a few lamps on the side. She did it again, like she still wasn't used to how much fun it could be.

"We gutted this place," she explained. "We basically built it up from the ground."

I wondered where this porn-loving husband of hers was, and how I'd compose my face, so soon after deciding his wife was too good for him. It would be inconvenient if he turned out to be insightful and kind.

My new housemate showed me the cabinets, the couches, the fountains, and the banisters. She told me how she'd worked out each design with artisans and tradesmen. She'd done so many careful things; and then she decided to share them with me. Of all the hitchhikers I have ever picked up, I cannot think of a single one I'd share my zip code with, let alone my living quarters.

We made our way back to the living room off the open foyer. In the morning, the windows would offer a near-panoramic view of the grounds around the house. The mist rising from the creek would look like gently heaving smoke.

"This is where Zack died," she told me softly.

It took me a moment to understand that Zack was the man I'd called a fucking douchebag. I remained silent as I slowly readjusted my perceptions. This home was a memorial, this room the last a flawed and dying man had ever seen.

We were standing in a vast expanse of exposed-beam loveliness. Reina was looking at me steadily. I realized then we'd come to a stop in a civilized place. We weren't speeding through the darkness anymore.

"I want to be careful to respect his energy," she went on softly. "This is Zack's house." A draft of cool air rose up from the marble floor.

Zack Hill had been a cardiologist from "back East," which in California can be as far west as Nevada but in his case meant the

Atlantic Seaboard. He was old money: a "big man," Reina emphasized. "He had very big energy," she specified meaningfully.

I understood at once that he was the kind of domineering rich guy my mother might refer to as creative and powerful. I thought I saw a hint of tightly controlled mania—or at least of calculating possessiveness, in how the dead man squinted at his bride in photos on the wall.

Reina was still telling me about Zack, still showing me her home. She was making friends with me. I tried to reciprocate by being a really good listener. She said her late husband wore pressed slacks and a starched button-up shirt to mow the lawn.

"And loafers," she added, gazing out over the grass like she could see him still, doing things his own particular way.

I could see him, too, his big face florid with too many martinis, his neck bulging masterfully above the collar of his shirt. His body was just swollen enough to inspire the kind of respect people have for a powerful, expensive machine. He was corpulent, it's true. But his bones were wrapped in succulent meats and delicate wines, the finest pairings of each. He was a libertine, not a Cheetos-chomping beer-swiller.

Zack Hill—if you slurred the name after a few drinks, it rhymed with jackal—had named his estate. And the name he gave the grounds, where oaks and manzanita spread their rich dark mulch in the shadow of the rolling hills, was Foxglove.

"Because of digitalis," Reina explained. The name had an air of secrets, and beauty, and crime.

The derivation of the name "foxglove" is shrouded, as death-obsessed people say, in mystery. The authors of the nineteenth-century classic, *English Botany, Or, Coloured Figures of British Plants*, quote the eminent Dr. Prior, an authority on the origins of popular names. The doctor claims that the original name was foxes' *glew* (which, as everyone knows, means foxes' *music*), because the flower looks like a tintinnabulum, or a ring of bells over an arch. Who but a fox, the reasoning goes, would be cunning enough to make a set of bells out of a poisonous plant?

Here the authors of *English Botany* exercise their right to disagree with the expert. They draw the reader's attention to the fact that "the name 'foxglove' is a very ancient one and exists in a list of plants as old as the time of Edward III (who reigned from 1312-1377)." It is touching to think of these well-mannered botanists handling such an ancient list, with the reverence due a long-dead specimen. They point out, with a briskness that belies a shy demeanor, that the name is "folksglove," not "foxglove"; and that the "folks" of Wales were fairies. With a certainty that is almost poignant, they go on to say that "nothing is more likely than that the pretty coloured bells of the plant would be designated 'folksgloves,' afterwards, 'foxglove.'" The fairies they mention, who sound like they would have devoured Miss Tinkerbell after roasting her on a spit, were said to lurk in the digitalis bell and use it to produce fairy thunder as an indication of wrath.

All these characters: the musical foxes, the wrathful fairies, even the ancient list, sound like fragments of some half-remembered folk tale, where everyone is panting for Freudian analysis, disregarding solemn injunctions, and falling prey to powerful potions. The foreshadowing of this malicious little tale grows darker with the mention of further names for the flower, which, like any charming psychopath, has more names than a nineteenth-century coquette had ribbons for her hair. They include: Bloody Fingers, Deadman's Bells, Fairy-folks-fingers, and Lambs'-tongue-leaves. They make Emily Dickinson's beloved perennial sound like an ingredient in a witches' brew that might also call for slivers of bone from a hanged man's skull.

The symptoms of digitalis are almost religious, in the way we've come to expect from medieval visionary saints. They include blurred vision, changes in color perception, and halos. There is no mention of the increased visibility of fairies; but mortality as always remains a primary concern. The literature notes that women and dogs are particularly susceptible to its harmful effects.

What was I doing in a place that was named after a poisonous plant, known for harboring fairies of uncertain disposition? If our origins have anything to do with who we are, didn't it matter that I was born into an anarchist collective in an old canning factory? My favorite thing to do as a child was roller-skate madly up and down the hallways, which were badly lit and wide enough for a team of Clydesdales and a couple of bulldozers to proceed abreast.

Now I lived in a doctor's mansion, where the floors were tiled in great marble slabs. They were a mottled meaty pink in the living room, and the bright glaring red of shallow wounds in the kitchen. What happened to that filthy child, that anarchist spawn with the tangle of unwashed hair in her eyes? I was such a genteel guest these days.

The fireplace was so enormous, it had a little porch that three people could sit on. Reina and I used to curl up in front of it, making beaded jewelry, sipping fizzy drinks, and dishing the dirt about men. The little porch and the mantle were made of thick black rock, dotted with trilobites and fossilized snail-shells.

What the hell was I doing in a place like this? In the years I lived on my grandmother's farm, I went to a one-room schoolhouse in a tiny town called Parkfield, where the only thing that ever happened was earthquakes. Because of the regularity of its temblors, Parkfield was the epicenter of earthquake prediction efforts for years. We took endless field trips to the laser station, where our teacher monitored the motionless hills with devices that made him swoon with envy for himself. I became a voracious reader, and lay in the shade of a tree that smelled like Band-Aids, gorging my young brain on books about horses and dystopian futures.

Now I lolled on deck chairs carved from wine barrels on someone else's lawn. A calico cat snoozed watchfully on a couch upholstered in soft burgundy leather. The anarchists and the earthquakes and the men were all gone, and we were still waiting, Reina and I, waiting for something to change. In the meantime, our life together was a string of sleepovers, one long girlish Friday night indoors. We spent hours at her hand-carved walnut bar, going over tales of Zack the philanderer, Zack the shrewd businessman, until the night yawned into morning and I missed the man as ambiguously as she did.

Zack had gotten brain cancer in the middle of a years'-long battle with his wife. It was unforgivable that he should end the argument that way, absolved of any obligation to apologize, explain, or divide his assets. I have promised, with every appearance of sincerity, that I would not tell a living soul what I heard in the course of a protracted slumber party at Foxglove.

"Zack was a pillar of this community," Reina explained. "You can't tell anyone!"

"I think I know when people would like to keep things private," I told her. I didn't add that I wouldn't know a pillar of the community if I were shackled to one in the marketplace.

Several beats of silence ensued. It was like one of those moments when everyone is making silly puns and someone suddenly drops a remark about how language makes us human. She assessed me. That's what she did. In the marble fossil fireplace, a handful of ashes held its breath.

"I'm sure you do," she responded evenly.

I tried to maintain an air of sympathetic understanding. That is what people do when they are so insignificant their only hope lies in being helpful or unseen. *You are a cream-fed cat,* I recognized. *And I am a likeable stray.* I knew that somewhere in those stares, I had finally been seen. Reina, I realized, probably knew that wasn't alfalfa in my hair.

I may have mentioned that Reina had a very fine eye. The pictures she showed me were composed with great dramatic flair around the large, lumpy, self-assured figure of Zack. He always sat, like an informal potentate or a charismatic leader, in a loose semicircle of people much younger than he was. If he was holding a glass, it sparkled and snapped with a double shot of something aged and burning. If he drank champagne, it was out of a flute; and if he held a wineglass big as a chalice, it was so the aroma of the deep red liquid could be properly released. And if he looked at a woman—

"Look!" Reina cried, tapping the screen with a manicured nail. She was a nurse, so really, her nails were maintained, not manicured. But they were very well-maintained, without a hint of cuticle or dirt. They glowed with perfect health and transparent nail polish, like they'd all been gently licked.

"Look at that!" she hissed. "Look at that *bitch!*" She tapped a few keys, and the image of a dark-haired woman with a cunning leer filled the screen. "She's standing—*here,*" she told me, angling her quick lean body into a doorway.

She crouched there, furiously exaggerating the other woman's posture. Then she leaped up and dashed back to the computer, as if the leering woman might have been up to something while she was gone. It occurred to me that it would be a very bad idea to pick a fight with Reina.

"Zack and our friends are sitting—*there*," she continued. She snapped the focus of the picture back onto Zack, and pointed at the patio. "And he was looking back at her—like this." She sketched a quick, invisible diagram on the bar and turned a triumphant, wronged glare in my direction.

"So you think—?" I ventured, not entirely sure if I was expected to be morbidly fascinated or politely interested. Here I was, in lavish surroundings with a sophisticated, savvy woman who was not my mother. She trusted me with her heartbreak. I was the recipient of so much generosity, and all I had to do was show up at the bar and be attentive, like a diligent scholarship student.

"Oh. I *know*." She sounded smoky and experienced, like a Washington insider encountering a young intern's horror at a senator's corruption. "Zack sent out mass emails sometimes." She paused. "He was too stupid to hide the recipients. Too stupid, or too arrogant." She paused again. Then, with the air of a forensics expert revealing the culprit, she declared, "This bitch was always on that list. And here she is—" She spun back to the computer, where she enlarged the woman's leer until it became a blur, a nonsense piece of information, like a memory that doesn't hurt anymore.

"She's at my house!" A howl crept into her voice. "She's at *my* house, looking at *my* husband, on *my* patio!" She was in a wide-legged scrapper's stance, strong bony hands balled into fists. The woman in the photograph leered on and on. "And he's looking back at her!" She zoomed in on Zack, who appeared to be smiling at a young woman lounging on the grass at his feet, like the youth of Athens being corrupted by a fat old man. "He could do that. He could point his eyes at you, and the whole time, he'd be scanning. Just scanning the room for some young cutie." She crept back to the leering woman, who was neither young nor lovely, though she did seem agile and willful enough to captivate a man.

"She thought she was getting away with it," Reina gloated grimly. "But I was up here, like this."

Abruptly, she ran halfway up the stairs. She peered slyly through the hand-carved manzanita banister. She hunkered and aimed an imaginary camera at the doorway where another woman had crouched in three-quarters profile, leering at a man who smiled at a girl stretched out on the grass.

"I ruined my eyesight," she told me soberly, descending the stairs like she was moving into the final act of a morality play. "Watching him around the corners of dumpsters, squinting at security cameras in the hospital . . ." She touched her glasses, which were checkered black and white and covered in tiny rhinestones. You will remember that blurred vision is a sign of digitalis poisoning.

The question remains: what the hell was I doing at a named estate, listening to a stranger finally tell the truth about a man I'd never met?

And now that the question has been posed three times, like a riddle in a fairytale, I have no choice but to answer it.

I was a scholar. I was a reader. I had retraced the journey my ancestors made—not to find out about my own past, but to abandon all traces of a pointless marriage to a man who should have been someone I knew briefly, a long time ago. I already knew about lusty passionate women like Reina and Caitlin, and how they fall in love. Their drama was a movie I'd seen so many times, I could sit in the dark alone and murmur along with the lines.

But I was going somewhere on my own. That's how it started. I was on my way, and I got sidetracked and confused and caught in simple snares. I spent a long time sitting stupefied. I made escapes that compromised my honor. I took shapes that weren't my own, and finally—well, you remember the lotus-eaters, don't you?

CANNABIS

ALL I WANTED to do was lounge around reading novels and recover from not being in Germany anymore. But I was not a well-born lady of the nineteenth century, with the option of soothing my nerves on a fainting couch indefinitely. I had to get a job, as horrid as that sounds. And there is really only one industry in Mendocino County.

Sure, there are ranchers and loggers and fishermen, too. But mention Mendocino anywhere in the world—which I have—and even the straightest stockbroker will raise his eyebrows and get a little grin on his face. When I came back to Northern California, my speech still furred with traces of German, I took a job in the industry. Specifically, I went to work in Alizarin Goldfarb's pot garden. I had a little bit of a fraught history with gardening, and a long history with Alizarin.

I met her when I was three years old and she and her daughter Jezebel moved into the canning factory. Jezzie and I were both in kindergarten when her mother and my father locked eyes across a Scrabble board and fell briefly and flagrantly, madly in love.

The thing I remember most about that time is killing snails in Caitlin's garden. The yard at the canning factory was a gaping wound in the middle of the parking lot. It had been ripped out of the concrete with a rented jackhammer and amended with compost from the sewage treatment plant. I don't know if you can still buy cubic yards of treated human shit in San Francisco, but in the early 80s, they were practically giving it away. The people in our building kept the chunks of concrete they tore out of the parking lot and used them to build rough benches and a wall around the wound, which they christened Jackhammer Park. They adorned it with giant aloe plants and red geraniums and two small plum trees with fruits as dark as scabs. A few of the women grew food. Someone rolled out a carpet of lawn, as severely groomed as a military haircut. The grass and I both flourished under daily ministrations from a sprinkler that had to be moved every five minutes.

But gardening is brutal business, and Caitlin wasn't one to spare a child. My task was removing snails from the glossy green leaves and stomping on them. I think I was supposed to find this gratifying, the finality of those hard brown shells as they broke into the soft flesh of my mother's enemies. "Even the babies!" she instructed gaily, like she was giving me permission to transgress some rule we'd all agreed on.

My mother's beans climbed up a network of salvaged poles and reached for the plum trees. Her melons twined around the headboard of a bed she had driven into the ground. An assortment of companion plants was supposed to protect them all from insects and disease. She had begun to draw a diagram of a medieval knot garden, where all the herbs were planted according to mnemonic devices invented by monks who knew the Bible by heart.

The trouble was this: my mother, a fighter to the core, was raising a wimp. As I re-create that era in my mind, it becomes almost clear to me that by the time we had our showdown in the garden, she must have known about my father and Alizarin. It cannot possibly have had anything to do with me or the snails. But there I was, refusing to accept her enemies as my own. She wanted us to stand together in Jackhammer Park, stomping on snails and lining the pathway with little dead smears.

Instead, I plucked them off the plants and held them in my hand. I understood how terrified they were when my enormous fingers wrapped around their fragile bodies. I knew why they vanished into their plain brown spiral shells. It made sense to me that they clung as hard as they could where they fed in the sunshine, oozing harmlessly along. So I put them in the pockets of my pink and white dress, dawdling as my mother moved ahead of me impatiently.

When I thought the snails were getting overcrowded, I wandered over to the other side of the giant aloe plant. The leaves were prickly, but not enough to hurt, if you were careful. I took a handful of snails out of their hiding place and began to arrange them on the muscular curves of the aloe leaves. Some I put in the sun, because I thought they looked pale and might like to get warm. Others, I concluded, preferred the shade, so I tucked them in close to the heart of the plant.

I was almost done when I became aware of my mother, standing above me with a trowel in one hand and an empty plastic planter in the other. She was wearing a large straw hat, but her bare shoulders were lightly sunburned. She watched me in silence for a long time. I began to feel a slight chill, crouching there in her shadow on what had been the sunny side of her favorite healing plant. I had set a clump of snails beside me on the grass, and they separated and began to stream away before she spoke.

"You really don't care at all about this garden, do you?" she said at last. "You could give a shit less if everything I've worked for"— she waved her arm, and bits of wet dirt flew off the trowel and onto my hair—"all this." She turned to look at the melons, the beans, the tender lettuce in the shade. Then she looked back at me. Her eyes were wet and fierce. "What the fuck, exactly, are you doing?" Her diction was precise.

She was much bigger than I was. It occurred to me that this no longer meant she was someone who would pick me up when I was tired; who would reach into the cupboards and give me things to eat. It meant she was stronger and faster than I was, and we were alone in her garden, and I had never seen her this angry.

"I'm putting the snails," I whispered, watching as my slimy little friends crept onto the aloe, inches from her foot.

"You are putting the snails," she repeated slowly. She crouched down beside me and brought her face close to mine. "Are you aware, you little asshole," she enunciated clearly. "You are actively destroying something that is very important to me." She took a deep breath. Then she stood up. "Fine. You stay here. Save the snails. By all means." She smiled brightly. "Have a great time," she added, and spun away. I saw her take off her hat and drop it in the parking lot.

I did not live with my mother for a long time after that. When I came back to San Francisco after years of tending bees, she was hard and bright and beautiful. Her mouth was always red. Her teeth were very white. Her breasts didn't move when she walked, and the planes of her face were flattened with powders and creams.

She told me her name was Lilith now. "Lilith was the real first woman," she explained. "Sometimes, you have to go all the way back to the beginning to find out who you are."

IN THE SUMMER of 2008, I began my education in cannabis cultivation at Serendipity Organics, courtesy of Alizarin Goldfarb. There were fires in the hills that year, fires so fierce people abandoned their crops and fled for the lowlands. Smoke hung heavy and blocked out the sun, like it was punishing the populace for violating federal marijuana laws.

Alizarin lived in an unincorporated community that was legendary for the beauty of the melons that sprawled across the valley floor. In 1852, when white men rode in on horseback, hunting for the headwaters of the Russian River, they reported wild oats that grew as high as their stirrups.

But nobody grows melons anymore. And wild oats are what a young man sows before he starts planting his real crop. A few organic farmers sell produce at the local markets. It's a decent living, because around here, people with acres of arable land buy fruits and vegetables at wildly inflated prices. With cash.

"Unincorporated community," in Mendocino County, means "wild west frontier town," with a few modernizing features. For example, cable TV is a lot more popular than it used to be, in the days of the swinging saloon doors. And there is a very high median level of education in hydrology, micro-economics, and soil chemistry.

After all, cannabis has its roots in the soil—even if that soil is trucked in by the ton because the native clay is too dense to support the root system of a healthy plant. By now, there are third-and-fourth-generation growers on a single plot of land, which, for people whose ancestors weren't even here before 1852, is a long-standing tradition. Some growers have strains they can trace back to seeds their grandparents smuggled out of Afghanistan in the 1960s.

In one of those instances of parallel development that has inspired thousands of hours of reverie, marijuana plants are charged with sexual tension. The females are hidden behind high walls like pampered virgins in a convent, provided with every luxury but freedom. Cannabis pollen is finer than thought, with the ability to drift for days on wind as soft as a sigh. Practically speaking, this means one vegetal pre-ejaculation can spoil the pedigree of every gently bred female for miles around. Because of this, almost all the males are pre-emptively destroyed.

Sometimes, a female plant will turn hermaphrodite and ravish all the females she can, like the plants have cast themselves in a cheesy all-girl porn film. Once, I heard about a grower who literally beat a hermaphrodite plant to death—to teach the others a lesson, he said.

At the height of their reproductive desperation, when their buds are full and firm and dripping with fragrant sap; when their fruits are covered with fine, crinkly hairs, the females are cut down like virgin sacrifices and hung up somewhere out of sight to dry. That means the next time you fire up a joint, you will be pressing your lips to the dried-up female genitals of a plant that never got laid. Inhale deeply, and let it out slowly.

REVERENT ANTHROPOMORPHIZING IS the order of the day on a lot of pot farms. But Alizarin was no outlaw hippie rancherette, watering her sacred garden with menstrual blood by the light of the full moon. She also didn't spend much time spinning her six-shooter and holding off the sheriff, who, in a story like that, would be torn by his duty to the law and his love for the woman who scorns it.

Alizarin was a highly respected professional in her field. She had an extensive portfolio and a pages-long CV. She was a working artist, which, ever since the DeMedicis retired from patronizing the arts, has most often been a euphemism for laboring in poverty and obscurity.

And no, her mother did not give her that name. No one—except maybe Alizarin herself—would do that to a defenseless human child. Alizarin is the name of a cool crimson, one of two colorants found in madder root. This, for her profound understanding of color theory and the inspiring power of rage, is the name her mother should have given her. Alizarin crimson is also an excellent mixer, which provides further commentary on the role of socializing in the life of a professional artist. And Alizarin was a consummate professional. She knew exactly what she was and was not doing, and why.

"I'm not growing pot so I can fuck around and buy toys," she explained, the first day I showed up to work for her.

In this field as in so many others, it is standard practice to head up an employee orientation with an emphatic mission statement. It was late August, and the plants were quivering in an unseen summer breeze. They were endearing, like wild-haired creatures in a Dr. Seuss cartoon, adorable and manic and not entirely predictable.

"I'm growing pot so I can work with kids!" she went on. "So I can give money to public radio and the SPCA and go to Israel . . ."

I stopped listening. It's what people do to women who talk too much. And I was doing that other thing, too. That thing that women do when they scrutinize each other.

I was trying to imagine how a man would see Alizarin. Specifically, a missing wire-walker, with scars on his back and memories of a long, uncertain convalescence. I tried to imagine the joy of renewed vitality pouring through a young man's healthy body. I began to understand how impossible it would be to defy this sudden power; the imperative to act, to love a beautiful, imperious woman.

A part of me knew it means exactly nothing when people come together for temporary mating purposes. I have a very clear memory of being eleven years old and telling my father what I'd read on the bathroom wall about a slightly older schoolmate. "But *I* know it isn't true," I concluded triumphantly. "Because she's dumb. *And* she's fat." I was deeply impressed with the solemnity of sex at that time. Girls who did it, I knew, were mysterious and knowing. They must be awe-inspiringly beautiful and expertly costumed to be inducted into the mysteries. In addition, they were required to be wise enough to comprehend the subtleties. I knew exactly no one who was qualified to conduct the activity on a non-professional basis, so I was forced to conclude that it was a very rare practice among amateurs.

My father waited patiently for me to finish my analysis. Then, exactly as if he were collecting data on a little-known phenomenon, he asked me this: "does she have a vagina?" Point made. She was fuckable, and that was that.

But daughters don't care how daughters are made. We don't care if our parents conceived us at the height of Tantric oneness or fumbling around in the bathroom of a Greyhound bus. We don't care that we exist, with broken hearts and sentience, because some guy had a hard-on and a woman happened to be ovulating. We want our daddies to be deeply impressed with our complexities, to know us through and through and love us anyway.

Alizarin was still talking. She was a tireless talker. "Look, I don't have the cash this time around. For house-sitting and, ah, *garden* maintenance. I *could* give you trimming. You'd have to wait on the payment, though. I usually give that to Jezzie, but she's fucking off somewhere, I don't know what's going on with her. She knows I have a guy in Marin who loves his lav—I don't know *why* they *call it that* it isn't *purple* not even *light purple* and it doesn't *smell* like anything, I mean it smells like pot of course but nothing *at all* like lavender. Anyway! He basically gets it on consignment. He's the *one* buyer I'll do that for because he turns it around so fast and I've known him forever. He just sent me an email: got any luv? (That's his clever code for lav)—and I *do*! It's just not ready yet. You could do a pound a day, right?" She gave me a stern, tire-kicker's stare, by way of assessing my competence at trimming weed.

"But, um . . ." Suddenly she was hesitant, the way little kids are when they present you with something they've made. "If it makes it any easier to wait around. I could teach you how to paint. Like a trade." I saw that she was trying to be casual. "*If* you're interested. Just something to think about." She led me out of the greenhouse and into the vegetable garden. "Now. There is *no such thing* as a green pepper. A green pepper is an unripe red pepper . . ."

I couldn't stop thinking about the pot plants. They were cheerfully miraculous. The only thing that could even approach their quality of down-home magic would be if one of the sheep strolled up to the fence and delivered a speech. The animal would have to fulminate on the most commonplace banalities, though, because really, the pot plants had no more access to mystery than that girl with her name on the wall. But, also like that girl, this didn't change the fact that they were utterly enthralling—even, in the end, mysterious.

They seemed to call down the light, like saints in a painting, and play an intricate, meaningless game with it. Every time we touched a plant, dozens of tiny goggle-eyed frogs burst into the air like slimy fireworks, then vanished like they'd been extinguished. As long as I lived among pot growers, I never saw another grow as covered with frogs as Alizarin's.

Or spider mites. Spider mites have mandibles to humble and inspire all the nightmare gods of Hollywood. They glow with a throbbing greenish light, like things on lonely roads that make people believe in UFO's and fairies. They weave diaphanous webs of spun glass cotton candy in the flowers of the pot plant, and they will bankrupt a grower whose vigilance fails.

This is where I found myself, after failing completely as an adult: standing at the end of a long dirt road, downwind from a reeking gray-water cistern in the doorway of a greenhouse made of scraps. I'd just received an offer for something with zero practical value, in exchange for the opportunity to commit the least glamorous crime imaginable.

Perhaps no other felony requires quite as many buckets as I used in my daily round of felonies that season. There were buckets with loosely attached handles that I would drag through fields of poison oak. There were cracked buckets, for hauling rancid gray-water from one patch to another. For most of the year, Alizarin's land had no water source, which led to complicated relationships with neighbors and a fervent appreciation for the nutrients in dishwater.

This precise level of knowledge was important because I was about to stay at the farm for two weeks while Alizarin traveled to Israel. She and a Palestinian artist would work together on a large mosaic with a mixed group of Jewish and Muslim children, just as the pot plants in northern California were reaching a crucial stage of development.

I would stay on the farm, because I had just received a detailed explanation of the condition of the tie rods and ball joints in the tired old pickup truck I had bought with my last financial aid check. This had been followed by a vivid description of what was likely to happen to that truck if I drove it seventy-two miles every day for two weeks, traveling back and forth between Foxglove and Serendipity. It would take several hundred dollars to persuade my eloquent mechanic that the dinged-up jalopy could handle more than one or two outings on the roads in Mendocino County, even the paved ones. And, of course, those funds were not available yet. I would have them as soon as Alizarin's retailer in Marin got rid of the weed I hadn't even laid eyes on yet, but which I would clean just as soon as I got around to it.

I would be stranded on the mountain, which should have made me nervous but didn't. Instead, I felt like I was about to be tested on some obscure subject that I hadn't studied for, exactly, but which I'd been prepared for by the circumstances of my life and character. I was ready for it, even if I wasn't quite sure what it was.

I would have plenty to do. There were sheep to move around from one pasture to another. There were spider mites to do battle with. And Alizarin would give me free access to her studio, while she did artistic fieldwork in the Holy Land, at the continental crossroads.

I saw pictures from this project afterward, Alizarin grinning with a bearded young man who did not smile. I saw the children squinting uncertainly, like children in historical photographs who are unaware of their obligation to be endearing. Behind this dusty exhausted crowd of humanity, the mosaic exploded with life, like the plants in her greenhouse. I learned that this was Alizarin's response to authority backed by guns: this exuberance, this show of strength in foliage and color. It was her way of outliving all decrees upheld by force. Her artwork had the appearance of uncontrolled, wild abundance, like an overgrown garden springing up out of some unseen water source.

The central theme of the design was children's handprints, which were made of clay and glazed in brilliant colors. The hands adorned a grim grey wall in a war-torn border town, expressing every possibility of human gesture. They moved across the concrete canvas like the lines of faraway mountains, their edges treeless and smooth. Aquifers and orchards and wise sayings in Hebrew and Arabic flowed throughout the gestural landscape, rendered in shattered glass and broken mirrors.

At that point, the plant husbandry portion of my résumé consisted of failing to kill the snails in Jackhammer Park and rinsing the dust from my mother's ficus. The *ficus benjamina* is called a weeping fig in the vernacular, which makes it sound like somebody, somewhere, has succeeded in doing it harm. In fact, it's a lot more likely that the ficus will be providing shade for the cockroaches after the nuclear holocaust has destroyed all other forms of life.

This is not to imply that my mother was only fit to cultivate a ficus. Like Alizarin, if Caitlin ever had to feed the world from a single plot of earth, there is no doubt the world would have twice as much as it could ever eat—plus a few ornamental shrubs to give the place a dash of color. Caitlin was an archetype, remember that, all holy whore and mother earth, raising the dead and bringing in crops, citing Joseph Campbell and *The Golden Bough* with inches of dirt in her nails.

Also: Caitlin Swift grew legendary pot. She grew in the days when legends were sung, because writing hadn't been invented yet. She grew when growers were drawn and quartered and their heads put up on spikes outside the city walls. I was starting to feel like it might be a mark of distinction, to be descended from such ability and daring.

So, yeah, I said to Alizarin. "Why don't you show me how to paint. I'll look after the garden for a while."

THE FIRST PAINTING lesson was learning how to look at color like I'd had a schizophrenic break with reality.

"What *colors* do you see in that teacup? Do you see the shadows? Can you see how green they are?" Alizarin made me paint a teacup, exaggerating every breath of color, every shock of light. "Paint it like you're on acid. You *have* taken acid, I assume . . . ?" She trailed off discreetly.

"Of course, the last time *I* took acid," she went on, like she was admitting that she herself might have been less than diligent, "it was that wedding gift from *our mutual friend*. Acid has quite the shelf life." She gave a light, throaty chuckle. She seemed to be permanently laryngitic, which gave her bossiest pronouncements a quality of intimacy, a kind of strident cooing.

The wedding of Alizarin Goldfarb and Morpheus Charnisse adhered closely to long-established Jewish tradition. They were joined beneath a chuppah in a ceremony where he stomped on a glass and solemn vows were spoken in a language no one understood. There was champagne. There were strawberries dipped in chocolate. And my father, gracious soul that he was, presented the other man's bride with a small quantity of high-quality LSD.

Alizarin's husband was an actor and a musician. He was widely read in shamanistic practices; in vision quests and dreams and eloquent animal spirits with a savage sense of humor. He wrote densely populated lyrics full of yearning and regret, and he set them to music with intervals so intricate that even he could only play them after weeks of practice.

Morpheus Charnisse may or may not have been the name he was given at birth. But Alizarin liked to call her husband M.C. Harness, perhaps by way of decorating the yoke of matrimony. He was Caliban to her Prospero, dependent and defiant. He would be lost in the dimensions of a gesture or the resonance of a particular sound, just when the dishes needed washing or it was time to feed the sheep. He especially liked the round wooden water tank, with its top like a stage and its slatted hull that produced a different medley of echoes, every time he struck it. Charnisse treasured the water tank like a custom-made musical instrument, but he almost always forgot to turn the water off when he watered the garden, which drained the tank and killed the living echoes. He was not competent. He showed signs of deep resentment and even alarm at the slightest hint that he should ever perform a disagreeable task. When, after several years of marriage on the mountain, he began to long for a single life in the city again, Alizarin blew the dust off a powerful spell and Caliban was quiet for years.

"It was perfect," she reported, of the journey on my father's acid. It may have been the weirdest educational product placement ever. "Just enough of that ooey-gooey connection stuff to make it clear that, hey, we're really doing something here; and then we sang "Tiptoe Through the Tulips," as the sun came up over the mountains. It was zany yet profound. That teacup is great," she added.

THERE ARE PEOPLE who grow pot because it is their calling. They might be serious-minded stoners. Many are brilliant geneticists with no respect for academic hierarchies. Quite a few are entrepreneurs, displaying the creativity and independence that fuel innovation. Some of them are sure that pot will save the world.

Alizarin was none of those things. Alizarin was a pot agnostic. She was as indifferent to the miracles of marijuana as an atheist Bible salesman to the Resurrection of Christ. For one thing, she was allergic to it. Because her endocannabinoids stopped short in her adenoids, she was immune to the passions of pot. She wasn't unaware of the fact that the drug war is an actual armed conflict. But when Alizarin got a flyover, she glared at the pilot like he was no more dangerous than a wayward husband, in need of a radical therapy session.

"Pour a little more of that right there," she commanded. She was leaving for Israel soon, and she wanted to make sure the plants got a good dose of fish tar while she was still around to make sure I did it right.

I would find out later that fish tar is controversial in pot growing circles, where a unique strain of geeky redneck connoisseurship has developed in the rigorously amended soil. Some smokers claim they can taste the fish tar in the final product. Furthermore, they insist that this assault on their delicate sensibilities is more than any discerning consumer should ever be forced to endure. There is something imitative about this analytical yet highly subjective savoring of flavor and high, some odor on the breeze wafting into Mendocino from the vineyards of Napa and Sonoma counties.

At Serendipity Organics, the plants got sizzled with a black syrup of liquefied fish bones that had been putrefying in a giant plastic tank all year long, waiting for its chance to unleash the regenerative power of death. There is no pot snob jargon yet for "aftertaste of rotting fish," so until there is, Alizarin will continue dosing her plants with fish tar. She couldn't care less about wannabe oenophile stoners, just as the plane at fifteen hundred feet was beneath her notice.

Not mine. I am quick to catch the implications of ecstatic violence in sleek machines and crisp formations. I was almost fourteen when I came home to the apartment I shared with my father and found a level of mayhem beyond even his particular affection for chaos. Mattresses were slashed, with the glee that follows a long session of patiently sharpening knives. Cupboards were ransacked, dishes methodically shattered. Heavy pieces of furniture had been flung across the room, and books were strewn all over the floor, their pages torn, their spines snapped. A list of confiscated items and a copy of the search warrant attested to the orderliness of the operation. But Alizarin had never been raided. The light plane, with its crew of uniformed savages, was a theoretical outrage to her.

"So, ah, what about that small aircraft that just . . . ?" I splashed a little more of the vicious liquid onto the roots of an innocent plant. I was trying not to behave like someone who expected to re-enact a childhood trauma any second now. Would they shoot the sheep when they came? Set the barn on fire?

"Buzzed us," Alizarin supplied, quickly, the way people do when proper nomenclature is important to them.

She pawed around in the dirt for a few seconds. Then she made a sound of extreme disgust—which made sense, considering the fish in the fish tar had been dead longer than it had been alive.

"They're from out of state," she said contemptuously. "From some Neanderthal province where they still spend thousands of dollars *a day* fucking up a few plants. Do you know there are children dying from abscessed teeth, right here in America? Infant mortality in our nation's capital is worse than it is in some Third World countries. But let's not pay for birth control. Oh, no. That would be un-*Christian*." She seethed, glaring at the rotten sludge like it represented all the corrupt political morals she could think of.

"So what are they doing here, if they're from out of state?" I persisted. "Are they federal?"

"No. They are from out of state," Alizarin repeated. She sounded like she might be getting cross, like a lady in a novel. "They can't bust us here, because California is semi-civilized. But they can send in their goons from Wyoming and Tennessee to pollute *our* air and *our* sound waves . . ."

It was training, I gathered eventually. Mendocino County was a training grounds for out-of-state marijuana eradication programs. The big game hunters couldn't shoot anything on the wildlife preserve, but they could roar around all they wanted, sighting their rifles and learning how to track down their prey. Recently, wildlife biologists have been studying the effects of a predator's presence on prey populations; how the expectation of a rattlesnake informs the movements of a gray squirrel's tail; or how the grazing patterns of the Tule elk adapt when all the wolves are gone.

"So . . . what if they *are* federal?" I persisted.

Gray squirrels twitch their tails constantly when they believe a rattlesnake is in the area. Scientists hypothesized that it might be a nervous tic, a squirrel version of post-traumatic stress from multiple brushes with death. But then videos with hundreds of frames a second showed that frequent tail-twitchers are far more likely to evade a rattler's strike than those with a more laid-back approach to things.

Alizarin flicked a chunk of something not quite liquefied out of the stew that was gurgling into the ground. If zombies didn't eat brains, I thought, this is definitely what they *would* eat. She shrugged.

"Then they're federal," she explained.

"Which means they can bust us," I finished, surging to the head of the class on a wave of inspired thought.

"Well, yeah." She looked at me like I'd just proven conclusively that fish tar stinks.

It wouldn't be exactly accurate to say that I was disappointed to be overlooked this way; noticed, then ignored, by a representative of all institutional violence. But it's a peculiar kind of suspense, to be tallied by some brazen, anonymous authority. It gives you an inkling of why some people believe being photographed is hazardous to the health of their souls.

Something intangible had been taken from us when that aircraft cruised across the sky above us; something that could now be used by someone whose purpose was hostile to our own. I understood that we hadn't been harmed, exactly, but we could be, at the leisure of that hostile purpose. It's the kind of awareness that can make a gray squirrel either twitch its tail to the exclusion of all else, or give up twitching altogether.

Alizarin's home was not inconspicuous. It was perched on top of a steep, alignment-wrecking hill that did not quite qualify as a mountain, nestled in between a couple of imposing formations that did. It could very well have been invisible. But Alizarin had painted it bright Ukrainian Revolution orange—just in case any rookie pilots looking for a pot farm needed a point of reference. I could imagine their dispatcher, directing them to fly east from the house that looked like a giant flotation device, with green trim and purple doors.

There was a theory at work here. I never did figure out exactly what it was, but I think it had something to do with theater, with sleight of hand, with chutzpah and daring and charm. After all, pot is magic; and what is magic if not the discipline of diverting attention?

Alizarin planted tomatillos in the doorway of the greenhouse, and their foliage poured into the sun. They were eye-catching, but you can't hide a family of pot plants behind a few vines with cheerful yellow flowers on them. Alizarin's pot plants were so exuberant, they were practically turning cartwheels in the driveway. Great waves of resiny scent gushed into the yard, as relentless as the smell of the ocean—if the ocean were contained in a tiny plastic shed and placed directly in the summer sun.

Compared to the greenhouse just a few feet from the front gate, the open-air patch was almost discreet.

"I'm hedging my bets," Alizarin punned, indicating the natural privacy hedge of coyote weed and manzanita.

I read somewhere that people who pun are incapable of murder; but the route to the garden was pretty unsafe. No European worker would ever tolerate conditions like that, unless it was within the context of an educational travel experience.

I should point out here that anyone who starts growing pot to make an easy living would be better off tending an irrigation ditch in small-town Mendocino County. The next time someone starts complaining about how pot growers sit around all day watching their investments grow, hand him a shovel. Pot is a crop. Crop cultivation is agriculture, which is a fancy word for work. Lots of work. And growing pot is a serious workout.

Alizarin and I slithered down a steep hillside, our path lubricated by a dense growth of shining poison oak. If we started moving too fast, we could always grab onto one of the slippery Manzanita branches, which extended helpfully into the path at about face level. This must be how all these leather-skinned pot growers stay so slim, I thought, panting.

Next, we struggled through a waist-trimming section of chicken wire, tied to a branch with a length of orange baling twine. There was something almost superstitious about the level of slapdashery to the arrangements here. It looked like someone really believed that the malicious spirit of federal law enforcement would look at this chicken wire baling twine mélange of an enclosure and say, *oh. This can't possibly be a criminal operation. It's much too slapdash. Let's go someplace where people have fences and dogs. All we got here is a bunch of big tomatillos.*

"These are my outdoor girls." Alizarin indicated a small orchard of quivering plants, their limbs outstretched like a distressing number of hands with too many fingers. Out here, in the semi-wild, they had a more serious look than their greenhouse sisters, less like pampered courtesans and more like rugged backwoods prophets. If they were humans, their cheeks would be sunken, their eyes a little crazed. We doused their dirt with fish tar, too.

NOW THAT I knew how to look at color like I was insane, the next lesson was learning how to look at shapes like I was colorblind.

"Everything is just a series of shapes," Alizarin assured me. "Like a jigsaw puzzle."

To illustrate the truth of this maxim, she introduced me to Enid, a lady who looked very much like she had been a garden ornament in her younger more beautiful days. Enid lounged nakedly in permanent contentment, like a nymph at the edge of whatever fountain she'd lost. Her plaster curls were piled high atop her plaster head. She could have been a Gilded Age goddess, pondering *Die Neue Sachlichkeit* as she faded into obscurity.

Alizarin slathered a canvas with burnt sienna pigment, made almost liquid with odorless mineral spirits. Burnt sienna is a color that does not quite occur in nature, but is the base note of any number of skin, earth, and wood tones. It is warm and touchable and living, with just enough fire to make you sit up and pay attention. Thinned to a watery consistency, it softens the screaming bright white of a fresh canvas. Its fleshy glow leaches into the colors that are layered on top, making them look as if they know what it feels like to hold their breath and listen to their hearts.

Alizarin used odorless mineral spirits instead of turpentine to clean her brushes and thin her paints, which was a relief, because turpentine, in addition to being highly toxic, always makes me think about ringworm. When I went to live with my grandmother, I had a variety of fungal and parasitic infections, which she treated with honey—to acclimate my system to its new surroundings and strengthen my immune response—and turpentine, which originally comes from pine trees and which, she reasoned, is therefore good for you. It's not the most exalted possible association for a budding artist, even one who is currently standing around making pictures of a naked plaster cast.

"You could *drink* this, and it wouldn't hurt you," Alizarin remarked.

She stirred the mineral spirits enthusiastically with her brush, as if she were creating a wholesome concoction that would give her the energy she needed to be plucky and successful. But those solvents could have triggered memories of every childhood fungal outbreak I had ever had. They could have promised every kind of cancer and brain damage and organ failure there is. I could feel my focus narrowing, the way it did when I was all alone again, learning how to talk. I didn't care how much it hurt. I wanted it, now.

Speaking German rearranged my thinking. It made me soften my throat, then called on muscles in my tongue I'd never used. It made me greedy for the day when I could jingle phrases carelessly, like people who scatter handfuls of coins because they have so many paper bills. I longed for the day when I would be skilled enough to say one thing and mean another; when I'd be good enough to spot the truth in a joke or a lie.

I never got that good; though I did develop some skill at eavesdropping, which is harder than it sounds. Eventually, I could even talk to people on the phone—provided the reception was perfect and they were neither very old nor very young, and they spoke only in High German, at a moderate pace, using grammatical but not overly complex sentence structures. If they managed to refrain from talking about numbers or giving directions, I could make it through an entire conversation without feeling like I had just had a stroke. My failure to establish myself at the lowest level of the German academic hierarchy was the worst humiliation I had ever experienced, for the simple reason that I had never tried anything particularly difficult before. I didn't know how to approach a challenge methodically, first by adjusting the way I looked at it and then by putting it together, one piece at a time, in relation to the pieces next to it.

But there was Enid, a series of shapes; and there was the teacup, with its riot of shadows. There was an alphabet in all those tubes of color; a grammar in the canvas and the brushes. There were inflections in the mediums that could be used to change the consistency of paint and make the brushstrokes watery or muscular, or so soft and pliant not a trace of the brush could be seen.

I could paint a mud pie if I wanted to. But if I rested a brush in the crook of my thumb—right there, where it jutted away from the paw and made it the hand of a human with something to say—then, I could tell a story. With a touch of green in the curve of a hip, I could make a thesis on the quality of light. With the angle of a brushstroke at a few key points, an assortment of facial features could become a character with a full range of emotion. It was as seamless and complex as turning a phrase in the language you dream in.

I wanted that. I wanted to try myself in a language where I wouldn't be derided by a cruel professor, lectured by a pedantic prostitute, or constantly remembering a husband I would always think of as The John. I wanted a language that couldn't be spoken, one that went deeper than words. I was ready to try again.

"Are you paying attention?" Alizarin asked sharply. She held a hard-bristled brush in her hand. "I'm talking about shapes. Do you see the *shapes* on our friend Enid here?" Enid was ignoring us as she contemplated the depths of her missing pool. "I don't mean the paint stains, or whatever the hell that is. Just pretend she has a rash or something. But you can see the shapes, right? The light and shadow shapes? See how you can tell one butt cheek is further away by how much darker it is?" She clacked the handle of her paintbrush on Enid's far butt cheek, which was mottled by paint stains or mold. "Of course, it's smaller, too, but that's perspective. We'll do perspective later. For now, just put the pieces together." She set the brush down, like she was in a hurry to get rid of it.

"I'd better go take some Hyland's," she said abruptly. "I think I'm getting poison oak."

Alizarin wore sandals, even in the garden, and her toenails looked like she'd been using them to claw her way out of a gravel mine. Contributing to this effect, the blue-veined skin on the tops of her feet was starting to display a garish rash. She left me alone in the studio, walking like she wished she didn't have to use her feet to do it.

I was alone. The drapes hung down across the windows, as motionless as if they might be waiting for the danger of the day to pass. There was no place cool in all the world just then. The sun poured in around the curtains, illuminating dust motes as they rained into the corners, down upon my scalp, and into the cleft of Enid's plaster ass.

I could smell the sweat of female plants, yearning with desperation powerful as grief. It swelled on the currents of unmoving air. Then, slowly, under its own power, it propelled itself across the valleys and the silted creek beds, over hedges and high wooden fences, in search of the vegetal love that tells us all our stories about who we are and why we die. Further off, in shadow, I could hear the clatter of a chopper, moving fast. There was urgency in that sound, a perception of terrible need. It sounded like the grinding of a hundred thousand teeth; of dumb erections bumping blindly in the dark; of searches for phantom seraglios and mountains of data that don't make any sense.

I picked up my brush and began.

THE ADULT BUTTERFLY has one task only, which is the creation of more butterflies. Each of these winged insects is a meditation on impermanence, as fragile as a watercolor on tissue paper. Some species don't even bother developing mouth parts or a digestive apparatus, as if processing food were too base an activity for beings whose one great purpose in life is the creation of more ephemeral beauty.

Other butterflies do eat, but should not under any circumstances be eaten themselves. Their participation in the food chain is reluctant, and conditional. For example, the swallowtail butterfly is toxic to predators because in its caterpillar form, it devours several times its body weight in leaves from the Dutchman's pipe, a member of the birthwort family of plants. The mottled red and white flower of this hardy vine is large and curved, with a blaring mouth at one end and a testicular bulb at the other. It looks like a cross between a sea horse and a tuba. The heart-shaped leaves are loaded with alkaloid toxins, just as scarlet oil paint is thick with mercury, those slabs of light, with lead.

When the caterpillar nestles into its cocoon, it digests itself with the enzymes it has made from all the poisonous plant matter it's consumed. This self-cannibalizing approach to puberty activates certain cell sets that were dormant in the larva and allows them to develop into the structures of the adult animal. These cells are called imaginal discs, as if the cellular fantasies of the chomping, heaving, defecating caterpillar envisioned a future where it would be lighter than breath, with sunshine streaming through its watercolor wings.

It shifts the focus on casual lepidoptery, when you know the social butterfly is either starving to death or is a deadly appetizer, desperate to achieve its purpose before it runs out of time. In Germany, where bedtime stories often feature little children being tortured, no one uses the term "social butterfly" to describe a human being with an active social life. It's as if all that enzymatic soup stuff were just a little grim for people reared on *Der Struwwelpeter*, with its whimsical illustrations of juvenile delinquents having their thumbs cut off and falling into wells.

Instead, if you know lots of different kinds of people in Germany, someone will eventually call you a colorful dog. It's endearing, if you happen to be a dog lover.

In the ancient beer-soaked German city, I caroused into the night with French law students, Rumanian pre-meds, Turkish philosophers, and even a few dreamy-eyed Germans. I smoked stinking Gauloises and drank too much Sekt and listened to my unshushed laughter ringing off the cold stone walls of castle masonry. I walked the way of the Philosophers and practiced academic arguments in a tongue that made me feel ancestral, and complex. My stunning humiliation—and my follow-up failure to recover—were as inevitable as Nietzsche and the death of God.

Now, on the mountain, everything went still. I didn't know anyone. There wasn't anyone to know, and nowhere to fall from. I shrank to my original size. I faded to my natural drab coloring. I retreated to my original monolingual thinking. And I began, very quietly, to hallucinate.

It seems very strange that in all that abundance, in the midst of so much offering, I lost all interest in food. Something about the smell of good things cooking caused a terrible sadness to wrap itself around me. I turned my face away from sun-ripened tomatoes and everything they stood for. I was drawing something else from the plants on the mountain, in the two weeks I was alone with them.

When I watered the squash plants in the brief cool sigh of dawn, I saw them breathe with deep relief, as if the short night, with only dust and dew to drink, had been too long. I saw how blue those deep-veined leaves were. I saw purple shadows in the yellow flowers. When I watched the glow of a far-off lamp outlined in equally distant window frames, I wondered how the painter made that light so shiny, made it glow like a lamp in the window of somebody's home. Something silent happened on that mountain, something only monks and outlaw mystics ever think to strive for.

I became acutely aware of exactly how many bites of food were necessary to carry out a certain set of motions. I could feel it, when my hand wanted to put one more cashew than I needed into my mouth. It wasn't a hunger cue, because the hunger quickly became something like a quality of light. It was a constant energy that animated and illuminated, but only as long as the conditions for it were absolutely perfect. The hunger itself was hungry, and I contained it with small pieces of dried fruit; with biscuits and berries and little arrangements of unsalted nuts. The hunger was a fire that I built just hot enough to temper a blade with an edge so sharp it would shatter if it ever struck a bone.

There is a slow-motion brinksmanship to giving up food, because you know things could get very bad. You could burn your house down. You could fall on your sword. But when you are hungry to the point of not being hungry anymore, you begin to think quite explicitly about the luxury of time. Things take so much longer than you ever knew. You have all the time you need to become something—to digest yourself in your own toxic enzymes and emerge as a poisonous beauty.

Alone on the mountain, I had long assignations with Enid and a pair of colored glass containers: a vase, I think, and a globe. I remember staring, for great slabs of time, with a brush in my hand and the rich, heart's-blood heaviness of oil paint hanging in the air. Everything was motionless, and silent. The world throbbed with secret significance.

"YOU WILL NOT," Alizarin cried, with her infallible instinct for entrances, "believe it!"

She dropped her woven testicle-shaped purse onto the counter. It slumped against the coffeemaker in a flaccid jumble of knick-knacks and chap stick and burst-open bottles of sunscreen. She turned to me triumphantly and announced,

"I finally found out what happened to Hannah!" She was extremely alert, the way some people are when they have just traveled at great speeds through multiple time zones.

"You remember Lillian," she went on, then changed her mind immediately. "No, of course not. I keep forgetting what a kid you are. Just like your dad, all that gray hair when he was only twenty-eight years old. Anyway. Lillian. She's calling herself something else now, what *is* it? I just stayed with this woman for three days on the kibbutz, come *on*! My *brain*! I *know* her name is not Lillian anymore, what is the Hebrew name for Lillian? Anyway. My good friend What's-Her-Name. Her stepdaughter's cousin Hannah, in Chicago? She would have been about the age you are now."

She shot me a sharp look, the way people do when they describe the horrible things that happened to someone just like you.

"Hannah started taking lithium, of all the horrible things," she went on, with angry gaiety. "Back in the 80s, when it was supposed to be this miracle drug. It sounds like nuclear waste, doesn't it. *Lithium*. Probably just about as good for you. But she was *so* miserable. She was in this *horrible* program at the whatever Institute of Higher Something or Other. And the expec*ta*tions from her family! Even Lillian! But she'd always been so good in school and then she went to work at this all-night diner and she thought, if she didn't get her degree, she'd be schlepping breakfast at three o'clock in the morning for the rest of her life. Everyone was sure she'd make it, just power through, better living through chemistry, right, and then, *BAM!* Just like that. Right out in front of a garbage truck. People on the sidewalk saw her waiting for it. I don't know why they didn't *do* something. People are always so afraid to interfere."

It was impossible to determine what level of interaction was called for here. I wanted to protest the implication, but I couldn't even be sure she was implying anything.

Her attention fell onto my canvases. "You're having trouble with your backgrounds, I see." She regarded my images of Enid, where the lovely adornment floated in unpainted space. She was languorous and unfashionable, like faded photographs of grandmothers, who always look demure.

But if Enid was an airy creature, dangling in streaks of burnt sienna without a point of reference, I was quite clearly made of clay. I was so dirty, my clothes all looked like they were the same color. I had surrendered to an unhygienic entropy, which has a certain voluptuous, falling-down feel to it, like giving up always does. Getting past the first stages of discomfort is a little like losing your appetite after you've missed several meals—though I will admit it lacks the quality of light, the frisson of burning houses, and shattering blades.

There is a peculiar sense of luxury in the decision to abstain from readily available necessities. It feels like willpower, but really, it's something else. When you begin to yearn for more self-deprivation; for more instances in which you must deny yourself; that is a form of greed. *More!* You whisper to yourself. *More less.* You begin to feel like someone you heard of in a story, a long time ago. *If this were real,* you tell yourself, *I would be one of the ones who lived to tell my tale.*

You begin to wake up very early, so you can go to sleep before you have to turn on the light. And then you work late anyway, in the glow of a lamp that casts a perfect circle of illumination, beyond which sometimes, when you finally remember to look, you think you may see fixed and staring yellow eyes.

"I was saving water," I explained. "For the ladies. For the garden."

AND JUST LIKE that, my two weeks on the mountain were over. I had another piece of something to tuck into my magpie's nest of a life, another shape with edges that might eventually align with something else. I had been collecting these shapes, but in a haphazard way. I was a hoarder, not a collector, because collectors seek out increasingly precise objects to create a coherent body of work, which they then archive in a tasteful and well-organized manner. But I had not even begun to apply the basic lesson about how pictures are a series of interlocking shapes. Even Enid, in her cloud of burnt sienna, had nothing to hold onto, nothing to indicate how large she might be in relation to mountains or mice; how far away she was from the horizon, or what she was doing on someone else's piece of canvas.

I swam in the river on my way back to Foxglove, where I lived my real life, with other human beings. Where I ate things and bathed and came inside when the sunlight dazzled my eyes. Where time faded into the background, like a radio that's always on, though no one ever pays attention to it.

By now, I was as impervious to cleanliness as a tar slick. Even after I dried off on my dirty shirt, I was smeared with oil paint. My fingertips were gloved with pot resin, hardened into crusts by the cold clean currents of the Russian River. I didn't bother trying to scrape it off. My stains were a badge, an indication that finally, I was being honest about who I was and what I did. I was a trimmer, and I was a painter. The signs were there to be seen, by anyone who knew what to look for.

I should mention that pot resin is basically raw hash, which is some of the most concentrated material in the cannabis plant. Smoking pot made me feel like I had the flu or a bad case of existentialism. It made me feel jet-lagged. I didn't like it much. What I did like was the transdermal buzz I got from cleaning pot without gloves. As my body heat slowly warmed the resin that got onto my skin from handling the buds, the active ingredients crept into my bloodstream and made themselves at home. The gradual come-on felt expert and subtle, like the photographic image of brilliant thoughts, slowly taking shape inside my mind. I didn't even feel like I was stoned as I sat there cleaning weed. I thought I might be cultivating a special style of mindfulness. Maybe I was even becoming enlightened.

My confidence receded as I drew closer to Foxglove. I began to find the signs of legal enterprise oppressive. I felt like a hastily prepared spy in the culture wars as I drove through town, past places where people received paychecks to do things they could talk about with anyone; where they lived by municipal codes and worked openly in gardens by the curb.

Foxglove was just beyond the city limits, tucked in between a disused logging road and a creek with shining stones. Trees with great mazes of exposed roots bent gracefully over the water, where steelhead trout flashed in the sun for several glistening moments a year. I parked my nearly crippled truck in the circular drive. It looked rude there, like it belonged to someone who lacked the common courtesy to show up in a decent vehicle. I grabbed my grubby bag and started down the flagstone path between two hedges of silvery lavender. Everything was hard and bright. I felt like I should have been wearing shoes from somewhere else to make the proper sound on those stones.

The windows at Foxglove made me think about light, how light could be cool as a corpse or hot as a murderous rage. Alizarin used the phrase "slab of light" when she showed me how to lay in clumps of high-calorie Titanium white, so creamy they made a person want to lick the canvas they'd been slathered on. "Slab of light," I whispered, moving toward the door. It sounded like the twist of fat on a marble statue's waist; like vistas of cleanliness or gravestones in the dappled sun. I opened the door and stepped into the slab of golden light, glowing Christmas-like upon the shining stones.

And then I felt it.

It rose with the cool air that swirled up from the marble floor. It wasn't fog or fainting spells or crackles in the sky. But those were its prototypes. It didn't have the savage joy of physical harm, the happiness of appetite. It was a wave of pure feeling that belonged to no one and everyone, the way the ocean belongs to every shoreline and none at all. It was everything a grimy little small-time criminal like me could expect from a fine upstanding pillar of the community. There I was, standing in his doorway on the floor he'd laid himself, basking in the light of the lamps he'd paid for. Me, with my artistic aspirations and my eating disorder, reeking of weakness, broadcasting ruin.

Reina always talked about her husband's presence; how Zack could fill a room, command attention, bully and charm and outwit any adversary. In the first year that I lived there, Foxglove was a memorial to Zachary Hill, M.D., Chief of Staff at the hospital and President of several boards. His photos gathered dust on the mantle, the bar, and a good portion of the wall space. The bookshelves were full of titles that breathed the dead man's politics and sense of humor, just as the bottles we opened released the fumes of his preferred intoxicants. I'd never even heard his voice, and I could recite dozens of stories about his cleverness, his power, his bold transgressions, and his acts of generosity. The rage that met me at the door was all those things, released from the confines of a body or a personality. And just as falling water in the ocean forces troughs into waves, all the things that Zack Hill used to be was rising into a silent crest. It was just for me, like a tiny localized expression of a continental shift.

"Zack?" I said out loud. I felt extremely stupid. "Is that you," I said to the presence, the way Caitlin asks a question when she knows the answer, without raising the inflection at the end. "Are you here, Zack?" I called out now. I sent my voice across the marble floor like I was standing somewhere classical and haunted, throwing down a challenge to the knights of days gone by.

The presence—I will not call it a ghost. I do not believe in ghosts—the presence, then, suspended its fury. This was a blatant violation of the laws of physics, because a wave that has risen by the force of its own matter slamming hard against the ocean floor is required to crash back down again. It's gravity. It's orbital motion, the waves bouncing off of solid ground and rolling toward the land and then back out to sea again. It is a rude interruption for it to simply stop happening.

"Do you know what, Zack," I told it quietly. "I'm here, too." The presence faded, like a photographic image that struggles to be seen but in the end is overexposed and fades to light.

I became aware of the shapes of my feet, bearing into the cold stone floor through my battered shoes. My weight became a solid thing, pouring into my bones. I could feel my own enzymes coursing through me, fed by all those colors, all those stories, all those mounds of neatly manicured lavender.

I took a long, hot bath that night. I washed my clothes and folded them carefully. Then I sat down at the walnut bar, alone, and selected a large sharp blade from the collection of Kasumi knives the surgeon had left his wife. Kasumi knives are made in Seki, a city known for the quality of its Samurai swords. I favor a seven-inch Santoku, with a deeply dropped point and a laminated wood handle. The action is decisive, the movements light.

I arranged all the sun-ripened tomatoes Alizarin had given me on a vast wooden platter. Their skins sighed open underneath that sweet Santoku blade like they'd been waiting for this moment all their lives. They glistened where they lay, a row of little hearts, winking in the slab of light that poured onto the lawn. I was very, very hungry.

ROCKABILLY CARCASS

THE MOMENTUM OF the growing season gathered toward harvest. Most people cut down their pot in stages, amputating branches only as the buds reach absolute perfection. This serves the dual purposes of turning out a high-quality product and minimizing the loss of an uninsured commodity in the event of a well-timed burglary. But sometimes, in a crop-punishing rain, a grower will cut down all the plants at the same time. Then the harvesters, embraced with sticky branches, look like the armies of MacDuff, trudging with the forest to a perilous encounter, where questions will be answered and heads might roll.

In early fall, growers crouch over their plants as anxiously as first-time fathers monitoring the signs of impending delivery. "These hairs . . ." they'll mutter, scrutinizing the crinkly auburn threads that look like tiny pubic hairs on the fruits of the cannabis plant. "Are these looking *red* to you?" they murmur somberly. "Yeah, but the *crystals* . . ." At this point, the discussion turns so technical, so mixed with quasi-spiritual theory, you begin to suspect that you might be witnessing the development of some new pseudo-scientific doctrine.

There is a specific fervor that comes over people when they talk about growing pot. In *Naked Lunch*, Burroughs writes about pushers who don't use heroin but get off on watching their clients shoot up. To the catalogue of complex second-hand highs, let's add growers who don't smoke but are high on the alchemy of growing, on the outlaw thrill of it. It takes a unique psychological metabolism to grow pot, one that runs on adrenaline but is patient as the seasons. Growers must be capable of soaking up vast tracts of non-narrative information about soil composition and ever-changing legal statutes. It's a cerebral, labor-intensive method of achieving a state of primal enthusiasm. Essentially, it's a slow-motion thrill-seeker's way to make a living.

There are plenty of drawbacks, aside from the obvious risks of prison time, asset forfeiture, and the lack of a small claims court if your business associates behave improperly with you. At this time, you can pay an as-yet poorly regulated lab to tell you that your bud is black with mold from some disease that only affects your pot plants and a few dozen sycamore trees in New England. The Board of Equalization is ready to collect taxes from you. A set of laws that sounds like a horrible bacterial infection is on its way to decriminalizing the entire medical marijuana industry. But years of paranoia and superstition have created a culture of farmers who place their faith in macho outlaw axioms, old wives' tales, and untested chemical compounds. In magic formulas, to put it bluntly.

The best dispensaries are run according to complex algorithms and shrewd market research. The temperature of the political body is taken by people with PhDs in economics, polling, and statistics. But growing pot still has an elf-spotting quality to it. In the absence of meticulous records, there is a reliance on intuition and rumor that borders on faith in an unseen god. No one wants the big-city buyers to find out that sycamore mold is floating around in the local microclimate. So the one or two growers who go to the lab are viewed as a disruptive influence on the fine tradition of making up a new solution every year, based on very little scientific information and even fewer reliable resources.

Alizarin was not an unqualified exception. But there was no room for mystic maybes in the magic practiced at Serendipity. Alizarin was unsentimental. That was what I liked about her operation. It was attractive because it defied convention in a way that felt like coming home; but also, it had an air of legitimacy to it, like something based in a well-established system of procedure and etiquette.

Alizarin grew Chocolate Thai and Golden Buddha, Bubba Kush and her own Serendipity Blend, a cross from a plant that had gotten fertilized by an unknown male.

"Someone not keeping an eye on things," she grumbled darkly.

It was a serious breach of protocol, the kind that can ruin an uninsured black-market farmer. A fertilized plant has seeds in it, a condition that causes a swooning horror in modern pot consumers. Normal plant parts, apparently, are highly detrimental to the healing qualities of a plant that is destined to be transformed into carcinogenic smoke.

But people are always developing new strains or improving old ones, which does call for the regrettable presence of seed. If a breeder fails to contain the producers of pollen, the plants are liable to explode with all the imprecipitate timing of frustrated young male lust everywhere. The most significant difference in premature ejaculation between the animal and vegetable kingdoms is that pollen can travel for miles, even on a summer day with no wind. Instead of one coy mistress, the triumphant male pot plant overcomes the resolve of every untouched female in the neighborhood. This is ruinous because, like an imperfect hymen in a savage country, the bud with a seed tucked into its folds is summarily rejected, unworthy even of burning.

"We always smoked seedy pot in the '70s," Morpheus remarked, as Alizarin and I hung weed from the rafters in the cellar. He was supposed to be fixing the fan, but his powers of analysis shone most brightly when he was probing the emotional life of a fictional character. Immediately, as if we were in a rockabilly musical, the two of them broke into song. The same song, at the same time. "Sittin' alone on a Saturday night," they twanged happily. They rushed a little through the first verse before giving full throat to the chorus, in perfect unison: "And I'm down to stems and seeds again, too!"

"Now *that* is an iconic tune," Morpheus declared, when they'd harmonized their way through all five verses. "That is what it *meant* to be a starving young artist in the '70s!"

"But the last verse," Alizarin protested. "Nobody who was a starving young artist in the '70s got their house repossessed. We didn't even have houses! That's a dejected middle-aged redneck song." And she hung a particularly phallic-looking cola on the line with the firmness of a woman possessed of good sense and a fine argumentative faculty.

"Kirchen's still married to his first wife. Bet you anything they have a house. And if he's not legit, I don't know who is." Morpheus was the kind of appreciative listener who reads all the songwriter bios. "And I'm just talking about the chorus, about being young and poor. In the '70s."

"Why don't you run into the house and grab your guitar, Harness," Alizarin suggested.

It was plain to see that Morpheus, defeated on the question of analysis, was preparing to retreat into his vast knowledge of music and musicians. He could base his interpretation on a subtle chord change or a biographical detail, and Alizarin would have no way of verifying her suspicion that he'd made it up.

"If you're not going to hang weed or fix the fan," she scowled, bringing the discourse back to the realm of practical housekeeping, "you could at least entertain us."

"Raining outside," he countered.

The "cellar" was really just a small cave under the house on the downhill side, so there was no way to get indoors without first going outdoors. He ran his long-nailed guitar-playing fingers over the titles in a small bookcase tucked into a corner of the pot cave. Spiders and earwigs scattered before his perusal, bringing a certain inclusiveness to the term *dank*.

"How about poetry?" he suggested, by way of compromise. He pulled a pair of moldering volumes from a worm-eaten shelf, which shifted and sighed before lapsing into silence again.

"We've got," he peered at the spine, then opened to the title page when the effaced cover failed to provide a clue, "the Oxford Book of English Verse."

He produced a comical grimace of impressed amusement, as if he were unaccustomed to the trappings of a well-read life. I was never sure if he was mocking the poorly educated when he did this or taking a stand with what he perceived to be the working class. I do know that his grammar was less than perfect; that he was known to use the phrase, *hoity-toity* with infinite disdain; and that he took a particular delight in announcing, "I'm going to go lay down," when he was about to take a nap.

Every single time he did that, Alizarin would launch into a furious explanation of the past and present tenses of the verbs "to lie" and "to lay." She managed the exact same level of frantic enthusiasm, each and every time. "It's just because you're doing it around all those kids," she'd finish desperately, as if he were indoctrinating them with principles of Fascist thought while chain-smoking and drilling for oil in a pristine wilderness.

Morpheus was peering at the other volume now. "You'll love this," he declared. *"Fleurs du Mal."* There was no comic acknowledgement of the fact that, aside from people living in certain regions of Continental Europe, only former French colonials, nineteenth-century Russian nobles, and the uselessly overeducated speak French.

"Something in English, please." Aside from a few phrases in Yiddish and a handful of Hebrew prayers, Alizarin was monolingual.

"Oder vielleicht ein bisschen Deutsch," I suggested, just to remind everyone that I was there, too. I hung a puny cola on the line, careful not to snap its stem.

Morpheus thumbed through the pages of the first volume, indifferently enough that it could have been his own idea. "The phrase, 'conversion of the Jews' has caught my eye," he announced at length. He glared sternly at us, as if he knew we'd come to class unprepared. "Any takers?" he inquired pleasantly. "Any *literary* people out there?"

I felt as if I were being drafted to bear witness to something. I hadn't decided if I was embarrassed or fascinated, but I could tell by the drop in atmospheric pressure that there would be a fight before the next rain.

"Andrew Marvell," Morpheus relented at last. "Sixteen twenty-one to sixteen seventy-eight. 'To His Coy Mistress.'" He squinted at the page for a long time. "Did you know he worked in Cromwell's government? When he wasn't contemplating the nuances of the human heart?"

"Did *you* know that, ten seconds ago?" Alizarin responded tartly. This was a long way from the Americana guitar serenade she'd been hoping for.

"And his housekeeper posed as his wife," Morpheus continued serenely, as if it were his policy not to encourage the class clown. *"Supposedly* to keep his business partner's creditors away from his small estate. Sounds like the slightly more respectable version, to me." He was very happy now. Marvell had joined Kirchner in the pantheon of artists he knew.

"Had we but world enough, and time," he began at last. He sounded like a first-rate rogue. By the time he finished enumerating the superpowers that would accrue to the beauty who seized the day, Alizarin was flushed and smiling.

"Should she sleep with him?" she asked, rhetorically, I'm sure, since we all knew the wages of male genius.

Morpheus exploded. "If she has *any* sense of decency!" he cried, smacking the unfortunate shelf with the even less fortunate edition of the Oxford. "She'll be humping his leg by the second stanza!" He shook the ragged volume like it was a pamphlet on how to change the world. "Any sense of decency at all!" he growled, and abandoned Andrew Marvell as if the dead man had done him a personal injury. "Now we're going to hear something good," he proclaimed. It sounded very much like a threat. "Enough of this sappy stuff."

He seized the Baudelaire. The spine flopped open of its own accord. "'*Une Charogne*,'" he declared, like he might really be an MC. "A Carcass." And he read us a poem in French, his voice dripping with sweet malevolence. "There's a romantic little trifle for you." He stalked out into the rain. Moments later, we heard him playing the guitar. It sounded like outlaw rockabilly. Alizarin sighed.

FALL IS THE most stressful time of year in Mendocino County. In mid-fall, I came upon a fragrant mound of uprooted pot plants, the little white fibers of their root systems plump and juicy in the weak September sun. All their limbs had been hacked off and placed in another neatly mounded pile about two yards away. I never found out whose pot it was, or who had savaged it so methodically. People used to alleviate this level of tension by burning a few witches at the stake. But what do you do when the witch hunts are over and the hills are full of dope-growing Wiccans?

You throw things at your husband. Your shingles flare up and you take too many painkillers and you work through the fog and you make a lot of mistakes. In the last few weeks before the rains begin, there is an exponential increase in cold sores and rashes and domestic disputes. Hardly anyone gets shot until after the trimming is done, when a few trimmers return to the scene of the crime to rob the grower, who shoots them.

Actually, that last scenario may have played out once or twice in the last forty years. But there are so many versions of the same story, everyone believes it's a standard occupational hazard. Even the trimmers think it's true, and each trimmer believes that he or she is a shining paragon of virtue for the lack of larceny in his or her stoned little heart.

In the fall, I walked into Alizarin's kitchen and noticed a great splat of something that looked like vomit on the refrigerator door.

"Someone not feeling too good?" I asked, as I rummaged for the grapeseed oil. Alizarin ran a strictly organic grow and believed that cleaning the scissors with alcohol would compromise the certification for which she planned to be first in line when marijuana was legalized.

"That's Baba Ghanoush," she corrected, taking a swipe at the vomity substance with a soggy rag.

The Baba Ghanoush had been liberally applied to a picture of Morpheus, who grimaced as a black and white collie mix nuzzled his sideburns. It looked like the image in the photograph was wincing as the semi-liquid food mass hit its face.

"I threw it at my fucking wonderful husband," she elaborated, with what appeared to be great satisfaction. "M.C. Harness himself."

I noticed she was carefully cleaning the area around the picture, but not the image itself. She seemed pleased with what the Baba Ghanoush had done for the composition. I was starting to experience something like envy for the passionate dysfunction of this marriage. Being married to The John had been so boring, both of us simmering with silent resentment. Would I be happier now if I'd thrown things and shouted? What if I had been able to muster up the ability to give a shit about Karen?

"I just don't understand what's going on with that guy sometimes," Alizarin fumed. She wrung a khaki-colored dribble of organic matter into the sink, then corrected herself. "It's his fucking ex. She let him get away with anything. I don't know how she could do it. She had a *job*! She used to be a damned good singer but then she got depressed and started taking some horrible medication for it. She gained a lot of weight and stopped caring about things. She just sort of flatlined. But! She kept picking up after him! She never made him *do* anything!"

I found the grapeseed oil and poured a few inches into a half-pint canning jar. I polished the blades of my Fiskars, which is the preferred weapon of choice in the trimming trade.

"I have *told* that asshole." She was seething now. "I have told him over and over again. But he doesn't even wear his hearing aids around me. He says they hurt his ears. They're *inconvenient*. But I have caught him wearing them at rehearsal. *That's* important. Just not what I have to say. And what I have to say is: the containers go under here." She indicated the cupboard where the Tupperware containers went—mostly to die, because they were crammed in so chaotically, no one ever bothered to use them. "And the lids go in here," she continued, with what was left of her fury. What was left, if it had been agricultural surplus, could have kept a few small villages going on modest rations for a year or two.

"He *says* Scott did it," she went on, as if she'd gotten to the bottom of a nefarious intrigue and was boldly bringing her findings to press.

Scott was another trimmer, the satori-prone middle son of a dermatologist and an engineering professor. He had rashes and eczema and obsessive-compulsive disorder and one day, without a word of explanation, he had set out on foot from Orange County and walked to Mendocino. In the spring, he'd refused to cut down the male plants, reasoning that he himself was male and if he deserved a shot at self-determination, so did they. He had the skulking posture of a dog that's just killed a chicken, and when he talked, his lower jaw moved up and down like a ventriloquist dummy's. Scott had removed all the lids from the lid drawer and all the containers from the cupboard. He had cleaned out the spiders and mouse droppings, and then paired up the lids with the matching containers. It was deeply satisfying for him to bring order to things.

"I'm sure he didn't do that on his own recognizance," Alizarin insisted. "Harness made a unilateral decision while I was at Beth's, and he deployed this *kid* to *fuck up my system*. And now he's trying to blame it all on a trimmer! As if I'd fall for that!" It was humiliating to reflect that if I were to be used as a proxy in the Goldfarb-Charnisse hostilities, the attempt would be derided on account of my insignificance.

"They don't come out of the dishwasher together, do they?" She wrenched the lid from a container, to demonstrate how nature had created things separate and distinct from one another. "And they don't go back together, either!"

With the fury of a woman righting one of the great wrongs of her time, she restored the lidless Tupperware to its cupboard and the lid to its drawer.

"He just doesn't have the patience to take a few minutes to find the right lid," she complained, as aggrieved as if he'd refused the peace terms of a civilized nation, on the grounds of a backward ideology.

"Maybe Wifey Number One had time to make sure the right lids went on the right containers before she put them all away in her spotless cupboards," Alizarin retorted, though nobody had said a thing.

Nobody was me these days, since Scott, shortly after his deployment in the Tupperware wars, had resolved to change the world through education. His parents sent him enough money to come home "like a civilized person," his mother told Alizarin, with a light embarrassed laugh at the foibles of her wayward son.

"I don't have the fucking time to be his mommy," Alizarin hissed, still ripping the heads off Tupperware and slapping them into the drawer. "His mother did everything for him, too. Do you know she made his clothes for him? She was sending him shirts she made by hand when he was *thirty-seven years old!*"

It was true. Stella Charnisse had a secret source for fabric in patterns of fanciful fish, photogenic predators, and flowers in colors that do not occur in nature. She also had a great disdain for buttons, which is why she sewed a single strip of Velcro right down the middle of her shirts, where a seamstress more easily intimidated by convention might have wasted time on buttons and buttonholes. Morpheus loved to rip open his mother's shirts, goggling his eyes like a maniac and grinning with unself-conscious joy as he exposed his startled chest hairs to static shock and sudden sun.

"Never laid down the law." She was working to a cadence now. "Never had the time to make *him* do the dishes. Oh, no. But there's unlimited time to do it yourself!" She scanned her sector with quick raptor-like movements of her head, seeking out any stray Tupperware that had been capped without prior authorization.

There was no sense of proportion to Alizarin's will. She had the exact same level of fury for the Tupperware as she did for the brutal triviality of the drug war. Every brushstroke was exactly as important as the rest. If the Tupperware drawer had been reorganized without her sanction, it was only a matter of time before the trimmers were getting stoned in her studio; before the Arts Council was walking all over her; before her vision dimmed into a placid thing and she was making watercolors of housecats and roses.

I remembered a story my father told me about a bear trainer, from his days in the circus. A few minutes before the end of every act, the clowns would gather in a chute behind the tent, so they could give the crowd a few laughs as performers struggled into costumes and roadies set the stage.

One night, as on every other night, the band began to play. The music tripped along, drawing closer and closer to the part that cued the clowns. It built momentum, sped toward the climax—then stopped and started building up again. The people didn't notice. They were looking at the bears. There is nothing like a couple of large carnivores in pink and yellow tutus to hold a crowd's attention. But in the chute, the clowns were getting restive. Someone passed a rumor that the bears had refused to do their next trick.

"Just let it go," the clowns began to murmur.

"But this was her life," my father told me, bringing the force of it up from his guts. He had been modulating his voice since well before I was born. "This was her heart, this was her soul. She would stand there all night long until they did that trick. She didn't care how many clowns were waiting in the chute. She didn't care if every single person in that audience went home. She didn't care if we took down that tent and left the country. The show was not going on until that bear balanced a ball on his nose exactly the way she told him how to do it." I have often believed that my father's favorite fact about human nature is the one about how people love to be just a little bit scared. And sometimes I wonder if Alizarin ever dabbled in bears.

I asked if the bears in their pastel tutus ever did the trick. "Oh, yes." My father smiled. "That was a long time ago."

MORE ON BEARS AND BUTTERFLIES

I THOUGHT I knew shamanic natures, with their sober reverence for Dionysian revelry. But Caitlin with her many names was no preparation for the husband of her former rival. Morpheus was not inclined to map the byways of his thinking. His thoughts would crop up suddenly, like unexpected landmarks in a flat terrain, reminding the traveler that something far beneath the surface churned, forcing up oddly-shaped formations.

He would passionately espouse some creed that was completely at odds with the last opinion he'd held, and which bore even less resemblance to the one he'd hold next. He knew more about the pacifist philosophy of Thich Nhat Hahn than anyone I'd ever met. But he'd be moved to poetry and song by some aspiring tyrant waging brutal revolution in the foreground of a far-off landscape. And, Jew though he was, he mourned the end of the Catholic Latin liturgy. "It gave the whole thing a sense of *mystery*." He sighed, dubious about the likelihood of revelation in whatever coarse vernacular the peasants used to curse the dog.

He was not a philosopher. But he could have been a courtier in a philosopher king's court. He would have been the deeply tragic comic foil of a stern protagonist. He was so often lost in the contemplation of symbols and dreams. He seemed like he was always waiting for a call from some fascinating force that would take possession of his mind and deposit insights there. It gave him an abstracted air of helplessness and profound concentration; of protecting his purity from vulgar worldly concerns. Of course, no one personified these worldly concerns more than his ball-busting wife.

Alizarin had a theory about the term ball-buster. She said it was a corruption of *Balabusta*, the Yiddish word for a virtuous, hardworking housewife. The *Balabusta* is not idealized as a silent drudge, like her suffering counterpart among the goyim. She would never stand for it. In traditional Jewish society, Alizarin explained, the men devote themselves to Talmudic abstractions, while women contend with the world. "That's the ideal," she emphasized. "In real life, well. Who has time for Talmudic abstractions?" And she shot a glare at Morpheus, who had been sussing out a single chord change for the last half hour.

Whatever it was the men were doing, she went on, the women were being effective: that is, being good *Balabustas*. They haggled with merchants. They kept a careful eye on the help. They had opinions and convictions and they always knew their worth. In America, the respectable *Balabusta* was corrupted to a term that old-fashioned feminists hate to love, though there may be a few in the ironic younger set who love to love it. Whatever the etymology, Alizarin was a muralizing, dope-growing *Balabusta* of the first degree.

"Hey, M.C.," she said jovially. There was just a hint of nervous warning in her voice. "I'm gonna need to you water the greenhouse for me." Morpheus stared uncomprehendingly. "You know, the tomatoes, the tomatillos . . . the pot? That thing that makes it possible for us to live out here in the hills where you can play the same chord for two hours without driving any neighbors crazy?" She was sounding less jovial by the syllable.

"What do tomatillos look like?" Morpheus inquired. He might have been having a dream about putting a question to the Sphinx.

"Oh, for fuck's sake, Charnisse!" Alizarin burst out. "I grow tomatillos every year! They're plants. With tomatillos on them. You know, they're round, they're green . . ."

Morpheus continued to stare at her, as if he were struggling to comprehend the truth behind the arbitrary symbolism of speech.

"Isobel," she appealed in exasperation. "Could you show Charnisse how to water the greenhouse? Just once, and he should get it." She made a laryngitic gasping noise that could have been laughter.

Morpheus followed me uncertainly, then dangled in the greenhouse doorway watching, like he thought I might be trying to trap him.

"It's not that hard." I smiled sympathetically. "The pot plants get a gallon each, and you just give the others a good drink. You don't even have to know what they are."

He moved cautiously into the greenhouse. He was wearing a broad-brimmed straw hat and a T-shirt with a picture of a mountain lion on it.

"She mentioned something . . . round and green," he murmured. "Do you have any idea what she was talking about?"

"Oh, those are the fruits of the tomatillo plant," I explained. "They're in the same family as tomatoes. But they're built differently." I compared a lacy tomatillo limb to a muscular tomato vine.

But Morpheus had found something truly enchanting: a small pillowy monster with eight soft loveable legs and a row of false eyes along its rounded length. An orange horn emerged timidly from its posterior, like the weapon on a child's plush toy dinosaur. Half a dozen armlike appendages opened and closed, like it wanted nothing more than three hugs at once.

"What is it?" he breathed, like I was the one who had lived here for years. With ineffable gentleness, he took the creature on one finger and lifted it to his bristling eyebrows, like an ageing satyr still capable of wonder.

Alizarin did not hesitate to denounce the ravenous beauty. "That is a tomato hornworm. It will eat everything in here in a day. Throw it outside. The birds will love it." She clapped her hands, like she was trying to encourage a reluctant performer to come onstage.

"I . . . don't . . . know . . ." He seemed to have found himself in circumstances that were not what they appeared to be. "I think I'd better put it outside," he concluded, after careful deliberation.

"Good idea, Charnisse." The plants in the greenhouse were not yet wilting.

"Where the birds can't get it," he temporized. "I'm not sure that would be the kindest thing to do to this little guy. He's a caterpillar?"

"He *or she* will turn into a hawkmoth. And then he *or she* will just fly around producing more hornworms. Put it somewhere far away from the garden, please." Alizarin gave the larva on her husband's finger a steady-eyed murdering stare. It curled its six little white-gloved mandibles under its chin and looked at her sideways with one row of false eyes.

"Let's find the perfect spot for this bright jewel of a being," Morpheus suggested.

I trotted along. The hornworm marched across his knuckles, officious and absurd as a tiny neon-green couch. It dangled for a moment from the end of a fingernail, then dropped with a multiply flat-footed flop in the palm of his string-picking hand. It *was* a bright being, green as poison, shining with excellent health.

"What do you think this little guy is?" He peered down at it, twinkling with chlorophyll and flexing its jaws.

"I think she said it's a tomato hornworm," I reported dutifully. "And that it's voracious."

"Voracious." He ate that word alive. I have heard actors say that playing a villain is more fun than anything. "I mean in terms of its significance."

He dandled the hornworm again, the way a courtier might dandle a second-born son. There might be possibilities, he seemed to imply; if something really interesting were to happen.

"Do you have a spirit animal?" he asked next.

I hadn't expected him to ask me that, exactly. But it was the least surprising thing he could have said.

"How would I know if I did?" I inquired. He scanned the horizon for a leafy birdless opportunity.

"It would be an animal," he began slowly, "that you dream about. Or that you have an affinity for. I mean, you could eat a bunch of peyote or fast until you were almost dead, to come closer to the spirit world. But that's pretty hard core." He sounded like a sedate bicycle commuter, disapproving the immoderate behavior of bike messengers. "We could have compassion for the birds," he said softly.

"So someone could have a special affinity for a hornworm?" I was trying to cast myself in the role of cultural investigator. I was trying not to be judgmental. I wanted him to be my friend.

"Oh, you could dream about it." He stopped walking. The hornworm swung from one finger to the next with dreary frivolity, like a poison-green child on the playground all alone. "But you have to be careful." He gathered his thoughts. "You have to be careful, because sometimes the animal is just a symbol." He regarded the hornworm, with its small soft horn and unseeing eyes. "Like this little guy here could symbolize, oh, I don't know . . ."

"Rampant consumerism?" I suggested.

"Yeah!" He gave me a friendly encouraging look, the kind I got so much from teachers before I wandered into Nietzschean metaphysics and indistinguishable umlauts. The kind of look that made me feel like a peer instead of a student. "Being enslaved to appetite. And for what? That's what I'd like to know. It's not like this thing turns into a beautiful butterfly or does anything for the environment, right? It's just an ugly moth." And he gave the would-be hawkmoth the kind of look I got after I ventured into metaphysics and complicated vowels.

"So it's just a gross bug," I concluded.

"Well." He took a few hesitant steps toward a patch of reedy grass, growing wild under an oak. "It could represent the appetite for being stoned, for never being happy with the way you are right now. Sometimes places have spirit animals, too." This was a long way from German higher education. It was like biting into something soft and yielding, after months of breaking my teeth on sea rations.

"So you think the hornworm is the spirit animal for the greenhouse, or just a symbol of society's insatiable hunger for luxury organic drugs?" I asked. He gave a small indulgent smile.

"The greenhouse already has a spirit animal," he informed me, as politely as if he were declining an offer with courteous regrets.

"So what is it?"

"I think it's probably just a caterpillar." He gave throat to this judgment with fulsome, gentle gravity, as if in the midst of inflicting pain, he hoped to offer some encouragement. "Unconscious of the role it plays in the dream lives of those who think symbolically." He was standing very straight as he delivered himself of this verdict.

"What is the spirit animal of the greenhouse?" In a country far away, I had developed the habit of assuming there were facts to be gotten down to.

He gave me a smile as resistant to skepticism as Teflon is to rust. "You know that big fat toad?"

"It's a frog," I told him.

I couldn't help myself. Frogs are completely different from toads. A toad will crouch inside a brick until the strong young man who made the brick has died of old age and his works have crumbled into dust. But frogs curl up and die at the faintest whiff of toxic brick-making materials. They stiffen into rigor mortis at the first dry breeze of climate change. My personal favorite thing about frog behavior is the fact that they eat their own skins, because they are constantly regenerating new ones.

"The spirit animal of the greenhouse is a frog?" I asked Morpheus. It took a few moments for the echoes of my doubt to croak away.

"I had a dream," he said slowly at last. He sounded like an up and coming prophet, would-be advisor to an Old Testament king. "It was one of those balmy nights at the beginning of spring, when the stars are so close you can almost hear what they're saying. Everything was ready and fertile and the earth was all dug up and black and open to the sky. The smell . . ." He shook his head, like a man trying to describe the scent of violets on the pulse points of his one true love. "And all of a sudden, there was this big fat glossy toad. She was sitting in a planter, looking right at me with those extradimensional eyes, and as I stared into that strange intelligence, she told me her name. Not in words. Just the sense of it."

There was indeed a great fat frog in the greenhouse, sitting underneath a pot branch. Sometimes, when the leaves lined up with her head just so, she looked like she was wearing a whimsical hat. She was so soft and liquid-looking, it was something of a lesser miracle that her insides were contained within her liquid skin.

"So what is her name?"

"Ardell," he told me, raising his satyr's brows ever so slightly, as if to remind me that he was just the messenger.

"Ardell," I repeated. "The greenhouse has a giant spirit frog named Ardell."

"It's not always what you might expect," he agreed, sighing like a man who's known for a very long time about the futility of expectations.

"What about you? If it's not too personal." I was feeling foolish for the first time since we took a bug on the run from his wife. By this time the hornworm had curled into a soft fleshy spiral as it studiously maintained an air of inedible watchfulness.

"Well!" He looked pleased and surprised that someone had finally asked. "I *think* so. I have a special affinity for insects sometimes. When I get high, I like to run out into the hills and channel this frenetic insect energy. I especially like to be a praying mantis. That's powerful stuff." I assumed he was a male praying mantis, and decided not to pry too deeply into how these sessions ended. "But I never dream about insects," he revealed, arriving already at the crux of the matter. "I don't know where I'd be without my dream life," he began, the way people do when they open a book of discontent with a proviso of love. "But I never dream about animals."

"So do you think your spirit animal is an insect?" I cast an eye—a real one—on the hornworm, which seemed to be languishing.

"I don't think so." And here it came: the crisis of faith. "It's so unsatisfying. Who wants to be an insect? They're the most common creatures on the planet. They're so undifferentiated."

I thought he was having a thoroughly good time with his contempt. He was so watchable, so undisguisedly performing. It gave his conversation a quality of impromptu ritual, enhancing rather than detracting from the truth of what he said.

"They just scurry around all the time," he complained. "No introspection," he muttered, like he was critiquing an offensively bad paper by a lazy student. "I'm more of a dreamer. For me, sleep is the greatest temptation. I *hibernate*. I take a long time to gestate my ideas. Like the mother bear," he added with tentative reverence. "Who gives birth in her sleep at the darkest hour of winter, dreaming and hidden away. Who comes roaring out of her cave with the return of spring, ready to seriously fuck up some food." He grinned, shy and triumphant. He was a bear. Maybe.

THE WOLF'S ACCOMPLICE

MY LIFE WAS so neatly divided then. By day, I apprenticed myself in the garden and developed an ear for distant aircraft. When the sunshine softened into evening, I retreated to Foxglove, with its acres of lawn and its wall to wall amenities. There is something snug and secure about leading such a thorough double life, like having a good spare tire that makes the rain a little less wet, the chances not nearly as desperate.

I especially enjoyed a scented bubble bath after a long day hauling buckets of scant recycled water through the poison oak. I was working with chiaroscuro then, enjoying the play of contrasts more than the shapes of things themselves. When the two halves of my life became incomprehensible to one another, I began to think of myself as doubly fluent, not easily caught, moving with singular competence between two worlds that were equally my own.

I knew exactly where to expect a man with an animal familiar. He would show up at Serendipity and have long abstruse discussions with Morpheus, which I would try to understand and Alizarin would disdain. But when Gregory showed up at Foxglove with Akana, the perfect alignment of my two worlds shifted, creating an effect that was like trying to observe an eclipse on a cloudy day. The contrasts were obscured, the line of sight disturbed. And when my eyes adjusted, I saw that a wolf had come out of the fog.

Reina was singing the day they arrived. "Is that you, Isobel?" she sang.

I was trying to glide past her door and make it into the bath before anyone noticed I was caked with marijuana resin.

"Would you come in here for a minute?" she continued singing, as if she knew I'd be as delighted as she was.

I saw Akana before I even realized Gregory was in the room. I could look at someone's new lover at my leisure. But I had never seen a wolf as white as a dove, curled up in a spot of sunshine on a dead man's Persian rug. It wasn't a pleasure, exactly, to observe a captive apex predator lounging around in a mansion, safe from everything except the loss of wolfish dignity. It's not a pleasure to see a car crash, either. It's just the most impressive thing there is. That's all. I stared at her. She met my eyes.

Akana's good looks were marred only by a slight crookedness at the end of her elegant snout. It gave her beauty a storied quality, like she'd been brought up short in full pursuit of satisfaction or revenge. She had perfect teeth and gleaming pink gums. With eight inches of immaculate white fur, she was lovely and innocent, disdainful and dangerous, like Marlene Dietrich as Catherine the Great.

White wolves are most commonly found on the Internet, in sentimental poses that are often enhanced by the addition of wings, smoke, or glowing eyes. But there was Akana, beautiful and trivial, an ornament in the life of a heavily tattooed chiropractor.

Gregory and Reina were lying in bed together, like liberated French people in a scandalized British lady's memoirs about Gallic hospitality. She was wearing a fluffy pink bathrobe, while the owner of a long-legged she-wolf reclined in khakis and a pale yellow dress shirt. They looked like people with two very different ideas about what to wear on Casual Friday.

"This," Reina announced, snuggling, "is Gregory." She beamed, in a way that let me know a true friend would be truly ecstatic about the presence of Gregory. "We're like John and Yoko. In bed all day." She flashed a peace sign.

Gregory looked chagrined. When he spoke, he took his S's in his teeth like he thought it might be rude to poke them with his tongue. He had a loose-lipped way of approaching plosive consonants, so Peter Piper picking his peck would be a spit-spraying mess before he was done.

"Except we're not naked!" he pointed out, shushing his sibilants and blubbering his plosives. Akana drew her tail in closer to her body, like a lady smoothing her skirts. I wondered if he'd gotten her spayed.

"GREGORY IS ONE of the finest healers I know," Reina told me quietly, late in the golden afternoon.

She'd prepared a voluptuous roast, soaking in blood and savory herbs. It was cooling on the counter, the one that always made me think of the phrase, "marbled flesh," because of how veiny and mottled it was. I tried not to think too hard about the cannibalistic implications of that. Gregory sat in the living room, beerlessly watching the game.

"The knowledge that man has," Reina went on. "He is one of the most knowledgeable men you will ever meet. He told me the reason he loves music so much is it's one of the few things he tried to do and wasn't good at."

I had no idea what I was expected to do with this information. Was Gregory simply aware of his brilliance, like he knew the color of his hair; or was he an insufferable know-it-all? I couldn't tell if I should sympathize, or congratulate. I kept my mouth shut.

"The power of his brain," she concluded meaningfully.

Gregory was a doctor, like Zack—but not like Zack was a doctor. It is unlikely that the next cardiologist who listens to your heart will be covered with inkstains from clavicle to carpals. It is even more unlikely that he will be ideologically opposed to antibiotics and painkillers.

Zack had been a lover of the newest drugs, the latest diagnostic equipment, and the freshest female pharmaceutical representatives. But Gregory diagnosed his patients by touching them. He asked them detailed questions about their phobias and dreams. He watched them walk. There may have been the slightest stiffening of the middle finger in Reina's decision to invite this tattooed healer to share the king-sized bed Zack Hill had bought.

"Healing is his *life*," she told me now. She said it fiercely, like she was taking a vow or daring me to find a flaw in her new love's diagnostic practices. When I maintained my policy of silence on the subject, she removed a slightly frosted beer from the freezer, popped the cap, and drifted off toward Gregory and the ball game on TV.

I sat tracing the angles of the joints in the bar. They were blended like brushstrokes into the grain. I thought about how I would make brushstrokes look like wood grain. Would it work if I dipped a stiff-bristled brush into lightly mixed colors? Or would it be more effective to layer the colors and blend them a little? It's hard to blend things without blurring them; but you have to maintain some kind of separation. I looked up.

The roast bled gently on a bone china platter. Akana was gliding across the red tile floor, as soft and silent as a single beam of light. When she reached the marble counter, cold and fleshy with its liver spots and veins, she stood up on her hind legs. The movement was so fluid, it looked like the first step in a transformation from ordinary household wolf to something enchanted, vaguely human, with unappetizing morals and undeniable appetites. She placed her tapered paws upon the countertop, like a lady testing the finish of her manicure.

She was believably tall for a very small lady, standing on long slim legs. But there is always a flaw in the enchantment, a crack in the fugitive's assumed identity. It can be as trivial as the mobster who was finally caught in a diner, exhorting the waitress in his own ringing tones to make sure his toast was buttered all the way to the edges. In Akana's case, the giveaway would be the tail. It was swinging very slowly as she stood there like a queen, surveying the view from her elf-wolf's height. It was her one bit of unsupportable vanity, the aspect of her wild nature that would get caught in a fence as she made her escape from the castle; would peep out unrestrained from underneath the ball gown; would catch the eye of the hunter who'd kill the prince's bride for her snow-white pelt.

It wouldn't be those eyes, as calm and calculating as a safe-cracker's. It wouldn't be the way she turned her head, cool and blond as Grace Kelly, pursuing a debonair thief. It wouldn't even be the telescopic ears, which flickered with speaking eloquence when she saw me watching her. It would not be the steady way she met my gaze when she dipped her graceful head and began to lap the cooling blood. The bone china platter gleamed. The round red haunch exhaled a rich perfume.

I slid off the barstool and made my way upstairs. I was a wolf's accomplice now. It cleared the fog a little, but didn't clarify where either one of us belonged.

THE MISTRESS OF THE WARDROBE

IN THE YEARS I lived at Foxglove, I dressed like an understudy for parts I was utterly unqualified to play. I was the object of sartorial charity by a high-end whore, a doctor's widow, and a pot-growing painter, none of whom was quite my size. So I rolled up the cuffs of my designer jeans and hacked a path through poison oak. I wore dress-sized Guatemalan shirts to dine by candlelight at Foxglove. And I wore Reina's sassy pre-enhancement blouses everywhere. My shoes still fell apart around my feet like they were allergic to me.

If getting dressed were a university degree like any other performance art, then every dissertation would revolve around the disposal of purses and shoes. As in any discipline, among the advisors on this faculty there would be classicists and modernists, old school and new. The classically-minded view on purses is that a woman should carry a clutch containing a lipstick, a tampon, and one or two love letters. Across the hall you'll find the modernists, who embody the belief that the woman who has it all is also nomadic, and should carry it with her wherever she goes.

"The tiny reticule," Caitlin held, "is a badge of femininity. It's like lacy panties without the itchy twat." And she smirked, in a way that is only possible when one is fully feminine without the torment of vaginal itch.

Reina belonged to the oppositional school. The doctor's widow packed a small duffel bag everywhere she went, jingling with buckles and straps. If Caitlin's purse was a badge of femininity, Reina's was the field office.

Costumes are strategic. Caitlin knew that. Reina knew it, too. Alizarin, with her closetful of woven things and slogan-bearing T-shirts, was also well aware of it. But I was barely beginning to catch on when the undisputed master of strategic costuming came to call at Foxglove.

Danica Morgan showed up at Reina's door decades after any mortal could expect to be forgiven for caving in a little; for settling down with a nice enough man and watching the sun go down with a glass of good red wine. Both women were from the hills of Trinity County, which sounds like the perfect place of origin for rustic saints and ancient wrongs. They were descendants of the few remaining Wintu, native people who survived the onset of disease, hydraulic mining, and indentured servitude that swept the nations of Northern California in the nineteenth and twentieth centuries. Their fathers chewed tobacco and their mothers wore boots, and even the children knew how to work. In their early twenties, they came to Mendocino County and began referring to their thrift-store finery as "consignment pieces."

When Danica Morgan came in through the gate beneath the climbing rose, petals tumbled onto her hair and her Burberry coat, which must have been a very good fake. She looked as capable of striding into a house on fire as she did of modeling the boots she did it in. She would teach her daughters the secret of elegance, and it would be an act of courage. She would show them how to dress themselves, and it would be a metaphor for self-respect, clean living, and the virtues of leading an examined life.

She paused on the walkway when Reina came out, and the two of them stood in the sun. There was a quickening of similarities, an apartness that identifies people who share something not easily identified. They were as tall as professional athletes, with posture that looked like they had spent their girlhoods pacing drawing rooms with Greek and Latin dictionaries balanced on their heads.

Like Gregory, Danica maintained a wolf that trailed behind her in the morning as she made her coffee; prowled at her side as she pulled the weeds around her daffodils; and slept watchfully at the foot of her bed. It's true that wolves don't bark. But they make wild desperate squeaking sounds when they are lonely or afraid.

"I don't *use* my sweetie boy for anything," Danica explained, airing her vowels like a woman who is used to being heard. "I keep him." She paused. "For my pleasure."

Meanwhile, the wolf at Foxglove plainly regarded Reina as a concubine, retained for her willingness to perform duties too indelicate for wolfish female dignity. Danica gave that wolf a steady-eyed stare, and Akana sat down demurely, in laughing imitation of what good doggies do. It was almost indecent, how graceful she was. She curled her tail around her slender flank and then across her paws, as if it gave her satisfaction to be touching it. As if it were not a part of her body, but a piece of finery bought at secret, devastating cost.

We had lunch on the patio, admiring the climbing rose. Danica sat down on Reina's right, Gregory on her left. I dangled off on Gregory's other side, a bystander in hand me downs who finally took a seat. I thought when Danica looked at him, the sharpness of her glance was softened by the interval containing Reina, so by the time it reached Gregory, it was shapeless and sad. I thought Gregory busied himself cutting his meat into a perfect grid of identical pieces so he wouldn't have to see that look; that he was startled when Danica asked him quietly if he would like a roll; and then again when she passed him the butter with flawless cordiality.

It's hard to say what motivates a wolf, if not the sight of yet another buttered roll passing in front of her face. Silently, Akana rose into a sinuous half-crouch between me and her master. She placed her dainty paws upon the tablecloth. Something in me leapt with joy to see what a marauder she was, with her air of wedding gowns and stolen diamonds. If Akana had a handbag, it would be a quiver full of arrows, lined with the skin of her prey. She began to angle her gently crumpled snout for Gregory's shining plate, with all its little meat bits lined up in a row.

Then Gregory did something that was frankly astonishing. He arranged his face into a caricature of rage. One feature after another was meticulously distorted. First, the brows came together like a thunderclap. Then the nostrils flared and the lips went taut and white. His hairline rose. He brought this mask of hypothetical fury very close to Akana's snout, with its long curved rows of sharp white teeth.

"*Noooooo!*" he cried, like his favorite pitcher had just walked a man, with all the bases loaded. He waved his arms like a referee gone mad, wildly indicating that the entire game was in ruins.

Akana flattened her ears and supplicated him with a liquid wail in her eyes, like a lady of great delicacy whose domineering husband insults her in front of company. Danica watched in absolute silence. Reina tore her roll into molecule-sized shreds. I watched the space between Gregory and Akana and tried not to breathe disruptively.

It was Danica who set the silence, and Danica who broke it. To the tune of a few clinking coffee things, she turned to her old friend and said, "Did I tell you I applied for a job at the Tribal Health Office?"

The atmosphere was choked with lupine shame. It seemed almost inappropriate to bring up something functional and sane, involving high levels of social responsibility and technical skill. But Reina lunged for it.

"Is Thelma still there?" she gasped, as if the presence of Thelma in her administrative capacity were the most pressing question that had ever occurred to her.

She turned to Gregory, who was now impassive, as if this awkward enthusing were clearly the result of low progesterone and should be passed over without comment.

"Thelma introduced us," she explained, with relentless gaiety. "When my Monya and Dani's Rita were going to the Tribal daycare. We both ended up working there, so we could be with our kids *and* bring home a paycheck. We had it all." She laughed. "Dani went to war when it looked like we were about to lose our funding."

"We both went to war," Danica reminded her friend, but it was clear by how those green eyes flashed who had led the battle. "Thelma's retired, but Denise is still there. Thelma's still around, though. She goes out riding sometimes. That big, huge, ugly . . ."

"Her Indian warhorse!" Reina shrieked. "Mister Lovely! Too ugly to die. She used to pile all those kids onto his back. I swear every one of them was asleep before he made it across the yard. Every time. Thelma!" She basked in uncertain happiness for a few moments, looking like she didn't quite know what to do with it. "So you're going back," she said quietly. "I'm sure they snapped you up so fast."

"Well." Her friend gave a slight, admonishing smile. "They haven't called back yet." Reina moved impatiently. "I had my interview," Danica went on, airing her vowels again. "And she asked me something I wasn't prepared for. I mean, it's been so long since I had a real job interview. But I could do most of it from home, and I'd bring in a little extra money if Zellie and Trey stay with us, which I think they will, because . . ."

"Dani. The question. At the interview," Reina pleaded, showing her teeth beseechingly.

"Oh," Danica started. "Right. So, not Denise, but this other woman, whose name—this is terrible. I can't remember. I wrote it down in my calendar, though, so I won't look stupid if she calls . . ." She made a quick lunge for her purse. "It doesn't matter right now." She caught a glimpse of Reina's tortured writhe. "So she asked me, to tell her, in my own words—" She paused.

Gregory gazed at her over his fork, as if he could not for the life of him imagine where all the progesterone had gone.

"What my greatest strength is," Danica revealed at last. "And my greatest weakness."

"Well, what did you say? Your greatest weakness." Reina scoffed, appalled at the temerity of this woman whose name was not even worth remembering.

"Well, I told her, it's a long time since I had a job interview," Danica reminded her patiently. "I have to think about it for a second. So I did. I sat there for a second, and then I said, I have to confess." She took a deep breath, like a woman who is undaunted either by the truth or the unknown, but takes a deep breath before them so as not to create hard feelings among the other mortals. "I'm not a very good speller. But: I have spell-check." We all breathed a sigh of relief. "And: I adopt children," she said next, with quiet, controlled ferocity. She had a trained actor's faculty for changing the shape of the space around her as she spoke.

"Is that a strength or a weakness?" Gregory quipped, as if he couldn't feel it, the sudden shift in the atmospheric pressure of the story.

"I believe that every child deserves a safe, clean, loving home," Danica continued, as if he hadn't said a thing. He withered into insignificance, but didn't seem to notice that, either. "And I happen to have a house with five bedrooms in it!" she exclaimed, carefully pointing her eyes away from the house that Zack built.

"I've seen it," Reina murmured, heartfelt as an amen chorus.

"What am I going to do with all that room?" Danica demanded, as if she were anticipating being called to account for her weakness and her sins. "I walk around asking myself: there are children *here in Mendocino County* who have nothing. Nothing! Rennie, you've seen them at the daycare . . ."

Reina nodded soberly.

"Coming in with no breakfast, snot all over their faces," Danica continued softly. Her voice was almost seductive as she described the wretched condition of the poverty-stricken children. "No spiritual training," she threw in, lighting her eyes on Reina, whose face made a motion of badly-suppressed distaste. "So here I am in this great big house with *acreage*, with *orchards*, with apples and walnuts and this vegetable garden that practically grows itself, and I'm not going to share that? With children who have nothing? Forget my lousy spelling. These kids are my weakness. I would lay down my life for any one of them." And she laid it down before us there, daring us to pick it up and be weak with her. "And," she added, defying any one of us to stop her, "I'm not done yet."

WHAT THE MISTRESS OF THE WARDROBE KNEW

DANICA MORGAN DID not divide her life into eras. She did not pursue a passion or a lover with single-minded zeal for years and then abruptly decide to do something else. But she had been a guest of honor at all of Reina's weddings. She'd sat in the front row when her oldest friend graduated from nursing school. When Reina ran marathons, Danica was there at the midpoint with a small cup of water, laughing and standing in the shade. And Dani was at Foxglove, the day that Zack Hill died.

"She knew," Reina told me, when Danica and Gregory were both gone and the place was a little less wolfish. "She walked in that door and took one look at him and she just *knew* that was the day. She put her hand on his chest and looked him right in the eye and whispered, *let's finish this.*" Her own eyes were brimming with secrets as she said it. "She helped me wash his body," she murmured, barely moving her lips so not a drop of those secrets was spilled.

Now she frowned into the fireplace, where the ashes of early spring were waiting for the fall. "She's really mad at me about Gregory," she ventured, after a silence long enough to contain multiple segues.

"Why is she mad?" I asked, aware that as I did so, I was falling into orbit around this woman whose generosity had a gravitational pull to it. It was the most natural thing in the world, to be this woman's sidekick; to involve myself in her alliances.

"She just doesn't think he's the right man for me." She gave a sluggish little sigh, as if the subject held no interest for her, though she had brought it up. "Did she seem a little . . . *on*, to you?" she asked suddenly, fastening her eyes on my face. I felt myself flinch.

"On to me?" I joked, to cover it. "What, she knows about my tax havens?"

"On a mission," she clarified, staring moodily into the fireplace again.

"She does seem a little mission oriented," I agreed, with some caution. I wasn't entirely sure I wanted to join her on another round of relationship crises. But I had gotten into the habit of being Reina's witness now. It was enervating and compelling, like binge-watching the third or fourth season of a television show without ever finding out how it all got started in the first place.

"She's always been like that," she said dismissively. "Laying down her life for the cause. Of course, she *would*," she hastened to assure me. "In all loyalty and fairness, she would. I used to be like that, too," she added, as if her younger self were an old friend whose company she missed. "But it's something else . . ." She was squinting past the ashes now. "The last time we talked," she went on, feeling her way toward an explanation, "she was literally yelling at me. I called her in tears and she yelled at me." We sat in lumpen silence for another shapeless length of time. It would have been the perfect moment to slip away. I didn't.

"I was upset about Gregory," she said at last. She sounded like she was forcing herself to tell the story. "We were way out in Grass Valley, and his friends were being really snarky to me and that man did not have my back. He did not stand up for me once. So I'm tromping around in the woods, alone, at night, about to be eaten by a bear, for all she knows, and I call my best friend for a little support, and she yells at me." She fumed for a few moments. "Danica Morgan's *opinion*, is that Gregory is a bad idea. Do you know what she said to me?" And now she brightened angrily, with the joy of taking offense. "She told me *to my face*—we were on the phone, but you know what I mean— she *completely* dismissed his skill and his learning. His compassion as a healer! *Knowing* he's brilliant. He's fixed her effed-up neck so many times and she goes out and effs it up again and comes crying to him and does he ever lecture her? Does he ever say, now, Danica, you're fifty-two years old, maybe you want to stop adopting insane children with oppositional defiance disorder and riding out into the wilderness on horseback with them? No! He does not. He lets her live her life the way she wants to. And she has the nerve to tell me to my face, and I quote, *that man is a fucking idiot*. This from a woman who calls herself a pastor. Judgmental Christian bullshit. I'm sick of it."

She subsided for a few moments. "And now, all of a sudden, it's like it never happened. No I'm sorry, nothing. She was sweet as pie to him. Not that she didn't have her chance." And she gave a quiet, brutal laugh. "He was just trying to make a joke. So he's a tiny bit socially inept. I know that. He's not an idiot—but she could have ripped him to pieces. I've seen her do it for less, and laugh about it. It used to be a blood sport for her, back in the day." *When we really knew how to have fun*, she did not need to add. *When I knew she was on my side.*

IF ONLY SHE knew her own daughter was on her side. Reina loved her friends and family with an old chivalric fierceness, the kind that showers its recipients with banquets and finery. It's an armor-clanking way to love, the kind that guards its bloodlines and requires periodic tests of loyalty.

There is no better way to fail a daughterly test of loyalty than by deciding, in your second year of college, that now is a good time to have a child with a man your mother never met. You could make it a double, by telling your mother's best friend before you tell the woman who gave birth to you. Then you and she could stand back and watch as your furious parent grasps how little you trust her; how certain you are to find your own way. Without your mother, who loves you so much the only thing missing from her life is the opportunity to die for you.

"My nineteen-year-old daughter fucks some random asshole sex fiend," Reina greeted me as I stumbled into the kitchen for a cup of coffee one morning. "Can't even take a twenty-first-century precaution like a grown-up woman who knows where babies come from," she seethed, fumbling around in the cupboard for the coffee beans.

She was including me in her life. It was an invitation from a woman who had never judged me; who trusted me for no good reason; who shared her home and her appliances and her personal weaknesses with me. For all that, I owed her the simple courtesy of hearing her out. I took a seat at the bar.

"And then, after she spreads her legs all over town, she asks her favorite Jesus freak: Can you think of any good reason I shouldn't be somebody's mother for the rest of my life?" She thrust her head into the cupboard, which only partly muffled her voice. "Maybe I should fuck up my entire life and raise a child on food stamps because, forget college, but hey, I'm a great waitress. Whatever we do, let's not *murder* this clump of cells that's growing inside my body because I let some guy fire one off at the wrong time of the month." She plugged in the coffee grinder and flashed a few furious air quotes as she said the word "murder."

I began to wonder if my own mother invited people to share her life by reciting the details of my sexual illiteracy. Was Caitlin drinking coffee with a sympathetic listener right now, explaining her theories about why my marriage failed?

"You know what I would have told her, if she'd had the decency to call her own mother?" Reina demanded. "Who happens to be a registered nurse, by the way: it is not a child. It is a cellular growth. That is science. She is supposed to be educated. She doesn't even need to be vacuumed right now. She missed *one* period. She can take a pill and go home. Not that she knows how to take a pill *or* stay home. Obviously." She seized a handful of coffee beans and slammed them into the grinder.

I tried to remember how much I'd told Caitlin about my periods and fears. Had I ever talked about boys with her? Or had I just listened supportively as she reflected on the deeper meaning of her clients' bizarre and horrible needs?

"And does my oldest friend, the woman I trust more than anyone else—does she call me? Does she say, hey, you have a situation here? Does she let me handle my family the way I think we all agree I have the right?" Reina prowled the red-tiled kitchen with her fluffy bathrobe on, hunting for the coffee press. I took it out of the dishwasher and handed it to her.

"Danica Morgan has been trying to get me to be a Christian since I don't know when. "She probably thinks it is her God-given duty to advise an impressionable young woman to bring more unwanted children into the world so she can save them." She picked up the pieces of the coffee press and glared at them accusingly, as if she were daring them to challenge her analysis. "It's not like she's stupid. She knows exactly what they did to us. With all her Native this and Tribal that. We're in California, for crying out loud. Where does she think all those missions come from? It's not enough my own daughter suddenly decides to be a Christian." She shot another bad-tempered glare at the coffee press.

I tried to remember if I'd ever read a book or seen a movie where the happy ending involved obedient adult offspring. Weren't we all supposed to fall in love with people our parents wouldn't have chosen for us; to disregard the way they raised us, and reject their spiritual teachings? Reina did not appear to know that. She was a mother, and I was a daughter. She was losing something I had never had.

"I told her I could call in some favors at the hospital. Honey, I said." Her voice when she said it was soft, like Danica's when she declared herself a weakling for children. "I said, honey. You don't need this right now. You have your whole life ahead of you . . ." She picked up the coffee things and surveyed them as if they had broken her heart.

"And you think Danica knew?" I asked. I began to heat a pot of water, in case anybody ever decided to have a cup of coffee around here.

"Oh! I *know* she knew. My Monya doesn't lie to me. I raised her better than that. She let it slip when she was breaking the news to *me*. Her own mother! And I said, Monnie. Have you spoken to Dani about this? And she said, yes, I did, Mom." She glared with triumphant anger, as if she had conducted herself honorably at a deposition and could now expect a favorable judgement. "And when I told her we need to get rid of this, she said, Mom, that's horrible and offensive and I'm getting off the phone right now. And she hung up on me. I raised her better than that!" She whirled in her fuzzy pink slippers and seized the milk from the fridge, as if she would force this maternal fluid to pay for all the daughters who had been well raised and insisted on their right to misbehave.

THE BEAR PLAYS WITH FIRE,
EXPOUNDS ON DEMON LOVE

IT WAS A season of rage, a monsoon of fury and hurt that battered the roses and pot. Alizarin used a palette knife to paint a towering piece. I wonder what the proper term is for a painting made with a knife. A knifing? She called it "The Patron Saint of Final Weddings"; rather ominously, I thought. The patron saint was leering from the bottom left-hand corner, with a bookie's gleam in his eye.

It was fall again, and by now I was such a fast trimmer, I could clean a pound in five or six hours. I spent every day inside, choking on wood smoke and resin. I think about that, every time I hear people talk about all those lazy pot farmers, sitting around watching their money grow on trees. I think about how many short fall days I turned my back on the final glories of the year and bent over my task like a data-entry clerk or a seamstress, working hard to make a living just like anybody else.

Not that work at Serendipity Organics presented unnecessary hardships. We ate homegrown produce and mutton, fattened on poison oak and blackberry vines. We listened to public radio—except the first few days of rain, when every DJ felt compelled celebrate the harvest by playing nonstop Grateful Dead. Sometimes, Morpheus played songs he'd written, with two-part harmonies and lyrics of confounding subtlety. When that happened, Alizarin would raise her laryngitic voice and sing, with unexpected perfect pitch.

There was something feverish about their singing that year. The more they fought, the more they sang. Their pitch took on the festive quality of an ER waiting room, where everyone is united in the glee of bleeding and endorphins.

They had too practical a sense of ecstasy to crave the shabby facsimile of drugs. But I think they were addicted to warfare, the adrenaline roar of the rage and the hurt. The wine at Seder and the hippie outlaw acid trips were ritual forms of defying the oppressive dominant culture. They had the simultaneous advantages of being really fun, and kind of cerebral. But for all the time we spent cultivating, handling, and prettifying the gateway drug to heroin, no one at Serendipity was especially interested in using it.

Warfare was the drug of choice. Alizarin and Morpheus fought with a single-mindedness that took precedence over everything else. It was needle and crack pipe and lines on a glass. Morpheus would roll in late to work, bleary-eyed and staggering, and weep in the teachers' lounge after a ferocious battle. Alizarin would skip board meetings at the co-op gallery in town. She showed up distracted and edgy at functions that should have been ideal hunting grounds for hungry artists. They worked on their relationship with all the self-destructive fervor of an alcoholic mystic, honing his crystalline visions of The One while marinating in his own urine.

And I saw Morpheus once, his eyes as crafty as an addict's. I saw him contrive a scene that could only be dreamed of by someone whose ability to think symbolically has swollen like a vestigial organ that should be operated on immediately.

In his own malleable realities, Morpheus created solar systems of intricate feeling, of thoughts informed by the highest principles of compassion. He was profoundly courteous to everyone he met in his mostly lucid dreams. Onstage, he was a tidal wave of nuanced tragedy, of joy with a shadow of pain. He was so captivating, no one else on stage existed as more than a moveable costume rack. I saw him play a dying man, rising to give voice to a last internal monologue. Narrative like that hardly ever works in live theater, not when everyone's ear is tuned to the peals of cinematic voiceover. But Morpheus was so vital, so dying, so private in front of the crowd, that I don't think a single breath was drawn until the lights went down.

And yet, I saw him drag his undreaming carcass across the floor at Serendipity and place a gasoline-soaked rag in the cold dead ashes of the wood stove in the living room. I saw him tuck it in behind a blackened log and softly shut the door.

As long as he'd lived on the homestead, Morpheus had never learned how to use a chainsaw. He was like some of the Americans I met in Germany, who bragged about how little German they knew, as if they'd proven their sturdiness of character by resisting some pernicious force. He was the only child of an unmarried schoolteacher, but Charnisse had a high-born horror of practical matters. He reminded me of one of Thackeray's noblemen, whose fortunes have fallen so low, they can't even keep a valet to help them dress. If Morpheus wore cravats and collars instead of velcro-fastened long-sleeved shirts, they would be greasy and askew. His wig would be utterly unkempt as he strummed his guitar, writing music madly by the stub of one last candle.

"If he spent as much time cutting firewood as he does playing with that fucking guitar," Alizarin complained, as if she were amazed he hadn't thought of it himself. She left the conclusion dangling, like this might soften the statement into something indirect, like a question or a hint.

She enlisted neighbors to offer him tutorials in manliness, but Morpheus would not be shamed. He would watch as some energetic competent man explained the workings of the chainsaw or the weed whacker or the diesel engine—and then he would take it in his hands and break it, or spill out all the gas, or leave the key in the ignition with the glow plug on until the battery died. Sometimes, he injured himself, and stood staring dumbly at the blood or the bruise or the blackening nail. The competent men would have known what to do if he had been playing gentleman farmer. They wanted to be gruff and good-natured, but he was semi-feral and didn't like them. They were too kind, in their way, to accuse him of faking it. And besides, he wasn't.

He was embodying it, like a professional actor who immerses himself in a role, fully aware of what he is doing; who discovers, too late, that it has taken over his life. He was like a man whose cognizance of gravity doesn't make him any less subject to its law when he throws himself off of a bridge.

That was what happened, the day he tried to turn the wood stove into a giant Molotov cocktail. I was at the kitchen table with my little jar of grapeseed oil, committing misdemeanors. Alizarin liked each variety of pot to have a slightly different trim, so I was trying to give a tray of Chocolate Thai a feathery, whimsical look. The buds this year were light and airy, and she wanted to imply that she had grown them that way on purpose.

Morpheus was interrupted as he sat on the floor, preparing to write a good song. His lips were moving. He was staring deep into the interior space where all the finest art resides before it takes its form. Every now and then, he stomped his foot or growled. It was a ritual for him, this demonstration of ferocity. He was showing the music that he was fierce enough to be worthy of it. And then Mike was there, with his big friendly ag-teacher glasses and his smiling sun-damaged face and his expertise in all things manly and mechanical. It was unconscionable.

"Charnisse," Alizarin said loudly. "Two o' clock. Remember? Mike's chainsaw lesson? You'll have plenty of time to practice before it gets dark."

Mike smiled encouragingly. Morpheus rose and took a very long time to find his shoes. In a very short time, something happened to the chainsaw, and the men came back inside to reconnoiter. I considered moving my trimming operation somewhere else and decided against it. I could trim an ounce in the time it would take to gather up the buds and drag the table out of earshot and set up the lamp exactly right. I seemed to be chronically witnessing other people's lives these days, as if, in failing to find a crisis of my own, I had a spare room in my life that I wasn't using for anything else.

As Mike conducted himself inappropriately—that is, taking stock of things with good cheer and rational thought—Morpheus began to move across the living room floor. He did this in a way that indicated impending disaster, by a number of cues too subtle to be identified. But if he were onstage, everyone in the audience would know that here was the guy who would get the message wrong, mix up the packages, leave the gate open, and accidentally set something on fire. The rest of us were moveable costume racks.

As Mike and I watched—because what else do you do, when a brilliant actor takes the stage?—he opened the wood stove, placed the gasoline-soaked rag inside, arranged it as if it were a piece of useful kindling, and gently closed the door. He was smiling.

"What the fuck is that smell?" Alizarin asked, appearing like a Fury in a play about revenge. "You guys aren't fucking with that chainsaw in the house, are you?"

Mike looked guilty and distraught. The young farmers in his classroom, with their simple rustic courtesies and sunburned faces, had not prepared him for a city-born lady homesteader who used expletives like commas. Alizarin, who always seemed to be suffering from poison oak, had finger smears of burnt sienna on her face and neck where she had scratched herself savagely. They made her look like she'd been pawed by something made of red clay.

"Well, we used some rags," Mike began with reassuring civility, "to clean up a little mishap—"

Alizarin zeroed in on the stove. "Charnisse. You didn't *put those rags in my stove*, did you? I *know* you didn't *put those rags in my stove*." The repetition heightened the tension, like a phrase that turns into a curse if it's said three times. "Because that would be a stupid fucking asshole thing to do, Charnisse."

When he answered, he spoke like he was unsurprised to find himself in a Socratic dialogue where no one else has ever had a single coherent thought. "We can't just throw them away," he stated, as reasonably as if he were positing a universal premise. His eyes were stubborn to the point of cruelty. "That's toxic waste."

"You want them to blow up in my face when I start the fire?" Alizarin was never mocking in her fury. That was Caitlin's weapon. Caitlin, who had even less sense of proportion than anyone else, would have created a scathing sarcastic fable, starring M.C. Harness as a bumbling Prometheus. But Caitlin regularly made herself ridiculous by turning Gatlin guns on mice.

"They won't blow up in your face." He sounded affectionate and exasperated, as if she'd told him the leprechauns were withering the kale.

He rolled his eyes at Mike. All of us, including Alizarin, heard the telepathic message about women and their whims. But Mike was rigid with fear, like a gentle wild creature suffering capture myopathy.

"You use gas to ignite an engine," Morpheus went on calmly, as if he had just discovered the principles of combustion and that was how they'd scare away the leprechauns.

What struck me most about the fury that followed was how unsurprised Alizarin seemed in her rage. She had been exactly this upset about the Tupperware. She'd come close when Morpheus had insisted, in an idle hour, that eggs are dairy products. No one has ever read the definition of dairy products from a 1986 edition of the OED with the passionate vindication of Alizarin Goldfarb at the end of that hour.

It was hard to imagine how the two of them had carved out a life together. They were always gathering momentum for their mutual destruction, always barely missing it for reasons that seemed to defy all natural laws. Their marriage was like a high-speed car chase in a movie, where no one ever gets hurt in a dumpy little sedan that corners like a race car after leaping over fruit stands.

But a car chase, highly staged or not, requires unrelenting concentration. Morpheus and Alizarin focused on the fight and kept each other close—closer than enemies, closer than friends; closer than lovers who cannot stand the sight of one another. I got the distinct impression that it would have been perfectly acceptable to them—not ideal, but acceptable—if the house burned down while they were concentrating on whose turn it was to clean the cat box.

And yet, the savagery at Serendipity did not preclude a sound artistic sensibility. One day during harvest, as we waited for the rest of the crew to arrive, Alizarin suggested I go outside and draw the bluebelly lizards. My drawing was stiff, she explained. The lizards would bring a sense of motion to my gesture as they skittered and flickered, ogling with golden eyes. "Plus, it's getting cold, so they're not moving that fast," she added, effectively strapping a set of training wheels onto my stub of graphite.

Lizards are pure motion, as simple as a song that is all melody. I approached the first one with an unearned level of confidence, noting with a higher hominid's contempt how little expression it had on its face. It retaliated by presenting two foreshortened limbs and flicking its tail out of sight, forcing me to render its quizzical saurian smirk. As if it were deeply invested in asserting its natural superiority, the creature suddenly performed about a dozen pushups in less time than it took to render it wrong, flicked its tapered tail again, and vanished.

I began to scribble in the margins of my notebook, hoping the crew would show up soon and save me from the mockery of tiny reptiles. I noticed Morpheus, running up and down the driveway with a small silver tarp in his upraised arms, like a purposeful madman in the background of an Ingmar Bergman film. Finally he gave up and stood in the shade of the house, panting and sweating and looking perplexed. He smelled like cardamom, I thought, like something green with seeds inside.

"I thought I'd lost that tarp," he reported. "But then I took all that gingko, and suddenly I remembered where I'd put it. I was celebrating just now, trying to make sure the gingko was circulating through my whole system." He glanced at my sketchbook. "Are you writing or drawing?"

"A little of both. Neither." I angled the book so he could see all my little reptilian abortions.

"Sweeter, more savage, than hope?" he read. "Is that the title?"

"I think it's the last line," I told him. "I'm writing a poem, I guess, about the lizards."

"Care to read out lout?" He smiled a friendly, unambiguous smile.

"Sure." At this, he turned his back and gazed out over the valley, where the only movement visible was the shimmering of heat waves.

It was a strange instinctive sensitivity, I thought, to take his face away as I read. I saw his hand half-curled at dog's-head height. About midway through the poem, Alizarin's big mutt Effie crept up quietly and placed his ears beneath that hand. By the end, the dog was pressing a ribby flank against the sparsely furred leg of the man. The two of them stared off in opposite directions, like they'd been thrown together in a crowded streetcar and the only polite thing to do was pretend it wasn't happening.

I rustled the page to let them know I was done.

"Ahl riiiight!" Morpheus exclaimed huskily, like a musician after a successful lick. I tried to look like I was thinking critically. "Do you have any more?" I did not. "Well, hey. Make a copy of that, and I'll try to set it to music. It's so weird and . . . spiritual, in kind of a sinister way."

I began to think rather highly of my poem.

He mused for a moment. "In a lot of places, people pay tribute to their demons. Or the darker side of life, if you want to be finicky about it. Not in a fetishistic way, like so-called Satanists here in the West. Who really don't know a damned thing about demonology. So to speak."

I could tell that if he ever watched a movie made from a book he loved, he would be tormented by all the ways the movie got it wrong.

"You love your demons like you love your children. You don't withhold your love from a child just because he's a demon." He was joking, but in the way that mystics do, when they believe the truth is contained in a great cosmic laugh.

"When I was in Bali," he went on, clearly about to illustrate the truth of what he'd just said, "I went into this tiny out of the way shrine. It was one of those little ramshackle places, more or less devoted to some local deity." He paid my worldliness the compliment of imagining I had a category for Southeast Asian shrines, full of gods I'd never heard of. "But really, they had a whole crew of deities, mostly different versions of The One. Beautiful women, all looking like Tara, and androgynous Buddhas and vicious little fat dudes with fantastic animal heads and claws and really horrible antisocial propensities. Like maybe they would tear your entrails out if you didn't invite them to your party or include them in your sacrifice or something." He paused to savor the possibilities. "And they were all decorated with fresh flowers. There was some gorgeous sexy pink flower blooming all over the place, and every one of these guys—and the Taras, too, especially the Taras—had flowers all over them. Imagine! This fierce little nasty baby-snatching demon with a delicate pink flower behind his ear. You wouldn't tell a kid he couldn't have something nice if all the other kids had it. Even if he *was* a demon."

"Don't they say Jesus is supposed to love you no matter what you do?" I remarked, unable to ignore the opportunity to play devil's advocate to his love-drenched demonology.

He winced, like Rudolf Lindt peering into a child's Easter basket. "That's so watered down. The only Christians with a real juicy sense of mystery about the whole thing were the Catholics. Before they pussed out, that is. I mean, come on. The cannibalism. The black-clad virgins. The shameless conspicuous consumption. Have you ever been to the Vatican? Can you imagine how many peasants starved to death to build that thing? It's the world's tackiest monument to human weakness. Those people knew all about blood sacrifice. It's what all the old gods went for. They weren't enlightened. They didn't give a shit about us. They were greedy and horny and jealous. With superpowers. But at least they were honest. They weren't paying lip service to some barefoot poverty-stricken rabbi and his sainted Jewish mother with her premarital celestial fucking around and that smug little smirk and her downcast eyes. Those people wouldn't even be a footnote in the history of the real gods. They would be beggars. No one would even try to pretend they gave a shit about them. With their one god." He made a furious sound, as if to say, had he been a god-fearing pagan in Constantine's time, he would have offered some irrefutable proofs and maybe changed the course of history. "Goddamned Christians," he muttered. Gathering his crumpled tarp, he stalked off down the driveway.

CHOCOLATE-COVERED ORANGE PEELS
BETRAYAL

MORPHEUS AND REINA obviously didn't care that they were acting like villains invented by medieval Christians. Morpheus appeared to be on the verge of conjuring a demon any second now. And Reina was a patriarch straight out of the Old Testament, with her towering rage and her vows about love and revenge.

"You are not going to believe this," she greeted me when I came home from a hard day's work on the pot farm. What part would I play in the movie of Reina's life? I wondered. I wasn't quite a friend. And I wasn't necessary enough to be a sidekick. I would be the hairdresser, with sympathy half a shade warmer than neutral and questions written in to get the exposition moving.

"What happened?" I asked obligingly, to move things along.

"Look at this." She had her laptop on the bar, like she was about to put on a slideshow of Zack Hill's indiscretions.

I moved closer. I had a sticky patina of pot resin on my hands. I could practically see the waves of fragrance rolling off of me. But I am absolutely sure that at that moment, I could have strolled across the marble floor completely naked with garlands of buds in my hair, and Reina would have beckoned me over to look at her laptop. When I think of how many crop circle hoaxes I could have perpetrated but didn't, I could cry my eyes out.

We were looking at Monya Harmann's Facebook page. I had gathered most of what I knew about Reina's daughter from photographs. I knew she was beautiful, dark-eyed, and slim, with long black hair like an Indian maiden in one of those offensive old Westerns. I knew her father, Matthew Harmann, had given her a Bible with a picture of himself marking the Book of Matthew. I knew she'd had braces on her teeth and that her mother thought she should stand up straight.

"Look at that!" Reina jabbed a finger at the collage of photographs and hastily composed remarks. The top knuckle of the finger looked a little swollen. The tip was slightly bent. "She's talking about the baby on her Facebook page!" Monya Harmann had 546 friends on Facebook. "It's all over the Internet! My friend Amy called me and said, is this true? Why didn't she tell me? I said, Monnie, it is unacceptable for you to treat our friends this way. *Our oldest friends* are wondering why you didn't tell them personally. I didn't teach her to be this disrespectful. Everyone's talking about the baby. And Amy and Max feel left out. They've known her all her life, and she couldn't even give them a call and say, hey, I'm pregnant. By some guy twelve years older than I am who hasn't even said one word about marriage . . ." She scrolled through the comments. Monya's friends were ethnically diverse and exquisitely groomed.

"Do you know what this is about?" she said suddenly.

I was just standing there. I have spent weeks of my life standing around passively, waiting for openings in conversations so I can slip away.

"This is about me not being ready to be a grandmother," she announced, as if the material had submitted itself to her analysis without the least resistance. "And she doesn't even realize that. She thinks it's all about her. So selfish! I don't believe this . . ."

I wandered into the kitchen to make a cup of coffee. I should never, under any circumstances, drink coffee after three p.m.

"What happened to the coffeepot?" I asked. The counters were bare. I had a brief image of Reina in a rage, sweeping everything onto the ground with both arms. But she was tapping keys on her laptop, on the verge of cracking the case.

"Gregory's spending the night," she said shortly, compressing her lips as she came across another offensively unscandalized comment from a girl with beautiful hair. "'Oh, Monnie,'" she read in a high, mincing voice, as if she'd never seen a more vapid remark. "'I can't wait to be an auntie. Luv, Serena'. I *know* Serena. Whose side is she *on*, anyway? He came up a few days ago, while you were gone," she elaborated.

I realized we were having one of those conversations where topics are addressed in a series of partly overlapping circles. Sometimes I wish I could just make diagrams while people are talking to me.

"He brought Akana, of course. He said she would never speak to him again if he left her. She climbed up on the counter and went through the cupboards. She threw a bunch of cocoa and chocolate-covered orange peels—the expensive ones, from Christmas—onto the floor and left the water running. I guess she was mad because nobody left a giant hunk of perfectly prepared meat lying around for her to gnaw on."

"Left the water running," I repeated stupidly.

"She bumped the faucet," Reina told me carelessly, as if this were not infinitely more interesting than partisan warfare over an unsanctioned pregnancy. I tried not to think about what it would take to drive an elegant wild animal to behave like a temperamental old maid with severe menopause symptoms.

GREGORY BROUGHT STEAKS. Akana scrupulously ignored them, surveying all of us with a wide-eyed imitation of innocence. She was basically a sociopath. Reina had spent the entire afternoon foraging around in Monya' social media, and now she was strangely elated. She didn't even bristle when Akana pressed her lissome fur-clad body against Gregory's legs and narrowed her eyes at the lady of the house.

Instead, she gave her furry rival an unprecedented friendly caress, while planting a kiss on her gentleman caller's ever-expanding bald spot. She presented him with a frosty beer in her non-wolf fondling hand.

"He's done it!" she announced, as if she had nominated someone for a special honor and he had distinguished himself.

Gregory held his beer uncertainly, like he thought she might be proposing a toast. Akana lowered her muzzle and rolled her eyes. She seemed to be conveying that she simply could not believe it had taken this poor daft human female so long to figure it out.

"Jeremy!" Reina cried. "Jay-Jay!" The tableau remained unchanged. "Monnie's baby-daddy," she relented at last.

"He cheated," I guessed. I felt like I'd heedlessly sat in the front row at one of those shows where performers heighten the tension by dragging audience members into the act.

"Yyyyyesss!" Reina made a fist and barely refrained from pumping it in the air. "He didn't even try to hide it! *Monya is crushed.*" She sounded like a citizen journalist reporting on the ouster of a cruel regime.

"Did you talk to her?" Gregory still looked puzzled. Akana was disdainful. *Her* people had ways of dealing with these things. "Did she say she was crushed?"

"I don't need to talk to her." Reina dropped her fist. "I *know* her." She looked like he had just asked her if she was sad when her grandmother died.

"So she didn't say she was crushed," Gregory determined, holding his beer a little more confidently now. He sounded very scientific, probing a hypothesis.

"She didn't have to." Reina was still astonished. "He is her boyfriend. He is the father of her unborn child. And now he's running around with this little junior-league hussy . . ." She had gone very still, though the impression she gave was not one of serenity. "I found a picture of her. They're friends on Facebook. Friends. She's just a skinny little blonde thing, nothing to her. Nothing at all. Just a scrawny, ugly, little . . . *thing*. With blonde hair. I bet you anything it's fake," she added savagely. Her own loyalties were starting to blur. "She even went to her page and said, 'oh, Monnie, I'm so happy for you, blah, blah,' and then she just struts off with her boyfriend. Doesn't even try to hide it." She had presented her evidence, and it was irrefutable.

Gregory took a careful swallow of his frosty microbrew. "Maybe monogamy is not their arrangement," he articulated with perfect clarity, looking steadily at Reina. I swear Akana smirked.

"You know what?" Reina replied. Her voice was several degrees frostier than that beer. "It's been a long time since I had a good run," she concluded in a tone that suggested it had been a while since she'd had a truly gratifying shooting spree.

Reina was a marathon runner. She had double D fake breasts and a lifelong intermittent smoking habit that cropped up in times of stress, the way it always will if you thought cigarettes were really cool when you were thirteen years old. "I used to train twenty hours a week," she reminisced one time. She sounded husky and nostalgic and a little mad, like she did when she told me that she used to be like Danica, laying down her life for the cause.

"That's a part-time job," I remarked.

"Yeah. Well. Zack Hill was a full-time job. And I already had a full-time job. So." She shrugged. "Zack liked to live well. We went out. We drank a lot of good wines." She looked affectionately into the bottom of her glass, the way you might look at a beloved child who has disappointed you. Maybe by being a demon.

Reina still drank a lot of good wines. But every now and then, like a bad habit she'd picked up in her youth, she'd throw on her running gear and hit the trails behind the house. Hard. "I have my own theories about fitness," she declared; and because she was one of those people who can leap up off the couch and win a marathon— though probably not a prestigious one—while chain-smoking and refreshing herself with a few good wines, no one ever challenged her. Least of all to a footrace.

She was forty-eight years old now. Age is just a number, they say; but whoever they are, they seem to forget that we live in a world ruled by mathematical algorithms. When Reina came back from her run, she was limping and clenching her teeth, like a horse that will die trying to conceal an injury. Akana was civilized enough not to demonstrate a Pavlovian response to that.

"I think I need the laser, Baby," Reina said in a voice that was soggy with pain. It would be weeks before she healed enough to hurt herself that badly again.

Without a word, as if this were their established method of abolishing the differences between them, Gregory produced two pairs of enormous old-man sunglasses. They looked exactly like the ones my grandfather used to settle over his bifocals when he thought he might be about to encounter a little sunlight. With professional tenderness, he gave his lady-love his arm and led her to an overstuffed couch. She reclined with languid primness, like a Victorian lady about to receive a treatment for female hysteria. With a stern expression on the part of his face that was visible beneath the shades, Gregory took up a small wand and massaged the air about an inch above the injured knee. They looked like they had found their bliss in some elaborate intergalactic role-playing charade. Feeling more like a voyeur than ever, I absconded. I had a few small yellow volumes to read.

"I WAS TALKING to Gregory last night," Reina mentioned the next morning. He'd left early with his wolf and his wand, like a recurring character in a story where archetypal healers show up with symbols of their craft, deliver messages hidden in riddles, and leave at dawn in the company of beasts.

"What did he have to say?" I inquired, as neutrally as I could. They'd sounded like they were moving furniture all night, so I was surprised to learn that things had taken a conversational turn.

"He just asked some interesting questions." She looked out at the lawn. "Did I tell you Zack used to mow that whole thing? In slacks and a button-up shirt? It's about two acres." She turned away impatiently, as if the recital were some boring thing her maiden auntie used to tell her all the time.

"Dani's mom has a saying," she began again. She spun her heavy clay mug slowly in her hands, so the cream made lazy swirls in the thick black coffee. "She says a house is not a home." She eyed the manzanita railings. "Until there's been a birth, a death, and a wedding in it."

Her gaze lingered on a photograph of her wedding day at Foxglove, gleaming in its frame above the fossil mantle. The laughing couple was wrapped in an Indian blanket. Reina, six feet tall in red cowboy boots, nestled into his craggy old shoulder like a soft little nestling cuddling her mate and protector.

"I guess I'm two thirds of the way there," she observed, and took her coffee upstairs.

A SILVER WEDDING RING
A SPIDER PLANT

THE SEASON PROGRESSED at Serendipity Organics. We hung the pot under the house, where we discovered the emotionally damaged cat had been hoarding dozens of small half-eaten rodent carcasses. We lost a lot of enthusiasm for the cat that season.

There was very little enthusiasm for anything at Serendipity that year. The mood in Mendocino County is heavily influenced by the seasons, as in any agricultural economy. Here, the paranoia reaches levels of ecstatic jubilation around the end of August. The plants are almost ready for harvest then, and they stay almost ready for a long, dangerous time when days are hot and idle, there is no more work to be done, and nobody has any money. People get restless in the long cicada days of waiting and the short, chirping nights of the same. Minor breaches of etiquette take on heightened levels of significance. Unmarked planes swoop lowest and oftenest then, like hyenas skirting the herd when the young are about to be born. The end of summer is a very bad time to go hang gliding in Mendocino County.

By mid-October, everyone is too busy harvesting and cleaning weed to indulge in a good bout of antisocial behavior. The pot harvest is Northern California's finest argument in favor of the mental health benefits of productive activity.

But at Serendipity Organics, there was a sense that everyone had just gotten sick of averting disaster. The water ran out and nobody cared. "The rain will come soon," Alizarin promised. One of the dogs tore the hamstrings out of a sheep, and the creature stood blinking until another dog finished it off, at a leisurely, methodical pace. "How horrible," Alizarin observed, before drifting away to sprinkle fish meal on the hollyhocks.

Things came into focus while hanging pot with Morpheus under the house. Alizarin was in the kitchen, over-indulging in trail mix and paging through a seed catalog. She was planning a flower garden that would be magically watered by moisture that came out of the sky.

"You were married," Morpheus remarked abruptly. He was examining the intricate geometry of crystals in the buds. "I met you once. With your husband."

"Could you tell he was an idiot?" I laughed, then stopped when I heard how bitter I sounded, how experienced, and therefore no longer young.

"I didn't notice very much about him. He was just a guy." He shrugged. "But you were a closed box. I said that to Alizarin. I said, 'I've never seen anyone who was such a closed box.'"

I was glad he didn't ask me why I'd married such a nondescript entity. I was grateful that he was discreet enough not to ask me if I yearned for children. I'm always tempted to tell people I have an obscure gynecological condition when they ask me that, but I worry about the details. It's a rare treat to find someone whose sensibilities are delicate enough not to inquire.

"So why did you marry him?" Morpheus asked now. "He seemed so nondescript. Were you yearning for children or something?"

"I have never wanted children," I began patiently. I always feel like I'm trying to explain some impenetrable cultural difference when I tell people that. But the fact is, there has never been a culture where women are allowed to sit around not having children without a proper alibi. There is something about unused feminine machinery that piques people's curiosity and causes them to form opinions.

If you are a childless, able-bodied woman with no sense of urgency about the fact that your child-bearing years are dwindling away, you have a number of options. You can join a celibate religious order or go to a country where you don't speak the language. You can say you were born with vaginal agenesis, and explain that while you have the external genital equipment and normal ovaries, you have no vaginal canal, cervix, or uterus. You could throw in a few details about menstruation and kidney function to give the impression that you have either received comprehensive reading material from your doctors, or you spend a lot of time researching medical conditions you don't have.

Of course, you could always just tell people you don't want to talk about it. This guarantees that they will then look extremely supercilious and say, "oh! *Now* I know why"; as if a woman who doesn't care to discuss intimate decisions with a stranger must be cold to the point of frigidity.

"He just knew I'd change my mind," I told Morpheus. "And then when I didn't, it was like somebody promised him a sea monkey and it turned out to be a brine shrimp. Only I never said I was a sea monkey. I said I was a small aquatic crustacean, and he was like, oh, so I get a monkey, right? From the ocean. What an idiot." I felt like an unsympathetic character in a sitcom.

Morpheus didn't appear to notice. "So why did you marry him?" It was a simple question, and he asked it like a sacred fool.

"Sheer stupidity." I flung a few branches onto the wire, and they shivered, all the way down the line. The John was just so undeniably *male*, after all those years of mystic yonis, sacred whores, and endless female emotional process. He had a quick dismissiveness that made things seem so clear and easy; a way of laughing things off that looked like intelligent skepticism, if you weren't inclined to look too hard.

I thought he was honest, a plainspoken guy who called it like he saw it. When the first wave of dot-commers swarmed my city with their money and their startups, he lived out of his car and built intentional communities where people lived collectively and grew organic gardens. The fact that he built homes and lived out of his car should have served as an important nonverbal communication from a guy who never stopped calling it like he saw it—even when I asked him nicely if he would please just shut the fuck up and let me hear myself think.

"Which tells you who the real idiot is," I acknowledged. "See, I'm supposed to be intelligent and educated, and he's a fucking troglodyte. Do you know what he told me? Stone cold sober: he said he thought my mom was a MILF."

Morpheus was mystified. "A mill?" His hearing really was deplorable.

"A MILF. Mom I'd Like to Fuck. I am one hundred per cent positive I did not ever say, hey, my partner and my helpmeet: how'd you like to stuff your dick into my mom?"

Morpheus gave the branch he was holding a light swing, like he was contemplating taking up golf. "I find humor that relies on acronyms tends to be un-witty," he reproved at last.

"I don't think he was trying to be funny," I told him. I was enveloped in unexpected anger and disgust. "I think it was just a piece of information he thought I might find interesting. I mean, what did he expect me to say? Thank you so much for sharing? Let's have more open discussions about our wildly offensive sexual fantasies?" Morpheus smiled discreetly. "So what was the genesis of your marital bliss?" I inquired. My hostility was already fading into self-consciousness.

"I was just . . . so impressed with Alizarin," he said simply. It was the kind of thing people say to someone they will never meet again. "She's just so emotionally healthy and fair-minded. And she's so responsible. When we first moved up here together, we weren't married." He glanced at me, to see if I needed a few moments to adapt to the idea of premarital cohabitation. "And one day she pointed her finger at me and said, I'm going to marry you. As soon as I pay off my debts. And I thought, wow. Here is a woman who takes responsibility." He sighed and shifted a little. The golf club pot branch was still hanging from his hand. "Plus I thought, I'm starting to get a little old and soft. Maybe it's time to settle down. Get married."

"And here you are," I said cheerfully. I have never liked enclosed spaces. The one I was standing in right now, with its reek of rotting rodents and fresh narcotics, was losing its charm in a hurry.

He nodded. "Here I am." He was looking at the pot branch like he could not even hope to fathom how to hang it on a line. "What exactly did you do when you left him? I mean, how did you go about doing it?"

"I put all my shit on the sidewalk and left the country," I declared.

It wasn't true. That was the impulsive, swashbuckling version, the one starring me as the great renouncer who gave it all up and never looked back. Morpheus waited patiently for the boring version.

I sighed. "I called a random guy off craigslist. Richard. That was his name." Richard was a paint huffer, and he initialed each clause of the rental contract with a giant novelty pen in the shape of a baby doll's arm.

"He had a rental agreement with about a hundred addendums or codas or whatever. He said he was a lawyer, but he never went to work. I think he got a law degree but never passed the bar or fucked up a case because he was high or something. So he just subleased rooms in his place in Lake Merritt. He had about nine people stuffed into a three-bedroom flat." There was gunfire at night, but there was also a balcony, so it was possible to stand above the sidewalk with a glass of cold white wine, listening to gunshots and imagining oneself as a glamorous foreign correspondent.

"That flat was nine point seven miles away from the shittiest job anyone has ever held in the civilian sector of a modern industrialized nation," I went on.

I covered that distance on a pink 1982 Bertoni racing bike. My mother gave it to me after I got hit by a car while riding an off-brand mountain bike, which was exactly the same shade of green as a John Deere. "You've gone from the tractor to the Clit Rocket," she remarked, after noting that I was sure to have a few scars. The Clit Rocket was light and fast. My thighs began to look like something out of a drawing by R. Crumb.

"I painted boats all summer long for twelve bucks an hour," I continued, feeling less like a swashbuckling adventurer with every word I spoke.

"Did you really put your stuff on the sidewalk, or is it boxed up neatly in your mother's garage?" I had the feeling I could tell this guy I had a trust fund or a love of forest fires, and he wouldn't hold either one against me.

"No! I did." After all, the great renunciate version was not *un*true, in the strictest sense of the word. It was just abbreviated. "And then I left the country as an exchange student. All you had to do to get into the program was show up looking like a Young Republican and not break down crying during the interview."

To my knowledge, I have never laid eyes on a Young Republican. And if it hadn't been for an uncannily prolonged endorphin high that bordered on mania, I never would have stopped crying. That, too, is an abbreviated version.

"So that's the story," I told Morpheus. I'd finished hanging all the Chocolate Thai in my box, and now I eased his carton away from him and began to hang that, too. He handed me his branch, like I was his pot-hanging caddy.

"Did it take you a long time to do it? Once you decided?" He was watching me hang pot the way a scholarly tourist might observe a native as she performed a picturesque ceremony. I could have been a Balinese worshiper, stringing garlands on my gods.

"Not at all."

This, at least, was mostly true. I thought of how I felt washed in cool water when I left him. At Lake Merritt, I tucked myself into a room that was barely big enough to contain a washer and a dryer. There was in fact a 240 plug in the wall. Boxy outlines from the missing appliances were pressed into the floor. A single long black hair was curled into the folds of the mattress I put away each morning.

"The space I lived in was so tiny, all my movements felt ritualized," I said. It's the kind of thing you only say out loud if you are trying to impress someone with how quirky and insightful you are.

"I've felt that way at certain times in my life," he agreed, as if he were recognizing me. "Like, oh, now I'm doing the breakfast asana." And he began to flip a pair of unseen eggs, as slowly and deliberately as a Tai Chi master.

"Exactly!" It was such an unforeseen pleasure, to be recognized by someone who could conjure an unseen breakfast using ancient esoteric arts. "And everything felt symbolic. We'd gotten a matching pair of beautiful ceramic mugs, and the first day I was at Crazy Richard's, I dropped mine and the handle broke off. I felt like it signified how the useful part of my life was still intact, but I couldn't be grabbed and held onto anymore."

He was nodding and laughing, like I'd shown unexpected improvisational skill. Then he took a branch and hung it cautiously. Hemp is barely weaker than a hank of human hair, but he handled it as if he thought it were as dainty as a spun-glass rose.

"Have you seen Alizarin's ring?" he asked suddenly, surveying his work as critically as a master glass blower. Her ring. Alizarin had extraordinarily long thumbs, but I could not recall anything about a ring. "Her wedding ring."

"Did she lose it?" I prompted.

"It's silver," he finally revealed. His voice sounded ragged, like a kid who's just realized that his mother is a playground laughingstock.

"They're usually gold, aren't they?" I ventured. I had buried my wedding ring in the soil of a potted spider plant. The plant had been given to me by a woman much more beautiful than I am, the kind of woman who gives thoughtful little presents to the wives of men who are enchanted by her. I allowed that plant to die a slow and horrible death.

Morpheus nodded. "She has a gold wedding ring. But she says she's wearing the silver one because she doesn't think my commitment to the marriage is worthy of a gold ring."

I hung the last of the Chocolate Thai on the line and wrote END CT on the back of a paper bag. I folded this over the wire and fastened it on with a clothespin. Very slowly, I drew an arrow underneath the letters, pointing to the last branch of Chocolate Thai. There were no more paper bags, so I tore a sheet of paper from my notebook and wrote DIESEL, with an arrow pointing in the opposite direction.

"What is your level of commitment to the marriage?" I asked carefully. *Not here to take a whore's revenge*, were the words that flashed through my mind.

"I'm committed." He stood as straight and proud as a man who is ready to die well.

"Are you happy?" I persisted.

"I don't know if happiness . . ." he began. He sounded like his inclination was to deliver a dissertation on the perils of hedonism. Then he rallied, remembering the credo of his generation and his duty to uphold it. "I've been having what I think of as a matched set of dreams."

"Do you think they have anything to do with your situation?" I asked. I began to hang the toxic-smelling Diesel briskly on the line, like an efficient housekeeper organizing the fruits of a long season's purposeful labor.

"In the first one," he said, and stopped. "I haven't had this one since I left the City. Seven years ago." I noticed that he referred to San Francisco the same way Caitlin does, with an emphasis on "the city" that can only indicate a proper noun. "And now I'm having it again. It goes like this: my house is on fire. I'm living in a tall skinny house with lots of crooked fire escapes, like a drawing by Roald Dahl. The flames are coming out everywhere and I'm desperately trying to drag this Old World-looking trunk with ornate silver handles down the fire escape."

"Do you make it?" I asked. Diesel fumes were raging all throughout the underside of the house, like something subterranean released into the air.

"I don't know. I've never made it by the time I wake up. *You* seem to be familiar with symbols," he added, like he'd found a Josephean dream reader in the garden with the pot.

"What about the other one?" I asked. Maybe I did have untapped talents. Maybe I was wise.

"This one I haven't had since I was a teenager." He was almost eager now. "I'm carrying my own dead body," he reported with relish. "I'm looking all over for a place to bury it, but it's like that old *Batman* episode, where he's looking for a place to throw away the bomb. You remember that one? He runs over to throw it in the water, but there's a mama duck with her ducklings, so he rushes over to this secluded woodsy spot, but there's this couple having a picnic, and then there's a woman with a baby carriage and over here there's a gaggle of schoolkids and nobody notices the guy in the Halloween costume charging around with a ticking bomb. It's like he's having a nightmare."

"So what happens?" I asked.

"Oh, I don't remember. He has to de-activate it in the next episode with a hairpin or something."

"I mean in the dream."

"I don't know." He frowned. "I haven't gotten that far yet. It's like it's on a loop. There's no good place to bury your own body, I guess." He prodded the box of Diesel with a curtain rod. A thick snarling wave of odor thrashed into the air. "Wow, that stuff really smells like diesel."

PATRON SAINTS & BEASTS OF BURDEN

I'M SURE YOU'VE heard of mules. I don't mean the dead ones you find in Southern novels. I mean the live ones you can visit—if you clear it with the right authorities—in any one of many women's prisons. They are the bad boy's lovelorn dupes, caught with a diaper bag full of cocaine. They are desperate village maidens who can barely write their own names, swallowing condoms full of heroin. They are hardly ever single childless women just a few credits away from completing a master's degree in comparative literature. There is a sense of being insulated when you are doing something completely unsuitable, as if you're safe because you're not really doing it. As if at any moment you could retreat to your proper destiny.

And besides, I was just going to the post office in Finley.

The Finley post office is a run-down little outbuilding on the edge of a pear orchard in Lake County. If it were fulfilling its proper destiny, it would be providing shelter to a few old garden implements. The postmistress can warm the whole place with a space heater the size of a milk carton. According to Google maps, it is forty seven point three miles east of Serendipity Organics. Mendocino County is vast, but not unlimited.

To the south, the famous wineries of Napa and Sonoma offer endless opportunities for high-end alcohol consumption. The vines of Bacchus reach for the horizon in orderly rows. The tasting rooms are eminently tasteful. But as you travel toward the setting sun, the hills begin to jumble together. There are vagrant waterways and broken fences. There is desperation east of Mendocino County. The meth labs are unrelieved by the presence of eloquent activists, speaking up on behalf of their most beloved controlled substance. No speed freak ever got up in front of the Board of Supervisors and delivered an impassioned speech about the medical or religious value of methamphetamine. Consequently, the District Attorney of Lake County is free to be an unreconstructed drug warrior, making no distinction between cannabis and speed. The sheriff is not required to satisfy a constituency that includes a large percentage of politically active felons. The chief of police does not hesitate to take action when he sees a cloud of fragrant smoke pouring out of a moving car.

However, as Caitlin used to say, I am the flower of white womanhood. "People who look like me *don't* get pulled over," she declared, when she wasn't plotting unlikely encounters with law enforcement. Simone de Beauvois asserts that successful prostitutes are fundamentally conservative, since their profession would be impossible without a profoundly unequal status quo. Still, Caitlin's copy of the Bill of Rights was bookmarked with a bright pink sticky note at the fourth and fifth amendments.

I'm not sure how many pounds it was. I do remember that we filled two coolers, both with Alizarin's full name and phone number written on them in black capital letters. Alizarin planned a lot of outings in her role as a community arts educator, and found it useful to identify her equipment.

When we finally took a break from our conspiracy to distribute a Schedule I controlled narcotic, we all gathered round to have a cup of herbal tea (caffeine was frowned upon at Serendipity Organics). The coolers were wedged against the door, so no one would forget them in the rush to meet the connection.

The buds looked impressively professional, now that they were properly packaged. It was like taking a painting out of the studio, away from all the dirty rags and scabs of paint; like putting it in a frame and hanging it on a clean white wall. Hey, that's a real painting, you say, when it's removed from the signs of the effort it took. The same is true of pot: taken away from the litter of leaf and the clutter of agricultural endeavor, it starts to look like a luxury product. Something seductive, worth thousands of dollars and the risk of several years' lost liberty.

"I've been driving that car," Alizarin began.

We'd agreed it would be unwise to transport the investment in my pickup truck, which sported bright red temporary registration tags and had developed a medley of inexplicable sounds. Instead, I would use Alizarin's royal-blue Prius. It was a solid, leftward-leaning, middle-class vehicle. With license plates bearing the name of a Mendocino dealership, it did hint at the fact that it had been paid for in full with undeclared cash. You will find imperfect reasoning at the heart of every conspiracy. The conspiracy to distribute is no exception.

For example: why didn't Alizarin drive her own damned pot into enemy territory?

The answer is simple and eminently sensible: the Hebrew calendar is lunar. That year, the month of Nisan fell in winter, which is the most logical time to dispose of a pot harvest. Regardless of the season, eight days of Nisan are given over to Pesach, a celebration of the end of captivity in Egypt. It would be a bitter herb indeed if Alizarin Goldfarb were sitting in jail, in the company of lovelorn dupes, instead of breaking unleavened bread with her people in the Promised Land. Alizarin was on her way to Israel again, just as the markets were opening up and she was ready to sell.

To be honest, we all thought of prison as one of those things that's always happening to other people, like getting old or being dead. It was tasteless and melodramatic to invoke the possibility. And besides, Mercury was only just now coming out of retrograde.

If it promotes my case at all, I'd like to make the following statement: while it is tempting to use a government agency as a black-market courier service, I was not premeditating the felony of sending controlled substances through the U.S. Post Office. No: I had an assignation there with Melanie.

Let's just say that Melanie worked in quality control and acquisitions at The Club. It doesn't matter which one; just that pot clubs were beginning to be the gold standard that year. The field was bursting with outlaws, longing for the respectability of country clubs and tasting rooms, where they would all smoke good cigars and build their business empires. Medical marijuana dispensaries had a superficial air of legitimate yet daring entrepreneurship, like the dot-commers of the previous decade. They were edgy and criminal-minded, though they would rather avoid the inconvenience of actual criminality. They were smart, and they were cool, and if you were a serious grower with quality buds, they offered a smooth transition from outlawry to industry pioneership. Placing your product in a well-positioned club was a huge indicator of success. Also, the clubs would buy large quantities, which cut down on the number of people like Melanie any grower had to deal with.

Melanie was how I came to discover my affinity with Effie the dog, because Effie always seemed torn between the options of biting her in the face and hiding under the house until she was gone. Melanie was a non-stop talker, constantly reciting self-evident explanations, unoriginal theories, and professions of loyalty to various causes. She gave the disquieting impression of someone with bad nerves and a good memory who is fully capable of making an accurate confession. She had a bouncy, cheerful ponytail, which made her look unnecessarily wholesome, and the exposed parts of her suntanned back and shoulders were covered with Sanskrit tattoos. Worst of all, she refused to conduct any business whatsoever while Mercury was in retrograde. When she considered the consequences of committing an ordinary workaday felony during this dangerous time, her voice reached a pitch of such frantic urgency it was difficult to refrain from biting her in the face.

However, as soon as Mercury was in a more permissive mood, Alizarin would be attending to religious responsibilities in the homeland of her people. That meant someone else would have to call upon the grace of Mercury, god of commerce, eloquence, travelers, and thieves.

"I've been driving that car," Alizarin began again. "So I know for a fact that it's fine. It really is. I was all ready to drive it into Finley myself, three days ago, but *fucking* Melanie . . ." The smell of burning plastic from freshly vacuum-sealed bags attested to the fact that no one had been ready for anything three days ago. But the implication was that we could have been, if Melanie had given us any reason to stay up after midnight stuffing bags while the planets were inauspiciously aligned.

"And Steve says it's fine," Alizarin continued. "Steve would not lie to me. He says as long as you're not taking it over the Sierras— actually," she amended, mid-quote, "it would probably be fine over the Sierras. It's stop-and-go traffic you have to worry about. It's not the clutch, thank God. He's pretty sure it's one of the slave cylinders, but if it's the master cylinder I think I have to replace all of them, don't I?" She appealed to Morpheus, who regarded her as if it were a serious breach of gender-neutral decorum to assume he knew anything about cars. "Anyway," she went on with unsurprised resignation, "there's only one stoplight, just as you come into Finley, and if you pop it out of gear and rev it just a little bit—with the brake on, which of course you knew already—I think it'll be fine. *Steve* thinks it'll be fine," she added, to strengthen her argument. "I specifically asked him if was safe to take it to Finley, and he said, oh, yeah, just don't try to take it through San Francisco at rush hour or anything." She looked at me expressionlessly. It's the way people look at you when they've just offered you a terrible deal and are curious to see if you will take it.

IN THE SHADOW OF THE MOUNTAIN

WESLEY, WHO MOVED through clouds of scented smoke with beaded dreadlocks clicking softly, spent his last hour of freedom sputtering up Dolores Street in a badly maintained VW van. He was conspicuously desperate to make it out of San Francisco with a suitcase full of cash and a binder full of blotter paper. He was nabbed by a beat cop who wasn't even looking for him. Many years later, I turned my headlights on at the precipice of dusk on a lonely country road in Lake County and got pulled over for a broken taillight.

It was almost a relief when the officer began the long, slow walk from his car to mine. Finally, I could stop worrying about what I would do. *I haven't been pulled over since I was seventeen years old*, I reflected, wondering if this bore any resemblance to what that sheep was thinking as the dogs removed her entrails.

"Licenseregistrationproofofinsuranceplease," he intoned.

I began to notice things. I saw that the officer's eyes were crafty, like the eyes of a girl named Heather I went to high school with. Heather would say things like, "Hey. Do you believe in *vibes?*" as her friends convulsed with laughter. She had an air of barely repressed violence, which heightened the sense that she was always trying to extract a compromising confession.

I handed the officer my documents. I remembered that I had said, "Why are you asking me that?" when Heather and her cronies cornered me. They were so disappointed, I almost felt sorry for them, the way I feel sorry for wolves in nature documentaries when their prey eludes them.

The patrolman strode back toward his cruiser. I began to think, for no reason at all, that I might be able to handle this. I waited, listening to my thoughts interrupt one another, until the officer returned with my documents.

"Ms. Ah, Ms. Reen . . . hard? Reen-heart," he tried again, before moving on. "There seem to be some irregularities here." He gave me several moments to absorb the news. "There's no proof of insurance in this . . . envelope." He regarded the packet of documents I had given him with a sad little smile, as if I had tried to bribe him, but the amount was so insignificant, he was willing to overlook it. "Would you like to take a few moments to check around for it?"

I could feel cold air on two inches of skin at my waist as I leaned across the passenger seat to peer into the glovebox. It occurred to me that I was halfway lying down at the feet of an armed man I'd never seen before. I could feel him glancing at my sudden skin, then glancing quickly away. I knew the flesh was taut from my regimen of hauling heavy buckets of amendments up and down the mountain. I knew it was sprinkled with cinnamon freckles, and so did Officer Mauer, whose name I read on a ribbon above his right breast pocket. The corners of that pocket were indifferently pressed, which gave me a pleasurable feeling of disapproval. I wondered if you got in trouble, in the CHP, for having a badly pressed uniform. I imagined him being scolded like a scruffy little kid, before strapping on his weapon to protect civilians from people like me.

"I'm going to have to ask you a few questions," he decided softly, after my rummaging produced no results. "Please step out of the vehicle."

The frost on the grass crunched beneath my feet, because the shadow of the mountain kept it cold, all day long.

"If you could take a seat in the back of the patrol car, please," he continued, ushering me in with a gesture of purest gallantry. "I'm going to shut the door. Just so you don't get chilled."

I settled into the bench seat behind the silent French braid of a female officer in the passenger seat. I noted with some surprise that it was very comfortable, if one were gracious enough to overlook the metal grille between the front and back seats; the heavy smell of well-oiled weaponry; and the fact that the doors could not be opened from the inside. But the cushions had just the right amount of bounce. The heater purred with odorless efficiency, unlike the one in Alizarin's car, which produced intermittent blasts of armpit-scented heat. I wasn't much more miserable than I've been on most of the dates I've had in my life.

Officer Mauer took his seat with calm authority and pulled his door shut with the same. "Cold out there," he remarked, rubbing his hands together in a way that was either gleeful or sympathetic. It was hard to tell in the dwindling light.

The French braid spun around, but only partway, like a mean little dog whose movements are restricted by a very short leash. I could see her in three-quarters profile now, but I couldn't make out her name tag. "We have a *problem, Is*obel," she snarled. I could see particles of saliva backlit by the pastel sunset as she hit the *b*'s in "Isobel" and "problem" with unnecessary force. "You don't have *proof* of *in*surance."

I found that I enjoyed the way she emphasized the first syllable of the word "insurance." It made her sound plebian, which was as obscurely satisfying as if she had suffered some small but significant misfortune.

"Well, Alizarin is very good about these things," I murmured.

I tried to convey the sense that I could not imagine how this creature had found her way into my drawing room, but had resolved to be civil until she was gone. I realized, in that moment, that I possessed an advantage I had never consciously exploited. It seemed somehow unsporting, though, as I sat there in the perfectly regulated temperature of the patrol car, it occurred to me, too, that I had never cared at all about sports.

My advantage had everything to do with how Mauer and the French braid wore heavy boots and used imperfect grammar; how obedient they were, like lesser wolves in a great pack run by someone they called "Sir."

But I was a high-born outlaw. I knew exactly how to mark my rank by handing off a menu to a waiter without looking at his face; to take my tickets from an usher and forget immediately that he ever existed. This particular weapon is a constant, demoralizing reminder to those who would establish themselves as your enemies. It's how you show the world that you are one of those who eats the tips of the asparagus and drinks from the headwaters and gets to hold the ornamental stick. Those who detain you illegally in the back seat of a patrol car on a lonely country road are a minor inconvenience.

"You need *proof, Is*obel," the French braid insisted, like I'd failed to back up some flimsy assertion about a great philosopher. "Do you know what *proof* is?"

In my mind, I cast her as a pitiable waif who had just offered to recite a few scatological limericks at my black-tie dinner party. *Your dignity is unimpeachable*, I told my outraged self. I waited as blandly as I could for whatever inappropriate thing it was she had to say to me.

Mauer looked up from the ticket he'd been working on. It seemed to be taking him a very long time to document a broken taillight and a missing insurance card.

"How do you pronounce your last name?" he asked, turning a face full of genial interest in my direction.

I wondered if he was the kind of guy who scours the Internet for tips on how to pick up women. I pictured him studying the articles in a men's magazine, chewing the end of a ballpoint pen as he put together a script. I pictured him next practicing his keenly interested facial expressions in a shaving mirror. It made me feel like I was invading his privacy, which produced a voyeuristic certainty that I knew more about him than he knew about me. I knew him, I decided. I knew exactly who he was.

"Rine-hard," I said, trying to sound like I was charmed that he'd been thoughtful enough to ask. It seemed like it would be poor counsel indeed to tell him the Germanic roots of the name Reinhardt, so I kept the manly virtue and the foxes to myself.

He smiled, with a steady-eyed stare that would have made me sure he was a serial killer if we'd been chatting in a bar. "That is *such* a cool name." He gave the rapport a few moments to expand, then asked, "How long have you known Alizarin Goldfarb?"

I couldn't help but notice that he accented all the wrong syllables in "Alizarin," in spite of the fact that he had just heard me say it.

"Twenty-eight years," I said, and saw him check my license to make sure I hadn't just told him I'd known her longer than I'd been alive. I decided to be flattered. The French braid was simmering resentfully, like she was sick to death of being interrupted all the time.

"So you grew up with Ms. Goldfarb," Mauer concluded, like he was in the habit of collecting sociological data on everyone he stopped for a minor infraction.

"Actually," I said, as if I were getting ready to present the officers with a fascinating little-known fact, "I grew up with her daughter."

I gave a perfunctory smile, like an English teacher who is unable to allow an imprecise construction to stand. Later, I would decide that I had carefully strategized the importance of my near-familial relationship with Alizarin.

"So where is she now?" Mauer asked softly, like he was Mata Hari and I was a love-drunk general, about to give away the coordinates of my troops.

"She's in Israel," I chirped promptly, and added, "for Passover," as if I only associated with people who took their religious observations seriously.

To my amazement, I realized I was having a great time. I was alive to every flicker of meaning and motion. I hadn't been this alert since I was nineteen years old, working in downtown San Francisco as a bike messenger. This moment here, with Mauer and the French braid, was more exhilarating than riding through the Stockton tunnel at rush hour. I could feel it in my teeth, like flying down Bush Street with no brakes, darting in between the cars and blowing all the lights and bursting onto Montgomery without losing speed.

A second patrol car glided off the road and pulled in beside us. I was savage with unreasoning invincibility, the kind that's only possible when all your tender flesh is exposed to crushing metal, every working minute of the day.

"Excuse me, please," grunted Mauer, lurching out of his seat.

He was ruining my beautiful danger with his beer drinker's gracelessness. Another officer, a little younger and a lot beefier, heaved himself out of the second cruiser. They were starting to look like highly ineffective villains. The two men met about halfway between the vehicles, alert and lazy, like a couple of unneutered male fighting animals who haven't thought of a good reason to attack each other. They stood for a long time by the side of the lake with their hands in their pockets, not at all like agents of other people's destinies. They could have been telling each other tall tales about the fish they hadn't caught. I could see their breath, warmed by the insides of their bodies.

The French braid began to flip through a manual furiously, fuming as the two men turned their backs on us. She gave every indication of bearing a serious, personal resentment for Isobel Reinhardt, whose name she had just learned how to pronounce. It occurred to me that she was just as likely as I was to be telling herself a story; to be casting herself as the victor in some epic battle between her people and mine. I thought I could sense the contours of her story. It was stiff and memorized, and every child knew it.

I began to look at her. I could see her slim, knuckly neck, bowed over the manual with the eager misery of someone small and weak and heavily armed. I suddenly felt very gentle toward this woman with her regulation hairdo, a few soft wisps escaping its severity.

I was overflowing with the sense that I had never known anyone as well as I knew her when the third officer approached the car. He had a sulky sneer on his fat pink lips and a look of flat contempt in his shiny black eyes.

"Forget about the manual," he said abruptly. He sounded like a varsity quarterback, giving orders to a socially maladjusted lower classman. "I looked it up on this." He held up an iPhone, diluting his air of athletic command with the boredom of a disaffected tech-savvy youth. "Write her a fix-it ticket if you want," he concluded, in clipped, dismissive tones. He jammed the iPhone back into his pocket and turned away.

I saw Mauer duplicate his sneer as the two men passed each other.

"Catch you later," the younger one muttered, exactly like a normal human being who is allowed to say things like that without terrifying large segments of the population.

And then an extraordinary thing happened. That little officer who peppered me with spit and fury and never got a chance to be a really good bad cop—she, whose name tag I never did see—scrambled out of her seat and pulled open my door. Now it was she who made the gallant gesture as she ushered me out of the car.

"You have a good night, ma'am," she said earnestly.

She sounded almost devout as she released me into her county, calling me ma'am and holding the door. I realized that she had a certain callow classiness, the kind that lays a hand across its heart and bows its head; that says its prayers and is moved by words like "duty," "honor," and "brotherhood." She was watching me.

"Um," I managed. "Sure." And I drove away with two coolers full of someone else's actionable felony.

A DIGNIFIED EXIT

I CALLED MORPHEUS at Serendipity to see if he knew anything about the proof of insurance. I didn't want to seem overly eager to obey the French braid and Mauer, but I thought I'd carried my advantage far enough.

Morpheus was smacking his lips with tremendous enjoyment when he picked up the phone. "What's new and exciting?" he inquired. He sounded like he was making out with a bowlful of grapes. Suddenly, I didn't feel like entertaining him.

"Not a whole lot," I replied. "Hey, look, I got pulled over and the cops gave me a really hard time about the insurance on that car. I need to get that taken care of right away."

"Oh. Yeah." He slurped at something with such ecstatic gusto, it made me not want to eat anything, ever again. "Chris called about that."

"Who the fuck is Chris?" I wondered.

"The insurance agent," he replied. He sounded like he'd just spotted the first signs of my impending dementia. "CHP in Lake County called him and gave him a bunch of shit and he called here to give you a bunch of shit. But you weren't here."

"How did they find out it was insured?" I inquired.

"They ran the VIN, or the license plate, or something." He slurped diligently, like he wasn't going to leave those grapes alone until they'd all had multiple orgasms. "Everything's all connected to a computer."

"Well, I got some fairly dire warnings about the terrible things that will happen to me if I don't mail them exactly what they need by some specific date," I remarked. "Is that pretty much what Chris said?"

"Yeah, pretty much. He said he mailed it days ago, and he couldn't understand why it wasn't in the glovebox, where it's supposed to be."

"He *said* that?" I could tell he was nodding by the way the grape juice sloshed up and down in his mouth. "Dude, he *scolded* you." It was not the right thing to say. I could tell by the complete cessation of all disgusting mouth noises.

"It was Alizarin's responsibility," he declared, in a tone of such dark melancholy I could only hope he was trying to be funny.

"Well, if he mailed it," I suggested brightly, "maybe it's in the pile of mail by the phone?"

"Oh, there's a shit-ton of mail here," he agreed, sounding as if someone had indeed deposited a ton of something disagreeable, right there in the kitchen, where he was trying to have an affair with his food.

"So . . . is it there?" I prodded.

"I have no idea." He sounded utterly disgusted.

"Maybe if you poked around a little," I tried, remembering that Morpheus suffered acutely from male refrigerator blindness.

"Aren't you coming out here?" he complained.

"I'm not. I'm looking for a job," I explained. "Like everybody else this time of year. Look." I sighed, wondering why the hell I had to explain this to a grown man. "This is a big hassle. I know. Maybe you could just run off a copy on the printer upstairs and pop it in the mailbox, to me, and I'll mail it to the CHP in Lake County and then everybody will be happy and forget all about us."

Happily ever after the end, I added like a prayer. There was a long, silent pause as he contemplated his role in this plan. It was the simplest one I could think of. I knew there was a scanner in Alizarin's office, but I also knew there was exactly zero likelihood of getting Morpheus to scan and email anything. He expected all electronic devices to respond intuitively to telepathic commands. When they failed him in this, as they did every time, he punished them the cruelest way he knew how, by refusing to talk to them.

"I can't," he said at last. "I'm eating soup right now." And then, no lie, he hung up the phone.

He was still eating soup when I arrived at Serendipity forty-five minutes later, which is how long it took to get there from Foxglove. He reminded me more than ever of Effie the dog as he hunched over his bowl, surveying me with narrowed eyes. He really did have very small eyes, I noticed. I saw, too, that he had drops of glistening broth on his chin and shreds of something in his teeth.

"Got it!" I called so cheerily that even I could hear how much it sounded like an accusation. He nodded sullenly, like he was busy coming to terms with the fact that all women are incurably passive-aggressive.

"Alizarin thinks you're mad at her," he muttered as I sailed toward the door, determined to be as annoyingly cheerful as possible. I paused. He offered a grudging explanation. "She called right after I got off the phone with you." He sounded like he'd been bullied into conveying the message and resented it deeply.

"Why would I be mad at Alizarin?" I could hear the hostility in my voice.

"That's what I wanted to know." He stared off into space for so long I finally realized he was waiting for me to answer my own question. "She thought maybe, because of the car . . . And the cops," he added, acknowledging the possibility that there might have been something distressing about my roadside chat with Lake County's finest while trying to commit a peaceful felony.

"I gotta get going, Morpheus," I told him. "I have to get this in the mail." And I concluded my dignified exit.

THE FACT IS, I was plenty mad at Alizarin. I thought having a husband who wasn't even functional enough to go through a pile of mail was in extremely bad taste. Never mind that I had been married to The John, who was goateed and flatulent and panting over my mother.

I thought Alizarin should maintain her vehicle and her paperwork to a higher standard. Never mind the weather-beaten registration extension tags on the bucket of bolts I was pleased to call a pickup truck. I thought if she really cared about her investments, she wouldn't drop them in someone else's lap and leave the country at a crucial juncture, like a hard-hearted criminal cutting her losses.

My mind echoed with doubts and complaints. Had I really traveled so far and studied so hard to risk my liberty on a lonely country road? In my interview with Mauer and the French braid, I had put together an act, starring myself as the outlaw princess I had always wanted to be. I knew plenty of people who treated reality like it was an ongoing improv gig. Remember Morpheus, throwing gasoline-soaked rags into a stove to heighten the dramatic tension of his married life.

But my playacting with the CHP officers—which was only half a shade better than theirs—raised a question I had always shied away from, because I thought it might make people sneer. The John, who fancied himself a populist, would have sneered mightily at the faintest hint of it.

What if I really am too good to be a petty criminal? The thought of it produced a deep unease, as if I were setting myself above a class of people who were well-suited to trimming and muling and going to jail. Who did I think I was, to set myself above them in this way? I hadn't taken the time to cultivate any special abilities. I had no ability to captivate the powerful. No one ever held his breath as I made my way across a wire or out of my clothes or past a police perimeter. I wasn't dangerous to anyone, which meant I had no right to command anyone's attention.

And yet: I was steadfast. I was trustworthy. In the cheesy Kung Fu movie that was not, after all, my life, there would be a special ceremony with flickering firelight and somber music. I would be pronounced ready for the next adventure.

But now, I wasn't even sure I wanted an adventure. I wanted something else. It wasn't a cooler full of someone else's deferred prison sentence. It wasn't a permanent seat in the audience to other people's lives. I was sick to death of being a sidekick.

I wanted my own life, with my own risks. And I had no idea how to go about getting it.

MONYA CAME BACK to Foxglove. She looked like a poor dishonored creature about to throw herself into a well, haggard and forlorn.

"She should be *glowing* at this stage of her pregnancy," Reina stated gravely. But Monya was singularly glow-free. Her hair was dull. Her skin was gray with yellow highlights, like she'd been smoking two or three packs of cigarettes a day since she was six years old.

Mother and daughter took long walks in the frigid garden. She may have lacked glow, but there was a steadiness to Monya Harmann, a calm as unalterable as the structure of her bones. She was a woman who could raise a child in the mouth of a cannon, and that child would grow up with a sense of ethics so refined, he'd have to write a book about it.

But Reina—fearless Reina, with lovers and marathon trophies— Reina Serrano was openly scared. She began preparing gourmet meals with lots of beets and chard and grass-fed beef. She insisted that Monya drink only distilled water, which she had delivered in hygienically sealed five-gallon jugs. The jugs were plastic, but Monya was only permitted to drink the water from metal or glass containers. She was forbidden all unpasteurized cheese, which, in the United States, is only commercially available in Mendocino county and certain corners of Maine. The fridge was papered with lists of the top ten fruits and vegetables that absolutely must be organic and the seventeen species of fish most likely to contain high levels of mercury. Finally, the anxious grandmother-to-be cross-stitched a baby sampler that read, in darling pastel yellow cursive letters, "Abuelita's Leetle Angel."

"That'll look great with puke all over it, right?" She grimaced and snapped it sharply. "I might make it into a bib."

"Abuelita's Leetle Angel," I said slowly. "Do you guys speak Spanish?"

"My mom *is* Mexican. More or less." She bristled. "And no, as a matter of fact, I don't speak Spanish. But I am *not* going to have someone calling me *Grandma*." I had the distinct impression that things were going to keep on changing, just when I could use a little stability in my life.

I wasn't lying when I told Morpheus I was looking for a job. I was several months behind my trimming cohort, all of whom had dispersed into miscellaneous endeavors with gentleness and grace, the way people do when they walk around with a working theory of the world. I seemed to be the only one left, like the last stubborn coffee grounds or particles of sand that simply will not be absorbed when it's time to clean up and move on.

It was the middle of Passover when I responded to a flyer in the window of a local art gallery. Alizarin was still in Israel. Reina was compensating for her earlier negligence by scouring the Internet for stories about horrible things that happen to pregnant women. The articles on the fridge ran the emotional gamut, from motherly concern to paranoid screeds, with a few humorous gynecological sidebars for relief.

Now that's the kind of work a girl can tell her mother about, thought I, as I tore a copy of an email address from the fringe along the bottom of the flyer.

RUBENS' WHORES

MY PROFESSIONAL GOALS have always rocked steady on one simple theme: *DO NOT be a whore.* But then I found myself married, and Caitlin/Lilith was clacking away about how I'd joined her in the world's oldest profession.

"You know that marriage certificate is just a plain old-fashioned business contract," she purred. "It's a simple exclusivity agreement. Now if he takes his business elsewhere, you can terminate and collect indemnity." I was wondering how moving it would be to watch that smirk as I concluded my marital arrangements. "What will you do about your *chattels*?" she cackled. "Did you provide security in the form of a *dowry*? What will your *logo*—excuse me, please: your *monogram* be?" My mother has achieved a certain amount of notoriety for her incisive commentary on Hooker.organs.org. The result is that she tends to forget the simple fact that it is not her sole responsibility to eradicate every unreasonable psychosocial sexual convention.

"Why don't you just pretend you've been hired to play the gracious girlfriend," I suggested. "Pretend my wedding is a workday, and one of the conditions of the gig is that you have to be nice to everyone." I tried not to think about how many johns had given her detailed role-playing instructions.

"Oh, so you want the fake me," she exclaimed, suddenly affronted.

"Yes, please," I affirmed. "I think that would be lovely."

Caitlin was not invited to the wedding. She did not once allude to the event or the missing invitation, a combined omission that shone like two black holes until I ceased to be married, at which point they collapsed and lightened to the darkness of ordinary empty space.

But now, I thought I'd like to have a chat with the real Caitlin. Maybe Lilith, if she could refrain from playing the pedantic oracle for once.

"Mom," I hailed.

I winced at the fake chumminess in my voice. Did I ever call my distaff parent "Mom"? I did not. I called her Caitlin, because she

wanted me to call her Katy; or I called her mother, because she would
settle for Caitlin. She was sure to be on her guard after such an artless
opening. I braced myself for cold exquisite civilities. My mother reads
vintage etiquette manuals, when she's not keeping up on the latest
happenings in the fetish community or scrounging around in feminist
herstories for sexy morsels about female deities. She has been known
to demand a level of graciousness that would not be out of place at a
Civil War-era debutante ball.

"Is that my Izzie?" she crowed. "My Infanta! My Isabella of
Borbon. *And* Borbon. Izzie, sweetheart, how the hell are you? You
haven't been disfigured, have you? I can still see you clearly in my poor
old bleary mind's eye?"

I hadn't told her what I'd done to my hair. It wasn't a real question,
anyway. Some people just think it's funny to joke about disfigurement.

"I'm in Mendocino County, Mom," I told her. That phony-
sounding Mom again. I could rip my tongue out. Isobel the First,
that weak-chinned, strong-willed Servant of God, would have found
that course of action ladylike and proper, considering all the Jews and
whores I hung around with.

"Menn-dah-see-know Cown-tee," my mother trilled rapturously,
then gave a lavish sigh. "Harvest should be good and damn well done
by now. Did you get a decent crop? Your first time out and all."

"Mother," I warned. "I am not cultivating marijuana."

"Did you hear that, boys?" she enthused.

Shortly after my father vanished, we concluded that our phones
must be tapped, so we got into the habit of addressing comments
to the agents who might be listening in on our conversations. My
mother, reasoning that the decorum for such things was not covered
in her etiquette manuals and therefore must be sanctioned, had never
hesitated to share the details of what she called "X-capades" with her
mortified underage daughter. After the invisible agents may or may
not have joined us, she began to include them by adding, "Did you
like that, boys? Both hands on the table, now, where I can see
them . . ." We never did get any audience participation, but once
established, this family tradition only increased her proclivity for
treating every interaction like a performance.

"Okay. They hear you," I said now. Certainly it was rude to refer to them in the third person; but I assumed that even the most exacting mistress of etiquette would grant me an extenuating circumstance. "And anyway, it's not exactly a crime around here. It's just a felony. Which doesn't matter, because I'm *not growing pot*." I paused, after this translation into the vernacular. "I'm modeling."

"Mod-ell-ling." She drew this out slowly. My mother tends to act like she is under the guidance of a director who is legally blind, might as well be deaf, and is committed to reviving vaudeville for a non-English speaking audience. At this moment, I was sure she was doing a saucy imitation of a Betty Page pinup pose. "Like Betty Page? Are you a pinup girl?" She sounded cautiously gleeful, like parents always do when they think their children might have stumbled onto a promising career track.

I don't know why, but every time I get on the phone with my mother, I find myself trying to make her hate me. I do it on purpose, but really, I can't help it. We are like a couple of alpha females in a nature channel documentary, prowling around each other in search of weak points and the most flattering camera angle. Just once, I'd like us to meet for coffee, get a pedicure, tease each other lovingly. Where did I even get this idea? I picture a montage, with background music. Maybe we'd be wearing scarves over our hair, like beautiful 1940s movie stars on a windy day. Instead, we show each other our weapons, rattle them menacingly, and then put them back with much fumbling as we retreat, pretending we never advanced in the first place. I took a deep breath.

"Mom," I said. "Caitlin. Katy."

She was silent. I imagine she didn't know what to do with her hands, now that she wasn't posing like a red-haired Betty Page.

"If we were living in Bangladesh. Or Thailand." *If there was nothing self-indulgent or amusing about anything we ever did*, I explained silently. *If we had nothing to renounce.* "And you were in a brothel. And then I was born." *Please please please*, I prayed. I guess that was praying. "Would you sell me, Caitlin? Would you turn me out?" *Tell me what you really think*, I thought at her. *Just this once, you loud-mouthed whore, shut up and be sincere.*

I thought she'd say, "Fuck yes," with such unshakeable certainty it would be impossible to believe her. I'd planned, already, to peek behind the laughing mask and watch a tear run down her face. I knew what she'd say and how I'd respond.

"Isobel." She sounded very tired. "Isobel. If I had a beautiful baby girl in a hellhole like that—" I could hear rustling as she shook her head. Her hair brushed the mouthpiece of the receiver. "I would wrap her in the cleanest blanket I could find. My beautiful girl. I would walk and walk until I was ready to die. I would do anything, Isobel. I would work, and I would die—" I heard more rustling; and then, like she'd found her place in the script and could stop ad-libbing, she chirped, "Oh, hell, Izzers. I could get a better price for you from some menopausal American lesbian couple. Wouldn't that be fun? No leg hair in the bathtub, ever." She cackled like a smoker, though she never was. "Just in case you think you could handle two of *me*. What kind of modeling did you say you were doing?"

Of course, I lacked the job qualifications to be a pinup girl.

"You got those from your father," Caitlin used to remark of the feminine accomplishments upon my chest. "Of course, Haley—you remember Haley, don't you? She had a classic Roman toe. Being on the Committee never hurt *her*." My mother laughed lightly, like a broad-minded lady observing the enormous genitals on a representational work of art. "Let's just say the Catholic schoolgirl uniform *worked* for her." The Committee, of course, was the Itty Bitty Titty Committee, and my mother's mind was as broad as the open field she worked in. "She used to wear pasties that said 'organic' on them," she went on, like I might benefit from the tip. "You know, like from the health food store. When she danced at the tamer places," she added, so I wouldn't think of Haley's pasties as an unbecoming affectation of false modesty.

"Mother," I broke in. "I am not a pinup girl."

"Nobody's perfect," she chirped, quickly, like a bratty kid getting in the last word before the bell rings.

"I am an Art Model," I enunciated loftily.

"Nude?" I couldn't tell if she was elated or aghast.

Sex work is more than a job for my mother: it is the thesis statement of her life. She is like a researcher who starts to analyze the world from the point of view of her extremely specific discipline. She thinks hiring pretty girls to work as baristas is a form of pimpery; that the girls themselves are underpaid whores. "Really," she'll sniff, if the sweet young thing who makes her nonfat latte has a winsome way about her. "That girl is worth a lot more than just a wake-up wood. I certainly hope she's getting *paid*." And she'll glare sternly at the girl (who may have overheard this market advisory) as if in matronly disapproval at the spineless apathy of today's youth.

"Yes, Mother." I sighed, trying to sound as if this were the most boring possible detail. "I pose nude. No big deal."

The first time I stood up in front of a class, I felt my face flush hotter than I thought my body could sustain. I wished I'd never shaved my head, so I could take a classical maidenly pose with a curtain of hair cascading round my downcast eyes. If I'd kept my long, thick, already graying red-blonde tresses, I would be less naked. I could gaze into my split ends and not those pecking eyes.

It was not like being ogled. The students didn't leer. Rather, they pecked, looking more at their drawings of me than they did at me. It reminded me of people who are constantly interrupting you to tell you what kind of person you are.

Peck, peck, peck, taking my measure in quick little pecks, except when they squinted to flatten me out and take a more precise measurement of how many naked head lengths I possessed, from the crown of my skull to my stained calloused heels. When artists measure a model, they close one eye and straighten the arm holding the measuring tool—usually a pencil—and they point it at the model. They want to make her two-dimensional, to bring her down to size. They want to see how many fractions of a pencil length her head is, if the distance from chin to breast is one full head, and how many heads from her nipples to her groin. Hardly anyone can close one eye without baring their teeth, so when they do this, they look like they are snarling as they take aim at the body on the stand.

It was a large classroom with a gray baseboard wall behind the podium, which was not a podium at all. A podium is where the learned and lovely stand. I displayed myself on a huge wooden slab of a table that the instructor and two of his students struggled to move to the center of the room. Someone had strung wire between the years' worth of tacks and nails in this wall, so I posed before what looked like an abandoned Paul Klee drawing, made of wire. I thought I might pass out. I hoped I didn't fall with my legs wide open, gaping at the classroom full of aspiring young artists.

"It's really not a big deal, Mother," I said now, hoping I sounded like someone who had lived in continental Europe. "It's not like these people are voyeurs. They're celebrating the human form."

My mother sounded like she might be choking. "Isobel Marie!" she gasped at last. "Don't you know that all of Rubens' models were whores?"

"Because whores in the seventeenth century paid so much to have their portraits done?" I retorted.

If only she hadn't picked Rubens. In my mind's eye, I could see the great man's drawing of a lady with a peacock collar, looking skeptical, amused, and sideways at the master as he took her likeness. She had a small, sharp mouth and a small, sharp beak of a nose. She had great thyroidic eyes and a forehead broad and bright enough to give a phrenologist heart palpitations. As usual, I could not remember names or dates. I would have loved to say, in a bored, even tone, "Mother. Are you not aware of the drawing commissioned by the Lord and Lady What's-Their-Name of the Whatever Court in the Year of Our Lord Sixteen Hundred Blanketty Blank?"

But my mother plowed ahead. "Oh, not the Ladies Whoozit and the bankers' wives and all those *mistresses* trying to buy their way into the aristocracy. I mean those fat-assed bathing beauties and the Venuses and Ledas and that *leering* Andromeda. Let's all celebrate cellulite, shall we? Will anyone ever render cellulite with that degree of love and care and—I mean, what a chubby-chaser. The original flab-fest fat fetishist. I'll tell you what he had in his other hand, and it wasn't a paintbrush. Honestly, Izzy, if you'd just pay the tiniest bit of attention to history . . ."

"So I could honor it by repeating it?" I managed to insert. That was a good one; but Caitlin didn't even salute me, like she would have if we were going about this honorably. "You sound unhappy, Mom."

"I'm not unhappy, I'm astonished. This is . . . *well*. Do you think for one second those high-minded artists aren't hiding hard-ons behind their easels? Why do you think they wear smocks?"

"I don't care if they are, Caitlin. It's not my business." I took a deep breath. "Since I'm not a whore."

"Maybe not," she said evenly. "But they only want what every john wants from one."

"Someone who will pretend she gives a shit? For a price?" I could feel my lips drawing away from my teeth.

"Ask any painter's wife or girlfriend or mistress if she didn't pose for him first," she commanded. This was her area of expertise. I could tell I was trespassing as clearly as if she'd squatted at the boundary and marked it. "They're shopping, honey. That's all they're doing."

"Do you know what you sound like?" I could hear my voice starting to shake. I had a logical argument. "You sound like a Republican." *The facts are on my side*, I thought triumphantly; but she refused to hear me out.

"Of course I can't prove what's going on in other people's heads," she allowed, as generous as only a victor can be, "but trust me, sweetie, there are some things a person just *knows*."

There are times when my mother's mix of perfect diction and vulgarity makes her sound like someone's stock idea of a naughty schoolteacher, all formal hair and high-necked dress, open to reveal her garters and her black lace peekaboo bra. Other times, she sounds like she's been driven to measures she would never dream of, the coarseness in her mouth as foreign as a shotgun in the hands of a well-born lady protecting her virtue. And, like that determined virgin, tightening her grip, no one is more astonished at her unexpected competence than Caitlin known as Lilith. Now she was ferocious.

"Men," she said, drawing the last word like a poisoned dagger, "don't *celebrate* the human form without a few emissions. It's about time you knew that."

"Not everybody has sex on the brain all the time." I knew I sounded like I was begging to be heard. I had expected this conversation to be very much like the one that preceded her absence from my wedding, the one where she cackled and called me a whore. Why did she cackle when I married, and then act like she'd have to cross my name out of the family Bible when I took a few classical poses at an accredited college? "You sound like some crazy religious fundamentalist. Why do you think women wear burqas? Because people are obsessed with the perils of sex." Too late, I realized I had left a few steps out of my logical argument.

"That is exactly what I'm saying," she said patiently. She sounded like a highly trained customer serviceperson—which is exactly what she was—deflecting the outrage of an unreasonable client. "I think I know a little bit more about this than you do." Her voice came down about a quarter of an octave, as if she knew a lot more about my marital problems than I did.

"Are you saying we should hide our bodies unless we're fucking?" I screamed into the silent phone line. "Because sex is all they're good for? How is that materially different from fundamentalists who say that sex is just for procreation?" But Caitlin, I knew, was brewing her tea. She had an herbal infusion for every emotional occasion.

I put the phone down. I felt like I'd spent my life decoding hieroglyphs, only to discover the cuneiform was full of pompous dirty jokes about the Lord and Lady Wee-wee.

"That answers that," I said out loud. I brewed a cup of strong black tea.

TUMBLEWEEDS AND DIM SUM

CAITLIN WAS AS easy to see through as a lace peignoir. She was just a cocksucking whore, and she knew it. She with her high-flown talk of temples and the Sacred Vulva had no secret message more confounding than the fact that people fuck. But I carried a parallel text in the stele of my own being, hacked in hard and deep, like an act of the most painstaking vandalism: *Do not ever be a whore.*

Not that I never wondered how it would feel to bring a man to his knees; to awe him with my power. Once, in early spring, I stood on the highway outside Soledad, watching white smoke and tumbleweeds and thinking, *I could fix this if I had the nerve.* The smoke was pouring out of a twenty-three-year-old Honda Civic I had bought with a year's worth of waitressing tips, and the tumbleweeds were tumbling because that's what spring is like in Soledad. A real season of renewal.

When the tow truck driver arrived, I tried to imagine how I would handle the situation if I possessed the proper secrets; if I dared to use the power that was mine. Did I have the brutal charm that Caitlin had? I did not. I sold him my car for three hundred dollars. Then I called my mother. I was crying so hard I was choking on snot. She dispatched a client, one she'd dismissed for the crime of falling in love. Marriage is a whore's retirement, but dating a man from "the office" is a failure of imagination. He drove from Hollywood to Soledad alone, from Soledad to San Francisco with the tear-stained, travel-smeared daughter of his one true heartless love. He was hygienic, discreet, and what ladies in the ads in free weeklies describe as "generous." Caitlin known as Lilith swore she didn't mind.

There was a reason I was so ill-equipped to take my place among the goddesses and archetypes who chomp the heads off little men and pick their teeth with bones. It is a reason that prevents me from enjoying several savage pleasures; from wallowing and plunging and generally abandoning all sanitary codes to embrace the unshaven and the slimy, the wild-eyed, graceless, and urgent. The truth is that I am equipped with a finely tuned instrument of revulsion. If I begin to realize that a man is attracted to me, chances are my instrument will home in with the precision of a surgical camera on some minor detail no one else has ever noticed. I become preternaturally alert to the horribility of his hands, the skin beneath his eyes, some fleeting moment of his facial features that seems furtive, guilty, or cruel. I was so unfit to flirt, it took me over a year of waitressing to buy a car that lasted less than that.

When Frank the plumber winked at me across a plate of eggs, I imagined his big meaty hands on the soft parts of my body. I felt my face freeze in horror and wondered if I was capable of fainting. When Jerry the veteran began to gaze at me earnestly, I noticed how the skin beneath his eyes made his cheeks look like a pair of melting candles. I thought about that skin moving close to my face and bolted for the kitchen with a stack of greasy plates. With the man I married, it was his chin. I didn't notice how horrible his chin was until it was too late.

The John's chin wasn't weak, exactly. It was just extremely small. Plus, at some point, he started smearing Vaseline on his mouth, which made him look like he had just been devouring something greasy and obscene. The lower part of his face began to fill my field of vision. I could not look at any other part of him.

Once, shortly after I almost had to stop looking at him entirely, I happened to notice that his face looked perfectly normal. We were lying in bed, and I sat up to brush my hair. I had hair then. It was oppressively beautiful.

"Hey," I said, surprised into affection. "I just realized that your chin is really not that small."

"What are you talking about?" He was falling asleep. He always fell asleep. He didn't care about clichés. And yes, I was having sex with a man I could not bear to look at. If I am not mistaken, that is exactly what my mother does for a living.

I decided an unadorned explanation was what the situation called for. The John and I cared about communication, authenticity, and respect. So, in my most reasonable, non-calculating tone, I began.

"I think, because of the difference in our heights, when I look up at you, I perceive your chin as being much smaller than it actually is. But looking at you just now, lying down, I realize that in fact you have a perfectly proportionate chin." I breathed evenly, like I did when smoke began to trickle into the interior of my car. I have always believed that a calm rational attitude has the power to banish disaster. But it's magical thinking, to believe that logic will prevail in a situation ruled by a heart gone numb or the installation of an after-market electrical system.

The John grew a mustache and goatee, which he tended like a hothouse full of orchids, and which made him look disreputable— but only like the villain in a children's movie, easily vanquished and bristling with endearing neuroses. He installed himself in a spidery black ergonomic desk behind a large computer screen. It was comical and sinister, indicative of dark disorders. It was exactly the kind of furniture a Disney-generated malefactor would use. Presently, he forgot the primary purpose of whores and became the avuncular confidante of several young women my mother was mentoring. "I like to keep my hand in," she explained. I did not ask her what she meant by that, mostly because I knew she would tell me if I did.

I reached a point where the sound of my own husband's breathing filled my heart with hate. I began to drink fizzy pink cocktails that made me feel like I had high-heeled Playboy bunny slippers on both sides of my brain. When The John went lobster diving with an American-born Chinese/Thai contortionist who called herself Dim Sum, I finally had enough.

I had been loved—I thought—by a man who was not moved by ordinary temptations. He taught yoga and drank tea with scholars of obscure religions. In an age of greed and easy money, he joined a tiny underground community that bartered goods for services; where people knew the names of springtime flowers and raised chickens in their backyards in Oakland and held forums on how to eradicate racism.

I married him without due diligence. But that was not the biggest mistake I made. If I wanted a shoulder to cry on, the dumbest thing I could have done was go crying to my mother.

I should have known immediately, by the way she occupied the seat across from mine. We were in the kitchen of the home she bought herself, when my father left her for a younger more beautiful woman. We were sitting at a table she had carried on her back from a garage sale where a dead man's heirs knew nothing about the value of his things. The walls were painted with colors Caitlin Swift had mixed, and the windowpanes were made of beveled glass with ripples in them. Glass, essentially, is slow-moving water. If you wait long enough, say, a hundred years, you will begin to see it swirl and run.

"What did you expect?" my mother asked me, when I'd poured out my tale of woe.

"I'm supposed to expect him to hop on a boat and go lobster diving with a contortionist?" I asked, just to make sure.

My mother smiled briefly. "It is the season. Tell me about this contortionist. What's her name?"

"Karen," I said. "Karen Lau. She's—"

My mother waved her hand. Her bracelets flashed. "No. What you said before."

"She calls herself Dim Sum," I muttered. "It's supposed to be a joke. Because you can have as much as you want of so many different things. It sounds like an insult, right? I mean, she says that to a couple of white people, and we're supposed to laugh? Like racial fetishes are funny or something. It's so awkward."

My mother was looking at me like she'd never seen me before. "And you think a white guy who collects Japanese swords might not have a tiny bit of a race thing going on? Let me ask you this: did you ever even try to find out? Did you—"

"That is so shallow," I protested. "And anyway, Dim Sum isn't even Japanese. I don't think she's ever been near—"

"She's highly intelligent, is what she is," my mother interrupted. She had clearly designated herself the dispenser of racist stereotypes for the day. "She knows how to do her research. She's not squeamish—" She held up her bracelets again, to forestall another interruption. They rattled up and down her forearm. "She knows how to pay attention." The bracelets went silent.

"Pay attention to what?" I asked in the hush.

"Let me ask you a few more things," my mother replied. "Why do you think your husband went on this trip with this woman?"

"I didn't have the money to rent the gear," I admitted.

Part of our marital program of equality and respect involved keeping separate finances. By that time, The John had signed on as a finish carpenter with a highly respected construction company in

Marin. I was taking classes at City College and working as a barista at a coffee shop that also sold Beanie Babies and collector's editions of Pee-Wee Herman dolls.

"Did you know Dim Sum was going to be on that trip?" she asked softly.

"I don't care about Dim Sum," I replied indignantly. "She talks in this squeaky stupid voice around men, and when it's just us, she sounds like she's been chewing rocks. She's so obvious."

"Karen's hilarious," my mother murmured. "I thought you'd like her. Look. I think what happened is this: Karen's playing with you. She's testing you. She wants to be your friend, and I told her you had a little more mettle than this. Maybe I was just projecting." She looked at me closely again.

"I don't think I really need a friend who finds it hilarious to walk around in a gold lamé bikini in front of my husband," I retorted. "And I don't think I need manipulative tricks to have an honest relationship."

"Do you think marriage is an honest relationship?" Her voice was very soft. There's a fallacy in argumentation called the fallacy of rhetorical questioning, which is a thinly veiled attempt to make a claim in question form. The implication is that the answer is obvious. "Don't you think your sainted husband might be just a little sick and tired of all this high-minded respect and understanding? People like to play, Izzie. Maybe he wanted you to dress up in a kimono and have a sword fight with him or something. Didn't you ever even try to find out? Maybe Karen is trying to help you. Can't you take it that way?"

I couldn't. I put most of my worldly goods on the sidewalk and left the country. I had a large red Samsonite suitcase and a fresh tube of toothpaste, the latter of which was confiscated before I was allowed to enter international airspace.

I had failed to maintain the interest of a man who was enthralled by the deeper meaning of Japanese swords and gold lamé bikinis. Next, I failed to shed new light on the metaphysics of a long-dead German genius. But I could keep my cool in the back of a cop car. I could ignore my aching muscles and maintain a graceful pose. Not bad for a fiscal year or two. But it was late April now. The students in the drawing class were working on their final projects, making copies of old masterpieces. It was time for me to put my clothes back on. The ground was heating up, and the days were getting long. The season was starting again.

PART THREE

MORPHINE

IN THE FEUDAL COURT
A MUTANT CAT AND IRON GOATS

"IT'S A PATCHWORK Mendocino lifestyle," I acknowledged lightly, hoping I could make "unreliable petty criminal" sound culturally relevant. A bland smile numbed my face as a stunted yellow tabby somersaulted onto my lap. The animal began to writhe in a way that was highly illustrative of why certain job sites are called cathouses. It looked very much like this particular cat was having an erotic interlude; which, if you think about it, didn't make me much more than a giant feline sex toy. I gave the top of her head a perfunctory pat. I wanted to give the impression that, in addition to overflowing with kindness, I was not the type of person who suspects a housecat of masturbating during a job interview.

I read somewhere that the yellow tabby gene occurs on the male chromosome in cats, so the little creature burrowing into my thighs was probably some kind of bizarre domestic mutant. It could only be an improvement on the basic design of a species that is deceitful, murdering, and extremely unhygienic. I told Fiona Jones I'd come to Mendocino County because I had a once-in-a-lifetime opportunity to work with the renowned muralist, Alizarin Goldfarb.

"You know," she replied, drawing it out slowly, like someone producing a weapon for the sole purpose of displaying the aesthetic merits of the blade. "I went to art school. In London." Her speech was full of faintly foreign idioms, of crisply enunciated *t*'s and *r*'s so softly rounded they emerged like well-dressed vowels. "But really, I don't care at all about art." Her tone was masterfully inoffensive. She smiled with her mouth closed, squinting into the past. "I only went because, well." And that "well" had a ripple in it, the kind that implies a sound like gentle laughter, without a trace of mirth. "Because I could. And—" She settled her squint on a poster with several dozen photographs of sheep on it. Each specimen was accompanied by a detailed paragraph about its region of origin and the quality of its wool. "Because, you know," she went on with a careless confidential something I would not quite describe as amiable; "it was a place where I could be a bit crazy." It was an unambiguous statement of intent. I hope I never have to come up with a story about why I ignored it.

I had developed a philosophy about job interviews in the back seat of that patrol car. After all, what happened in the shadow of the mountain was a job interview. I was being interviewed for the job of not being in prison. My desire to get that job enhanced my awareness of social cues to the point where distinctions between me and my enemies evaporated. It was a standard mystic revelation, with pragmatic applications.

For example: people talk about applying for a job as a matter of selling yourself, which means you have to win people over. You have to convince them that you are right and others are wrong. But I had learned that I would know exactly what to say, in the moment when everything hung in the balance. I had learned the special knowing that comes with danger, and how to breathe into the pause that invited me to plunge. It was dancing in between the raindrops, a spell that lasts until the sun comes out or the rain comes down. It required perfect concentration, a variety of luck with just a pinch of skill. I may have been a kingpin's daughter, but that kingpin was a wire-walker, and wire-walkers fall.

That is how I found myself on a narrow dead-end road that ran along the river, in a valley full of coyotes that sang in wild harmony when the night was full of stars. I was there to make sure I never had to talk my way out of a cop car again. If I could do that, I decided, I could talk my way into a job.

Fiona Jones was screening applicants for a caregiver's position. The client was old and sick and not likely to recover. It was only a long slow dying, not a reckless risk. Optimism can be a very grim thing, when you are abandoning a life of illegal enterprise.

When I pulled into the long, dusty drive, I saw a metal sign on an arch above the entrance. I took it as a signal that I was in the right place. Two rusty iron Billy goats butted horns against opposite ends of a wrought-iron phrase. *"Marianas Hof im Tal der Berge,"* it announced. German can be so redundant. Where else would a valley be, if not in the mountains? I knew for a fact that I would be the only applicant who could translate that sign. After all, I had crossed the ocean twice to read little yellow books in tiny print with vowels that had dots on top of them. I told Fiona Jones that "Hof" has feudal connotations; that here we were on the estate, or in the court, of Mariana in the valley of the mountains, where I could be useful in more than one tongue.

"I always wondered what that meant," Fiona murmured. She sounded like a great lady, idly waiting for a peasant lass to bring some lowly needful thing.

Fiona created an air of stillness in a place that was indeed very much like a Hof. The grounds included spacious gardens, several outbuildings, and tenants who generated income from agricultural activities. For many years, however, Mariana's estate had consisted solely of her bed. She lay there wearing headphones, watching television, and eating very slowly with her hands. If there had once been plate and silver; if her father was a *von*; it didn't matter anymore, because Mariana Blanchefleur no longer had the use of them. Her speech was slurred. Her hearing was bad. When I tried to speak German with her, I heard, to my horror, only an infinitive verb at the end of a jumble of sounds.

"Well, if you like her." She smiled in English at Fiona.

"I think she can hear us," Fiona replied gravely. "We should wait."

They didn't wait long. Fiona called me at Foxglove, where I was paying my rent by digging bull thistles out of the lawn. In inland Mendocino, almost all the pot is grown outdoors, which meant the only thing scarcer than the demand to see me naked was the need for the only well-honed skill I had at the moment.

"Hey. Listen." She sounded reckless, which, in her nasal English accent, was thrilling and unladylike. It sounded trashy and classy, at the same time. "Do you really get *into* things. I mean, when you decide to do them do you just say, hey, let's get this done; and really do it."

She had Caitlin's habit of making a question sound like a statement. I began to speak enthusiastically about my great love for gardening and art; but she cut me off.

"Because. Because, if you do, I think we can make this thing work." She sounded like she was organizing an event where ticket holders could expect some kind of illicit excitement. "But," she continued, like her principles demanded that she make a full disclosure, "I don't know what you'll do all day. When you're here, I mean. It can get quite boring. I try to interact with her, between about ten and ten-thirty, and then again at three; but there's quite a bit of, well, waiting. D'you see?" She did not say what she was waiting for.

"I could paint," I ventured, feeling virtuous and forthright.

Painting, after all, is not like reading a book, which is how I have compensated myself for the majority of brainless jobs I've held in the past. You can't sneak off and while away the badly-paid hours with an easel and a palette and a sloshing jar of solvent and your carefully constructed lighting situation. You can't just heave it all under the couch, grab a duster, and pretend you've been busy all day removing dust motes from a few acres of knick-knacks.

"You're not allergic to oil paint, are you?" I inquired. That was a good touch, I thought.

"I don't know," she said dismissively. Maybe she had been a sculptress, when she went to art school in London. "I have a device," she murmured. She sounded like she might have been reflecting on whether it was a good idea to tell me that or not. "You just plug it in. It cleans the air." Her voice quickened a little. "It charges the atmosphere. Like lightning. It really cleans out the negative ions. You'll see."

I did not see. Fiona must have thought better of her decision to show me her device, which should have made me nervous but didn't. What I did find alarming—though I decided to regard it as a test of my courage—was the mass of flesh beneath the pastel comforter. The sheer indifference of this unstoppable human machine as it churned out waste and fragments of thought; as the eyes blinked and the mouth chewed and the hands crawled slowly back and forth across the counterpane: any part of it should have made me run; and not one part of it did.

Mariana Blanchefleur was tremendous. She was imposing. Worst of all, she was completely helpless. She gave the impression, in her hospital bed, of being perched on the crest of a mountain with her hand on the brake, contemplating the scenery below with faded blue eyes. There have been a lot of pale blue eyes in my life, but I have never gotten used to them. They tend to seem a little blank, the tiniest bit fixed, like the intelligence behind them is liable to mania or idiocy or a perception unclouded by the need to understand.

Fiona's eyes were pale blue, too. I began to realize that her stillness was that of an indrawn breath. She was waiting for the body on the bed to die before she could continue her own life. If I had had the capacity to be nervous about her unseen ion-cleansing machinery, maybe I would have been horrified by the fact that I envied her.

When I was fourteen years old, wearing floral-patterned Spandex leggings like a Russian dowager, I wished more than anything that I had the right to be as miserable as I was. Somehow being fatherless and unattractive, at an age when girls are obliged to be pretty, lacked the dignity of proper misery. I always suspected that I didn't deserve to feel the way I did, as if unhappiness were a luxury a person had to earn. I was sure some vivid, authentic person was going to find out that whatever I was doing or feeling was not the real version of it. What I wanted, then and now, in Mariana's Hof, was to be seared by something real; to serve in a capacity that was beyond the endurance of an ordinary human being.

And so I began a course of instruction on the quantities of shit a human body is capable of generating. We had a form to fill out, regarding the frequency, consistency, color, and amount of a substance that disregarded diapers like a river leaping its banks. The bedding was fouled beyond belief, every single day. The shit coursed into the folds of Mariana's flesh like something geological, filling in spaces and smoothing terrain.

We had detailed instructions as to allowable quantities of sugar and fluids; which television programs were appropriate; and how long the patient was to lie on which side every morning. I was shocked to see that these instructions were full of grammatical errors; that the patient was to *lay* on alternating sides for twenty minutes; that she was to have an *amount* of something clearly numbered; and that errors in parallelism abounded. I suffered from the poorly articulated notion that good grammar signaled organized thought. Fiona's British accent had seemed to indicate that all suffering would be conducted in well-spoken dignity. It was a hard blow, to find myself elbows deep in shit with someone who had never heard of Schiller.

Still, I descended into the valley of Mariana's Hof three times a week, for the remainder of spring and into the summer. Mariana continued to eat extremely slowly with her hands; to greet her dentures every morning with a rusty but serviceable, "hello there, teeth"; and, once they were glued to her gums, to grin in an unsmiling way that was far more reassuring than the empty black hole of her undressed mouth.

And then one day, everything changed.

THE TRAIN DEPARTS

"MARIANA HAS SHARED something with me," Fiona reported when I appeared at eight o'clock one Friday evening. "I've spoken with her son about it. Also, I spoke with His Holiness." She gazed off into the near distance of the far wall. She was poised and inscrutable.

"Who is His Holiness?" I inquired, feeling my tongue shrivel with the alliteration and hoping I sounded graceful and neutral, like Fiona, when I said it.

She turned her pale, protruding eyes on me. I saw that the irises were separated into sections by thin black penstroke marks, like the spokes of a wheel. The sections were pulsing at what appeared to be slightly different frequencies, like the engine behind them was firing on a set of poorly synchronized cylinders. "The Buddha Maitreya," she said gravely, like she was actively forgiving me for not already knowing that. "I don't know how much of this you care to hear"—she smiled faintly—"or how much you know about Buddhist cosmology."

Where was I while this was going on? I was standing around waiting for something real to happen. That's where I was. And I think Fiona sensed it, in the uncanny way that crazy people sense the things about us that are most embarrassing, most trivial. Most real.

"It really is real," she told me now, with the same brittle, peremptory briskness that crept into her voice when she insisted that the inner leaves of a head of lettuce cause cancer; that vegetables need to be hermetically sealed in large Tupperware containers so they don't absorb the harmful chemicals inside the refrigerator. "It really is real," was a common refrain, if you cared to hear what Fiona had to say.

So what had she discussed with the Buddha Maitreya? "Mariana has opened her heart to me." Her voice was so cool when she said this that she might have been discussing the state of someone's linen closet. "She's done. She really is. Do you understand?" Again, the pulsing in the wedge-shaped sections of her pale blue eyes.

"Done," I remarked thoughtfully. "With . . . what?" I have always prided myself on my ability to ask incisive questions.

"Done with all of it," Fiona replied.

Her English rose complexion was dotted with freckles, doubtless from a wholesome outdoor childhood. Her auburn bangs turned up a little at the corners, because she didn't waste her time and money on regular haircuts. She looked like an aging dainty tomboy, the kind who wears a rumpled frock and isn't scared of frogs, but who won't go so far as to get into a fist fight with the boys.

"She's sick of lying in bed all the time. She's sick of eating and she's sick of drinking. It's really hard on her. Don't you see?" She was finally starting to sound a little heated. "She's in pain all the time. She's bored with the television. She can't understand the way people talk these days, and she's seen all the classic films. I try to plug her in to nature programs, but there's only so much beautiful scenery a person can take, you know?"

"What is it she would like us to do?" I asked this very clearly, like I was conversing with someone who did not speak my language; someone with whom, therefore, it was useless to attempt verbal communication.

"She doesn't know yet." Fiona gave every impression of herself as a simple servant, standing at the ready. "I requested a special audience with His Holiness, when we celebrated the Buddha's birthday last weekend . . ." She subsided momentarily. I remembered I had seen a box of hair dye next to the denture cleaning tablets. I had been touched by the poignance of this harmless vanity, on the part of one so devout. "He says we are to respect her decision," she finished, like she was repeating something she'd heard in a dream.

"What is her decision?" I persisted.

I had a mental image of myself, running alongside a train departing a station, desperately trying to scramble on board. Modern trains have been designed to discourage this dangerous yet highly cinematic practice, so the vision must have come from one of Mariana's classic films. And then I made what felt like a tremendous leap.

"I'm not comfortable doing anything," I blathered, so hastily I heard my consonants jumbling into one another. I felt like the one kid who won't light up in the girls' room, the one whose frightened rectitude probably has something to do with how unattractive and badly dressed she is.

Fiona regarded me with cold politeness. I never think that would work on me, when I see a movie where some high-cheekboned villainess is wielding hostile courtesy against a lesser character. It seems so false, so *posed*, like fight scenes in cheesy martial arts epics where the combatants aren't even touching each other. But why don't *you* try facing someone delicate and British with your big chapped hands, your subordinate loneliness in someone else's home. Try *that*, when you've spent your whole life in a snarling standoff with someone who uses the word cunt in casual conversation.

But I was in the middle of explaining something. "Until I've talked to someone. I mean someone . . ." I couldn't bring myself to make sense. I wanted to say, "Until I've talked to a qualified medical professional who is not a member of a cult," but how could anybody die in peace if I went around insulting people's dearly-held beliefs?

I felt like we were standing right in front of something huge and recognizable and impossible to explain, like elephants or icebergs; that Fiona kept looking around with annoyed polite confusion saying, *where? whatever do you mean?* as I struggled to describe it before running out of time.

Incidentally, I was not that kid who wouldn't smoke in the girls' room. I was the kid who stole the cigarettes and smoked them in class if the teacher was a few minutes late. I knew exactly how I felt about the ugly dweebs who broke into a clammy sweat at the sight of my self-destructive defiance. Now Fiona was me, and I was all those quiet cowards, and I did not even reflect until just now upon the limits of a person's character; how little childish defiance prepares one for a situation where character tells.

Meanwhile, Fiona had clearly cast herself as the one who is endlessly patient with those who are ignorant, stupid, or otherwise disadvantaged. "Her decision is that she doesn't want to do it anymore." Her eyes were flat and elegant as only the eyes of a girl smoking in a public toilet can be. "That's all I know right now. I'm sorry. I know as much as you do." Then she doled out one more tiny morsel of information. "The hospice nurse is coming out. To have a look."

DO YOU REMEMBER Grace Poole, from *Jane Eyre?* She was the hard-drinking minder, secretive and careless, the one who failed to keep Miss Eyre's imprisoned rival from burning down the house. When I think about what happened now, I think about Grace Poole, driven to drink by terror and tedium. I think about the inevitability of fire in a lonely attic room. It makes me hate that Gothic heartthrob Mr. Rochester more than ever, when I think of the hatchet-faced Poole, whose shift never ends, who must have wondered now and then if she was doing something terribly wrong.

"So you called hospice," I confirmed. I felt like I had just awakened from a harrowing dream about pounding after trains to find myself seated in a noiseless German Bahnzug.

"Well, yes." Fiona blinked at me. "I've pasted their card on the fridge." She had. It was bright yellow, with letters about two inches high. "Reuben's coming out just as soon as he can. They'll stay in their cabin up in the mountains and make a bit of a vacation out of it."

What could I have expected of poor Fiona, who was not a saint but was sufficiently good for this world? Did she not give every indication of disinterested compassion? Did she not consult the experts, spiritual and medical, and paste the proper notice in a highly visible location? It is sane and just and timely for a bed-bound woman in her eighties to surrender. Right?

How the hell should I know? I don't know what happened when the dying and the mad were all alone in the cool, blue-shaded room. I was not privy to the murmurs underneath the ceiling fans. I only know that Verdelein the mutant housecat purred as steadily as if she were under a hypnotic suggestion to do so.

But in addition to sane, just, and timely: what could be more poignant than a final visit? The dying woman would have one last chance to press her family's hands, to gaze into their eyes. They would bid farewell with the eloquence of grief: her son Reuben, a pilot with a radio announcer's voice; his slender wife Colleen the stewardess; and Hunter, their ten-year-old son with his head full of baby-doll curls. They would make a bit of a vacation out of it. They would take a few drives along the coast, all the while touched with the gentle sorrow of impending natural death. They would all clasp hands as they offered an ecumenical prayer to a genderless deity.

"BUT MRS. BLANCHEFLEUR . . ."

"DO YOU KNOW," Mariana said, in a way that indicated she was sure I did not, "they named that child *Hunter*." She glared at me as if I might be a spineless sympathizer. "They *know* how I feel about hunting. *She* says it is a family name. That I am to think of Hunter *green*." At the notion that she should be told what to think, she curled up her mouth in disgust. "*I* call him Reuben, because that is his middle name. Lots of people go by their middle names," she informed me, as if I were the foreigner, not she. "I do not send him money for his birthday," she continued, still as if she were explaining the local customs to a newcomer without a lot of native intelligence. "Instead, I make a donation in his name—which is Reuben Daniels, like his father—to the World Wildlife Fund, of which I have been a member for many years."

When I scurried away from Germany without so much as completing a single academic year, I did so with one small triumph only: my ability to line up parts of speech in a foreign language in a coherent sentence. I saw now that this triumph never faded: that Mariana Blanchefleur would continue placing parts of speech as accurately as notes in a waltz until the day she spoke no more.

And then her eyes fell on the dinner I held. I had made it according to precise instructions from Fiona, who knew how much the patient hated pepper; how she liked lemon, not lime; who knew, in short, exactly what Mariana Blanchefleur wanted at all times.

Tonight, a small round hump of glistening white fish had come to its eternal rest on an even whiter plate. It was accompanied by three dainty broccoli florets, each of them easily grasped by a clumsy dying hand. I'd arranged them so they looked cheerful and springy, delighted to be of service.

"And so," she concluded, regarding this arrangement. Then she looked back at me with eyes so blank I wondered where the opinionated supporter of wildlife had gone. "What am I supposed to do with this?"

"This is your dinner," I explained. "I thought you might like to eat it."

She waved her weak right arm to the furthest extent of its mobility, which wasn't very far. "How do I do that?" Now the eyes were frightened. She was about to be very angry.

"Well," I proposed, "you can pick it up with your hands, and then, if you want, you can put it in your mouth, and chew it up and swallow it."

She was looking at me so attentively she could have been memorizing the instructions for cracking a safe. I had the distinct impression that I was handling this exactly the wrong way.

"So!" I exclaimed, remembering how hopeless I'd been as a waitress. "Would you like to give it a try?"

And I actually gave that plate a little shake, like it might be more enticing if the broccoli bounced, if the dead fish quivered livingly. She looked at me like I'd just filleted a live snake, right there on the pale blue coverlet.

"Why should I do that?" she demanded now, mastering her revulsion. Her voice was strong and steady, as if she were bravely questioning an unjust order.

"Because you've barely eaten anything all day." I might as well have told her she should eat her supper because that's what good little girls do.

"But why eat?" she persisted.

"Because," I told her. "Because. If you don't eat, you'll starve."

And that's when I knew that it really was real. Here was a woman who had been incontinent and motionless for years upon years; who no longer knew how to read; whose friends had all forgotten who she was or ever had been. She was lying in a narrow hospital bed, exactly as she lay there yesterday and the day before that, trapped, excreting, and losing her senses as the weeds in her yard crept up to the door and the lingo of badly-dressed young people began to sound like a foreign language, all over again.

"It's very nice food," I went on without conviction. "It nourishes your body."

I looked outside, where the basil and tomato plants were leaping greenly out of the earth, delighted to nourish themselves with worm shit and the bodies of weaker plants. I was working every weekend now, plus one or two days in the middle of the week, so Fiona could go to classes at the Center. There was another part-time girl, but both she and her vehicle were extremely unreliable. I often found myself filling in for her, now that I had gotten my truck fixed.

"What happens if I nourish my body?" She looked a little less bleak now, more sure of herself. She looked exactly like she was laying a trap for me. So I walked right in.

"You feel better," I admitted. I began to feel like I was doing something devious, trying to trick a helpless old woman into making an investment with no chance of return.

She paraphrased my argument neatly. "I eat, so I can"—she waved her hand again, as if it were a dreadful bother to remember my trivial words—"nourish my body; so I can just do it all over again?"

I realized I was disgusted by the triteness of this epiphany, as if despair required originality or eloquence to earn the rights of pity. As if it didn't count, somehow, if it had all the literary merits of a slogan inside a depressive's greeting card.

"So I live to go on living?" she concluded, as if no one else had ever noticed that this was indeed the case.

Suddenly I wished desperately that I believed in God; that I could say, "but Mrs. Blanchefleur. That is the will of the Lord," and smile with dazzling confidence as I rebuked her in the knowledge of my perfect certainty. Instead, I stood there and waited.

She stared at the food in numb horror. "Take it away," she mumbled, exhausted by the battle of wits she'd just won.

In the craigslist ad describing the job, Fiona had written that Mariana suffered from Alzheimer's. Aside from the fact that I would never admit it if I'd lost an argument to someone with a degenerative brain disease, I don't think I did. I think Mariana Blanchefleur was a tired old drunk. When she was seventy-one years old, she was pulled over half a mile from the only bar in town and arrested for drunk driving. Everyone knew about it before lunch the next day, and everyone but Reuben was strangely thrilled, the way people are when they see a woman beat a man, or when someone very proper starts screaming obscenities. The people in town felt that a point had been scored in favor of something fierce and independent. They admired

Mariana Blanchefleur, who made grand entrances then, swaying in doorways with the folds of her great purple fat lady wraps billowing around her. She was one of theirs, subject to the same indignities they faced and always ready to prevail with an insight or a quip. She paid three times the going rate to have her ceiling painted, "like the sky"; and when she found out she'd been cheated, she bragged like she'd done it on purpose. Like she only ever paid top dollar for the finest craftsmanship, when everyone knew the painters were speed freaks who worked under the table to get out of paying child support.

I remembered a photograph I'd seen of her when she was almost young: "thirty-two or thirty-four," she said with great precision, as if no one would ever believe she was German if her random certainties did not sound precise. We were trying to find some pictures of a trip she'd taken to San Francisco in pursuit of Reuben's father. "I was chasing a man," she declared, smacking her lips. She was a woman of tremendous appetite who had always known exactly what she wanted. In the picture, she was straight and strong, like all those Greatest Generation types who smoked and ate red meat and wore high heels and whose bellies were perfectly flat; whose arms were slim and taut. She wore a yellow dress with pleats in the skirt and a tightly cinched waist. She was not in San Francisco. She was standing on the stones of a street where black-haired people wore the clothing of their ancestors and smiled shyly at her.

I turned to the next photo and saw the same nearly youthful beauty. She was sitting in a field beside a picnic basket, holding a cream-colored sandal with a two-inch heel. She could have been giving a lecture on the lesser-known methods of drinking champagne from an open-toed shoe. To ensure maximum attentiveness on the part of her audience, she had removed her blouse to reveal a pair of suntanned, buoyant breasts. "That was before I had babies," she remarked. "Hah." Her eyes were carnivorous with remembered satisfaction.

FROM FOXGLOVE TO THE FEUDAL COURT

IT REMAINED UNCLEAR how Mariana Blanchefleur would choose to die. One thing, though, had become completely clear: there was no way an unemployed model and part-time caregiver could continue paying rent at Foxglove.

Foxglove was no longer a gathering place for women bereft of their men and their dreams. Reina took down a large framed photograph of Zack and replaced it with a soft-lit image of Monya caressing her rounded belly. A wedding picture disappeared, and in its place, she hung a playful shot of Gregory, spraying Akana with a garden hose.

"I hate to do this to you," she told me. "You're my friend." Her voice was tender. Her eyes were liquid velvet.

"No!" I exclaimed. "I mean, of course. The baby . . ."

Reina nodded, like I'd just convinced her with the best possible argument. Who needs a verb when you have a baby? The sentence doesn't even bear completion.

"The baby will need a room," she agreed reluctantly. This was the house that she and Zack had rebuilt for their wedding. She'd let the grounds go wild to commemorate his death. And now, for the birth that would make this house a home, she was ready for a sumptuous nursery.

Monya was already installed in the room she'd occupied for the few short years of her teens, when her mother was married to Zack. She'd rolled up the posters of boy bands and horses, taken a few swipes at the cobwebs, and pronounced herself fully nested. She was beginning to exhibit a slight gleam, if not quite the prenatal glow that was expected of her.

"Where will you go now?" Reina wanted to know. "Do you have any plans?"

I wasn't showing enough spirit to reassure her that she was well within her rights to give a tenant six weeks' notice to vacate. I should have been vigorous and cheerful. She would have known exactly how to respond.

"I *have* to get started on the nursery," she reminded me. "I can't have Monya thinking that it won't be done."

"I have friends," I pointed out, trying to be dignified.

My former landlady gave me a hard, grateful hug. It was not the least bit grandmotherly.

"WHY DON'T YOU move in here?" Fiona suggested. It made perfect sense. "My back is in really bad shape right now, and that other girl . . . well. I think she got into some goddess-y stuff when she was living in Sebastopol. D'you know what I mean? She's been giving me a bit of the fishy eye."

She gazed off into the long-legged weeds as she said this, as if she preferred to be absent while unpleasant inferences were being made. I felt so much more tolerant than that other part-time girl; or, more to the point, as if my ability to endure had been taken up and noticed. So I left the hardwood marble fantasy of Foxglove. I packed my bright red suitcase full of yellow German volumes and moved into the sewing room, in the back of a house where a woman of enormous appetite lay thinking only of her death.

IT WAS LIKE she was waiting for me to get there. It did not occur to me at the time that Mariana Blanchefleur could have been made to wait. But then, I never really knew the dying woman, with her name like a troubadour's love and the scar on the left side of her chest where the breast used to be. I just happened to be there as the life was fighting its way out of her body. I only knew her like a squatter knows the layout of a house, with special attention to exits and weaknesses.

If I had known her, I don't think I would have liked her. She had a commanding, performative quality that tugged on several memories but failed to evoke any pleasant feelings of nostalgia. She would fix her eyes on her captive—and that's what it felt like, when she told a story—like she needed, right now, to inflict this particular narrative on me and no one else.

Not that they were boring stories. But listening to them was a little like being force-fed a fine meal in a small room with no windows. For example: when she was eighteen years old, she worked as an interpreter on an American air force base in Germany. Her name at that time was Nicki, because her boss had very particular ideas about what was American and what was not. So a woman whose name was infused with a long and ancient history was christened with a nickname that wasn't short for anything: not Nicola, not Veronica, not Dominique or Annika. She was Nicki, because a spunky female military contractor thought it sounded American in 1943.

Mariana always began the tale of how she got her alias by explaining why she'd never reveal that boss' name. "I will not tell you," she'd declare, as if she saw me preparing to make a record of it, "because she was sleeping with a priest!" Every time she broke the news, she watched me very closely, as if she could find out who I really was by how I responded. I always feel like people are digging into me when they examine me with such open shrewdness, as if they don't know that I can see them, too.

Fiona, on the other hand, seemed to think it would be vulgar to show that she was paying attention to anyone, ever. When I arrived at Mariana's Hof with my suitcase and my books, Fiona was lounging on the bed she had assigned me. She looked like she'd been there some time, gazing in perplexity at a point on the opposite wall. I was embarrassed by the stains on the mattress, though I hadn't even used it and no one could attribute them to me.

"I haven't used that mattress," I said. I frowned at it, as if I found it highly indiscreet.

"That information isn't really useful to me," Fiona murmured coolly.

And then, in one of those moments that people spend the rest of their lives trying to explain, I was seized with the absolute conviction that I must not ever, under any circumstances, be honest with Fiona. It was a certainty that slipped over me like a net, like a chain link fence. I would guard my thoughts and feelings like a silent junkyard dog, slinking and grinning and always unsure. It was a terrible submission to a haughty, skinny woman who referred to a living human being as His Holiness; who believed that the inner leaves of a head of lettuce cause cancer; and who did not even know that the past participle of the verb "to lie" has nothing to do with the present.

As I embarked on my campaign of secrecy with this dangerous, trivial woman, I had the sense of something slow and irretrievable beginning to move. The moment I became a liar, I began to feel like I was always running downhill, losing my footing; that the only way to avoid falling was to keep running faster. It enhanced my sense of myself as agile, leaping from rock to rock, missing ditches, dodging trees. If I was not in control of my situation, at least I could take it as it came, with grace and wit and what my mother might refer to as a certain *je ne sais quoi*.

I began to arrange my books, as if I simply could not rest until I'd brought some order to my surroundings.

"I'd like to share something with you," said the woman who was preventing me from lying down on my bed. "Is it okay if I do that."

She looked at me as if securing my consent might be of passing interest to her. I remembered that in the old demon stories I used to read as a wholesome alternative to watching television, vampires could never enter a mortal's home without permission. I do not recall what measure of consent, if any, was necessary from those who had no home except the one the demon offered.

"Of course," I said, abandoning any pretense at bringing order to a room that was not, after all, my own.

"Mariana hasn't taken any food today," she said evenly. I noticed that she had begun to say "Mariana" in a solemn, worshipful tone, the way she said "His Holiness."

"Well," I began, nudging forward with extreme caution, "there *have* been a few days like that. Haven't there?"

She took a moment to remind herself that I couldn't help it if I lacked a few refinements. "This is it, Isobel. She's told me her intention. I don't think you know this, but I have a real connection with her. I've been here a year and a half, and we've developed quite a bond. When I first got here, she was wearing this awful plaid night dress and there was all this chaos going on, the television at top volume and dogs running in and out and people shouting at one another. I've really worked with her. I don't think you understand what that means. I called Reuben and I told him, I'm just in pain all the time. We've got to do something about this. So he gave me permission to try the headphones, so I wouldn't have to hear that dreadful television all the time, and I worked hard. I worked really hard, to bring the level of this place up. I worked my *ass* off." The abrupt vulgarity was stabbed into the monologue with what sounded like reckless delight.

"I don't think you know how bad my back is," she went on, beginning to sound rather fierce; "but I worked terribly hard. I said, I can't live here if there's not going to be peace and quiet. I think Mariana wanted that, too," she added, like a woman who is ready with her evidence. "People don't like to live like that, in squalor and, and, I don't know, in chaos. I focused on nutrition," she went on, as if I'd asked her to enumerate the things she'd done for the woman who lay before the television, watching manatees at play in a vast and photogenic sea. "I don't think I've told you this, but that's one of the ways we express our intention at the Center. It's really quite powerful. I've weaned her, very gradually, you know, off those awful anti-depressants. The ones that just flatten you. I have some very strong feelings about that. I'd like to talk to you more about it later. I've brought her back from a lot of confusion and anger and I really do think there might still be time for some breakthroughs." Her eyes were sparkling with such intensity they could have been the headlights on the spaceship in her brain.

In the popular imagining of the brain's topography, there are mountains and valleys and culverts; cities that light up in the night-time of our consciousness. One of these features is the uncanny valley, a scary little sweet spot tucked into the shadow of those two very similar neighbors, the mountains called empathy and revulsion. The effect of that valley is what people feel in the presence of clowns, androids, and human beings who have something terribly wrong with them. I began to feel very gentle toward Fiona Jones.

"Has the hospice nurse been here yet?" I asked, as if the dying could not possibly begin without official sanction.

"The nurse was here," Fiona admitted. "She checked her vitals. So"—she flashed an experimental, conspiratorial grin—"we know she's not dead yet. Right? But tomorrow"—and now she became grave again—"the spiritual care advisor is going to pay us a visit. I guess that's what they call the chaplain, or the vicar, or whatever." Again, I caught a flash of something experimental, a probe for anything with a molecular structure resembling sympathy. "His name is Randall," she went on, with a peculiar trancelike calm that was beginning to look a lot like its exact opposite. "I think he just wants to make sure we're not completely crazy out here in the woods, all by ourselves." She tossed off this possibility with a breeziness that could only mean it was tormenting her. "I think he'll be impressed."

SHE TELLS IT ONE MORE TIME

THE SPIRITUAL CARE advisor from hospice was not impressed. He was enraptured. Mariana was a raconteur, remember: theatrical and war-torn, with a damned good story to tell. Fiona smiled like a stage mum as the dying woman told her story, one last time.

Randall was a tall, soft-bellied man. He had an air of gentleness so elaborate, I thought he must know what it was to frighten someone who was dying; someone who would never understand that he was only living; only shedding particles of excess life like all of us who have more strength than we can save.

"I built this house," Mariana began, when Randall had seated himself with the tenderest possible regard for the dying woman's furniture. "I have lived here twenty-seven years. Which is a long time. Even when you are eighty-something years old."

Randall nodded with more kindness than anyone has ever brought to bear on such complete neutrality of agreement. Something about him seemed to expand. And then he said softly, without a trace of malice or sadness, "And it's the house where you're going to die."

The old lady looked startled, but only for the briefest spasm of her helpless claws on the comforter that no longer comforted. She was the boldest thing I ever saw.

"You wanted to know my spiritual history," she began.

Anyone could see that she was gathering the remnants of a strength that had once been unstoppable. It was like the rumble of subterranean forces, slowly bringing sightless eyes to bear on one last telling of a story that was almost done.

"I was born in Germany, in a lovely little country place. My mother Carlota was not French, but because her maiden name was Blanchefleur, she loved to have everything—*so*." She covered this inadequate description with one of the expressive gestures that will always be part of an immigrant's vocabulary.

"Mama wanted her home to be a *salon*," she explained, charming the spiritual care advisor as she examined him with the secular eyes of a hawker at a fair. "She always had dancers and painters at our house—sometimes for months. And there was always an uproar. Always, with artists. But my father: my father whose name was Rudolf—much too much like Adolf, so he always went by Rudy, after the war. But he was very German. He was a *von*, which means, you know, *sehr arisotokratisch.*" She gave a thin ironic smile to let everyone know this simple cognate had not left her aged mind. "He said, to Mama's favorite painter (he was a pet of hers. Ladies did that in those days): if you are going to be here, drinking my wine, you can work. So he made him paint portraits of my mother and me." She drew our attention to a pair of highly competent likenesses, one of a simpering blond child and another of a woman with luminous skin, gazing thoughtfully at something lovely, just outside the frame. She looked exactly like the gentle Francophile wife of a German country squire.

"When I went to work for the Americans, I used my mother's maiden name, because, *well!*" And she allowed a great angry laugh to rumble up from her tremendous depths. "I do not think she would have minded," she declared, enunciating the conditional perfect form with the deftness that belongs to scrupulous practice, not natural-born talent.

"She died when I was eight years old. Carlota, like the Empress." She flashed the ghost of a grin at Randall from hospice, to see if he knew which German-speaking Empress she meant; if he was ready, perhaps, to joke with her about the loneliness of exile in a country far warmer than where she was born. But he only made a sympathetic noise, which seemed to disappoint her.

"Yes. Well," she replied, briskly, as if he should have known better than to comment on a linear narrative with sympathetic noises. "She missed the war. Not the first war, you understand. 'The war to end all wars.' Oh, no! She missed *the war.* Oh, God! Hitler! Worse than, who is this? In Libya? *Gaddafi*," she breathed. "Only let me cut off his head. Oh, God. And why? What for? Let me tell you something. My father was in Adolf's army. My father, who was only strict with painters. And me, because I was so much older than my sister. But by German standards, let me tell you, he was most indulgent. *Most* indulgent. But let me tell you something now. He was a widower.

With two little girls. So they were very good to him, considering they were Nazis." This was a joke, but nobody laughed. It may have been kinder, in that moment, to choke out a laugh at the goodness of Nazis. "He only marched around and around in his uniform, looking very fierce, and I want you to know something." Her strength was leaving her, and she paused as she surveyed the terrain before her.

"He used to take us into the woods. Germans are always walking in the woods, you see, so no one would think. And he led us deep into the woods, and he explained things to us, very quietly. So no one would hear, because if they did—" she drew a close-clipped nail across her throat. "He wanted us to know they were all murderers, that no one had a right. And soon the whole world would know, and we should never be ashamed, because we knew, too."

Randall from hospice was utterly transfixed.

"And so I went to work for the Americans." She was hauling herself along now, rushing past the sights along the way, the unnamed boss who was sleeping with a priest, the horse that kicked her when she was thirteen, her habit of always riding coach when she traveled so she could pick up the local language.

"I married very young, and I was disappointed in love." She said it like it was a formal diagnosis; but she did not tell this kind, soft-bellied man that her husband had his teenaged bride committed to an insane asylum in Nazi Germany. I began to believe that I knew her, because I knew so many biographical details that Randall who was not a priest did not.

"So I came to America." She made it sound like it was a logical sequence of events. "It was easy, because I worked as an interpreter for so many years. I married again. Another disappointment. But I had two sons, and they are both married now. I made my younger son marry that girl . . . Kathy, I think her name is. I said, do you like her? And he said, yes, I do. So I said, well, let's get you married. And now he has someone to take care of him. So, I feel my work is done. I have never done anyone any harm."

She watched her visitor like he was a customs official, some petty bureaucrat she had to convince in order to get on with her man-chasing, her languages, her appetites and trying to forget. She had left out quite a lot; but she showed no sign of disappointment, only the anticipatory contentment of someone who has always had her passport stamped.

"What a life you've led," Randall finally managed.

"Yes." The lady laughed shortly. "It has been a life. A very long life."

"Do you feel you've left anything undone?" Randall inquired. His compassion was almost indifferent.

"I have two good sons. They are both married. They are not criminals." Even with her fading powers, she was gauging her audience and keeping him enthralled. "This house," she relented, judging that he would not be satisfied without some minor misery. "I built it. But it is not a home." At sundown, when she grew restless and confused, she always spoke of going home. The metaphors of death are unsubtle in the extreme.

"But it is the house you will die in," Randall persisted, with the soft persistence of someone determined to lead a stranger to the very banks of the river Styx and urge her into the boat.

"Yes." The dying woman looked around and sighed, as if this were a matter of unfortunate décor and there was nothing to be done about it now. "I got that beautiful bathtub put in," she said suddenly. "And now I am the only one who cannot use it." She looked at Fiona and me with good-natured hostility. It was a badly-kept secret that we'd been using her bathtub while she lay in the unsatisfying cleanliness of twice-weekly sponge baths.

Randall sat patiently, alert and soft and very much alive. I thought of all the thousands of corpuscles swarming like red-hot ants through a living person's body; of the pumps like oil wells, constantly pumping away at the juices that never stop squirting through an intricate system of canals and irrigation ditches. It struck me then that there was something, not quite obscene, but highly inappropriate, about all this business of being alive; all this industrious clench and release; this self-perpetuating frenzy that sends us hurtling along no matter what the needless horror.

Mariana plucked at the comforter, as if its freshly laundered warmth had suddenly become impossible to endure. Her eyes wandered, as if she were in search of an answer to a question she'd forgotten. Randall stood with heavy-bodied grace.

"Mariana," he called, demonstrating an uncanny ability to speak loudly without losing any of the softness from his soothing demeanor. "I'm very glad I got to meet you."

Mariana smiled weakly at him. Her dentures were slipping. We could see her pink scalp gleaming through the sparse white hair. It reminded me of baby bird's skin, before the feathers start to come through.

"I'll be back next week. I hope to see you again." He paused, waiting for the aroma of his own desires to evaporate before he went on. "But if you're not here anymore," he said, with such perfect clarity I think I would have understood him no matter what language he spoke, "that's okay, too."

Mariana continued to display her dentures and her bravery, as if she were about to embark on a rollicking adventure and could not wait to get started. She was a damned good liar.

RANDALL FROM HOSPICE never did see her again. By the time we cancelled his next visit, most of what would happen had happened and she was lying in a coma with the air whistling in and out of her lungs like a teakettle, whistling forlornly in a lonely, empty house. She was almost safe.

MARIANA'S JOURNEY BEGINS

I HAVE TO say that waiting for someone to die is more boring than anything else I have ever done in my life. It is more boring than memorizing lists of irregular verbs.

At the same time, death has a slow-moving urgency that cannot be conveyed. Neighbors and friends find it neither neighborly nor friendly. Dying, after all, is the height of anti-social behavior. Mariana is extremely ill, we said. You're supposed to call anyone who might want to say goodbye, which sounds tragic and dramatic, but it's not. It's just making travel arrangements, a process that always involves some degree of miscommunication.

Oh, right, the friends and neighbors said, the way people agree with you when they wish you'd stop talking about weird sexual practices or corporate malfeasance. Death is like that. It has a built-in selfishness, a whiff of shit and decay that all the ailing beauties of literature and film cannot deny. She's been down a long time, hasn't she? they said. We felt like whiners, like people who detect a deep malfunction in the most minor inconvenience.

It doesn't look like it's going to be much longer, we tried. We could hear the puzzled living frowns on the other end of the line. Everyone in the valley of the mountains has a landline. Only death is reliable there. Only death can always reach you, no matter what the disposition of the mountains or the clouds. How *much* longer? the friends and neighbors persisted. It is the height of rudeness to drop an unscheduled death on people, especially as a national holiday is approaching. The Fourth of July is coming right up, they reminded us. We have a lot of people coming over. Are you *sure* about this?

There are those who know how to insist on reality when the opposite is so much more reasonable. But I have fallen down and I have fallen short. I couldn't tell a dying woman she should eat her dinner, and I couldn't tell her friends that everything would be okay. "Mariana has accepted what is happening to her," I said quietly. "She's at peace with it. If you would like to come and say goodbye, today would be a good time to do that."

"IF I EAT," Mariana said to me, "will I be late?"

I hesitated.

"Will I miss my appointment?" she insisted. "With . . . the guy?"

Fiona watched with shining eyes from the kitchen. There was a cutout in the wall between the rooms, so the person cooking could continue socializing with people in the main part of the house. Dishes could be passed back and forth, without the hostess being relegated to a position of servitude. It created an air of openness and diminished secrecy.

"You can eat whatever you want," I said clearly. I felt like I was handing a syllabus for next semester's swim class to someone who was drowning. "Would you like something to eat?" I asked, with the hypocritical gallantry of holding an unpassable door. "I could make you something easy to swallow."

Fiona watched us both. Her eyes were almost invisible beneath her overgrown bangs.

Mariana began to pluck the comforter. She shook her head, and her hair streamed down around her shoulders. She looked like a woman driven mad by grief, mourning a fallen hero. "I don't want to be late," she murmured. She was deep inside the dark Teutonic woods, where madness and desire dance upon the grave of secular enlightenment. Someone told her something deadly there, and no one could know that she knew.

Fiona moved to the bedside as smoothly as if she'd been on wheels. "This is entirely up to you," she said softly. She placed one reddened hand on Mariana's chest, where the old, strong heart was beating hard beneath a vicious purple scar. "Is there anything you need me to write down for you? A message for someone special?"

The old woman's hands relaxed. She lay back on her pillows and fastened her faded blue eyes on Fiona's freckled face.

"Just . . ." she breathed. "Just tell them . . ." Her face began to gladden. "I don't want a lot of crying and carrying on. My father said the same thing: no crying. So we all gathered . . . like-minded people,

you understand . . . and we agreed: no crying. Just . . . raise a glass . . ."
She sank further into the cushions.

If she'd had the barest shred of respect for literary or cinematic
conventions, she would have slipped away right there. Fiona and I
would have shed a few forbidden tears and stepped into the sunshine,
just in time for Independence Day.

But life is utterly without propriety or pride. It is humiliating,
how life goes on in spite of everything, like it has no sense of its
own worth. Mariana sipped cold water with a cautious air, as if she
were satisfying a religious duty. For a soft-lit time of indistinct hours
or possibly days, she lay with a gentle smile on her ruined, hollow
mouth, casting shiny eyes around her like the dusty objects of her life
were a source of wonder and delight.

AND MINE, TOO

DURING THE PERIOD of this initial vigil, my mother sent me a photograph. She sent it the way people used to send things, in a large manila envelope, so it looked like a college admissions packet or an invitation to a sweepstakes. My mother has always said that "virtual" is a little too much like "virtue" for a lady like herself. The implication is that certain incompetencies are key to a true understanding of the mysteries of physical love. Therefore, instead of making a few keystrokes so I could have the images instantly, she sent me physical photographs in a materially existing envelope, which took a week or two to arrive. My mother has a thorough understanding of the power of delayed gratification.

She had written the word *PHOTOS!!!* on the envelope, in large, imperious, fluorescent orange print. I would recognize that handwriting anywhere. The letters were slanted at angles so precise she could have used a ruler, though I know she didn't. *DO NOT BEND!!!* the handmade italics continued. She had made little marks around them, like lines in a cartoon, indicating movement or a terrible stench. The rest of this extremely physical communication was covered with stickers and stamps and orders to forward until finally, in a hand I did not recognize, the address of Mariana's Hof appeared.

I stood in the sun beside a stranger's mailbox. The sweat poured off my face and smeared my mother's hand. I fingered the corners of the hastily-licked stamp and thought, my mother has sent me a DNA sample. I'll thank her for that in a letter, I decided. She loves an unexpected bodily reference.

"The mail is here," I told Fiona, in the subdued tone she found most suitable for maintaining a calm atmosphere.

With Mariana disintegrating in a contentment that was almost amiable, I was developing an intricate consideration for Fiona's well-being. It made me feel profound and nurturing. She was meditating several times a day, and I found I was grateful for her spiritual refreshment. When she emerged from her room, which she shared with a large, geometrical sculpture made of copper rods and artificial gemstones, she held herself as straight as all the heathen priestesses who ever marched into the flames. Her back, she said, was spasming every few seconds. It was all she could do to keep from crying out. I placed the mail on the partition between the living room and the kitchen, as carefully as if I were making an offering. I stepped away so courteously I might as well have bowed.

"Listen," she said. I listened, although I had absolutely no desire to find out what she was about to say. "I think we should come in the side doors instead of always using that awful squeaking front door."

I had the impression this was something she'd wanted to bring up for a long time.

"It's much quieter, you know, and I feel it would be much less alarming. For Mariana. We're very much on the same wavelength, as I'm sure I've mentioned to you several times." She paused to favor me with a look of guarded reproach, in case I'd forgotten this vital piece of information. "And I think it's very disruptive for her when people come crashing in using that big noisy wooden door."

I felt a mask of immovable neutrality come down over my features.

"I'll come in through the sliding glass door in my bedroom, and you can come in through the living room. I'll leave it unlocked for you." She regarded the dying woman with a look of grave compassion, as if she were assessing the effects of my brutal entrance and finding that this time, at least, I might not have damaged anything.

"That's fine," I assured her, in my most agreeable, soothing tone. It was slightly soporific to speak in such a soft monotone all the time.

"And," she persisted, "that includes that awful door there between the sewing room where you're staying and the rest of the house. You'll have to go out the wheelchair door onto the veranda and then come back in through the sliding glass door when you want to come into the living room. If you need to go into the kitchen for any reason, you can knock on my door and then come through my bedroom—I don't mind. I'll let you in."

"Okay," I said slowly. My brain was rapidly generating reasons not to speak frankly to this woman I found so uncompelling and yet whose whims I followed without so much as a questioning squeak.

It seemed so inappropriate to intrude on someone else's suffering with an objection about a door. I wasn't suffering enough to have the right to complain about something so inconsequential. But Fiona had been in seclusion for months, watching a stranger die. She deserved a little consideration.

"And about the kitchen." She sounded almost panicked now. It made me want to place a hand on her heart and speak to her softly. "I really want to focus on nutrition with you. I don't think your nutrition is very good."

I watched her, strangely unaffected by something any self-respecting adult would find incredibly offensive.

"I don't know if I've shared this with you . . ." She was starting to sound very sure of herself. "But, well. I've really studied good nutrition. It's something of a passion for me. It's well, it's really important for physical well-being, but also for emotional and, and . . . spiritual well-being, too, if you really want to know."

Meanwhile, my unhelpful brain was churning out excuses like a paper shredder. *She has been doing this twenty-four hours a day for longer than anyone else*, it pointed out. *She just needs to feel useful.*

"I think it's really important for everyone to be on the same wavelength," Fiona was explaining anxiously. *She doesn't know how to communicate*, my brain informed me, with great complacency. *All she wants to do is help.* "I think we really need to eat together. I mean eat the same thing. No pigging out on a bunch of carbs, okay? It really disrupts the natural thought process . . . so I've made some food for both of us." With an almost embarrassed flourish, she indicated two matching plates.

"It's just some fish," she went on eagerly, "and a bit of organic salad. Something simple, really. It's not some wacko vegetarian diet where you're not allowed to eat anything that tastes good." She smiled superciliously.

Quickly, I altered my impression so I saw uncertainty, and the desire to do something kind. I began to flatter myself for the subtlety of my perceptions.

"I've put some nuts and parmesan cheese in the salad. Also organic," she explained.

We made our way to the table on the veranda, beneath the gentle wisteria.

"So we've got plen-tee of protein," she exulted.

People come to California from all over the world to lecture the native-born on how to eat organic vegetables. *It's just because she's British*, I sympathized, as I placed my napkin on my lap, just like Fiona.

"Well, I think it's good for us to spend some time together. I'll be happy to eat with you." I took up a forkful of salad and brought it to my lying mouth. *Where did I learn how to be tactful?* I marveled.

"Mmm. Those cranberries!" Fiona exclaimed.

I was beginning to get the impression that it was a top priority for her not to respond to anything I said, ever.

"I forgot to tell you about the cranberries," she told me, like she'd neglected to mention an especially important proviso in a contract we'd both signed. "They're organic, too. I'm really . . ." she gave a thin, wry smile, like she was about to reveal a loveable quirk about herself, "well, I'm really into eating organic. I don't know if you know that about me. But I think these cranberries." She held one up to the light on the end of her fork. "I think they really give a bit of tang to the salad. Don't you?"

I nodded. It's easy to look neutral when you're eating. You have to move your face when you chew, so no one suspects you of having a facial expression that might be the result of an opinion.

"Do you know," she began, after a few moments in which the wisteria was gentle and a few distant firecrackers went off prematurely. I wondered what would happen if I put my fork down and said, "No, Fiona. Obviously, I don't know anything." It's what I would have done to my mother. But I didn't feel sorry for my mother. I wasn't half afraid of her. My mother, for all that might have been wrong with her, was not insane. I began to eat rapidly, making little yummy noises of appreciation in hopes of ending the meal as quickly as possible.

Fiona sat back in her chair and surveyed the distant hills, with the satisfied smile of a woman who has found the one thing everyone wants. "I want to share something with you," she said with gentle urgency, turning her eyes away from the hills with grave, composed regret. There was always someone needing her, that look seemed to say; something preventing her meditation from achieving the fullness of its potential. "You know, this is really important to me. I think you should know this about me, since, well, since we'll be living in the same house for however long this takes."

I am always apprehensive when people announce that they are about to share, like they have declared themselves the MC's of the heart's most cherished possessions. All I wanted to do at that moment was curl up on my disgusting mattress, with its unspeakable vintage stains, and read my mother's letter. Caitlin's letters reminded me of my favorite children's books. They were tender and wise and deeply funny. Once, she wrote a riveting page and a half about how she went to the store, saw a dog with a funny look on its face, and got a run in her stocking. I was almost moved to tears. I didn't need to be sitting here having a discursive heart-to-heart with Fiona Jones and her dead fish and her fucking organic cranberries. I thought regretfully about the high-fructose peanut butter I could be eating directly from the jar while pondering trivial events in the life of someone I fought with constantly.

But Fiona was settling back in her chair, ready to exact payment for the meal she'd provided with such thoughtful generosity. And here's a thing I will never understand: I did find it thoughtful. I did find it generous that she'd shared this simple meal with me, in spite of the fact that her presentation resembled a particularly unpleasant form of discipline.

Did I really see through her so clearly, even then? I remember distinctly that I did; and I trust my memory, because it doesn't do me any credit. You never see people in the witness stand saying, "Yes, Your Honor. Of course I knew that!" People will swear under oath that they are too stupid to live before they'll admit they knew better and went along anyway.

I remember my father warning me that the weakest people are the most dangerous, because they are the most unpredictable. I remember, too, that my greatest weakness that summer was simply that I was strong, and that I was ashamed of my strength. Every breath I took, every concession I made, every excuse I invented, was part of an elaborate apology for the fact that I was not debilitated the way Fiona was.

I never felt like having a good cry. It didn't horrify me that soon, a human being with a history and a consciousness all her own would simply cease to exist. It barely horrified me that all I wanted was for this woman's life to be over so I could finally get some sleep. When Mariana screamed in the darkest part of the night, I staggered to her bedside and said mechanically, "there, there. There, there." I was fully aware of the fact that this was not a comfort to a soul in mortal dread. I just didn't have it in me anymore to give a shit. The warm, tender feelings of connection that tormented Fiona were not available to me. What tormented me was the revelation that I was not authentically compassionate. I was refreshed by YouTube videos of drunk comedians insulting hecklers. I wanted to lie around reading mystery novels and eating Nutella right out of the jar. I was definitely missing out on the majesty of this experience. Fiona removed the napkin from her lap. She laid it on the table next to her plate. She was graceful and careless now, like we'd just concluded a quiet enjoyment and were ready to move on to cognac and billiards.

"I don't think I've shared very much about my history with you," she began. She had the serious, apprehensive air of someone who finds herself at a point where it would be an act of pure selfishness not to share what she knows. "About my . . . journey, I guess you could call it." She chuckled a little ruefully. "And really it is a real journey, too: I mean, a physical journey, because I am in fact an immigrant. I don't know . . . have you ever been to England?"

I shook my head. It may have been the first time since she'd interviewed me for the job that she'd asked me a direct question.

"Well . . . have you ever heard of Glastonbury?"

I recovered my power of speech enough to tell her no, I had not ever been to England. I did not know about this region, the last syllable of which she pronounced like it was a soft French cheese.

"Well, Glastonbury is a bit like . . . Santa Fe," she explained, savoring the comparison. "Only it's medieval, of course. It's one of the major energy centers of our world. There's this great old cathedral in Wells, just a few miles off, and there's this ruined abbey . . . King Arthur is supposed to be buried there," she added eagerly, as if the presence of Pendragon's bones were an all-purpose authenticator. "And of course it draws all kinds of spiritual leaders and people who are sensitive to that kind of thing." She gave me a searching look. "I ended up there," she went on, after a pause wherein much was implied. "It's a long story. I was young, and well, I was really fucked up, to be honest with you. I smoked a lot of cigarettes, and I was just depressed and mean to people all the time. *Because* I was depressed, of course. *You* understand. I didn't eat right. I don't really need to go into it.

"My parents were terribly unloving," she continued, by way of elaborating on a subject that didn't bear going into. "They fought all the time. They didn't know how to communicate lovingly. My mother, especially . . . she was so hard on my poor dad. They were ignorant, really, and I think they resented us for disrupting this beautiful love affair they had before we came along." She scanned my face again, a little sternly this time. "It's an awful thing to say about your own mum and dad, but I'm quite sure it's true. My father died without ever once saying he loved us." She was going red around the eyes and her nose had gotten moist in a way that was not pretty to look at.

"So I wound up in Glastonbury." She recovered herself and became almost lively, the way people do when they summon the strength to haul themselves through the same old origin story they've told a thousand times. "I think I felt the energy, and I wanted some help, but I was too mixed up to understand how much I needed it. So one night, I didn't have anything to do and I thought, well, why not walk around a little. Smoke some cigarettes, eat some crappy food. I was so awful to people all the time, I didn't really have any friends. So I went into this place."

I could see that the place was vivid in her memory, down to the dusty tables and the crumbling medieval stones. But she was a storyteller who relied on tone and implication; on emphases, omissions, and prolonged eye contact to convey the significance of things. So the pivotal location remained a simple noun. It could have been an open field, a live volcano, or a corridor in a house of correction.

"I thought it was a club," she explained, "because there was all this noise, like there was a party or maybe a fight going on. But it was an American man, speaking to this crowd of, well, freaks, I guess you could call them. He was creating quite a stir, as I'm sure you can imagine."

I decided that I would not under any circumstances imagine this stir, like a child who's been forced to go to a party and refuses to have a good time.

"He was there to clear the place out." She was in something like an excitable trance, telling tales of heroes from the days before the world as we know it began. "The whole place, all of Glastonbury."

I began to get the sense of something dreadful and historical taking place before me, there in the past where nothing can be changed. People always talk about suspense as if it were a type of deadly serious coyness about the ending, like no one really knows what's coming for them; but I think suspense is a quality of dread for what you know damned good and well is coming up.

I knew who this man was by now. He was the con man out of every legend, pettiness transcended by sheer force of personality. He was elevated to a tawdry godhood by the number of times his smirking image was reflected in his followers' eyes. He could have been any charismatic outcast, leading misfits to their doom. He could have been Erik the Red, rounding Cape Farewell, exploring Greenland in the loneliness of exile.

By now, Fiona was transfixed by the memory of what he'd faced. "Of course, when you have a place like that, with so much energy swirling around, you're going to attract the forces of darkness, too."

Remember that Erik the Red was banished from Iceland for the crime of double homicide.

"And he was there to clear out all the negative energy," she went on. "To let the seven rays shine through directly. Like light through a window."

And Greenland, the cold enticing fraud, is covered in glittering snow.

Fiona was explicating the nature of her leader's adversity now. "Anyway, he was extremely unpopular, because the forces of darkness had got quite a hold on the place." She seemed unaware of the fact that she was quoting a synopsis for every fantasy thriller ever written; every script for every bad idea that calls for a following, ready to die or give up and pay and pay and pay.

Erik's father Thorvald was a killer, too. People wander for a reason.

"And me, too," Fiona said quietly. "I was just so angry, all the time. I heard him speaking, and I thought, this guy is a kook. You know?

And that's what people were saying. *You* know how people are. They'll say anything to deny the truth."

Like calling it Greenland, to entice the livelihoods of people who don't even know enough to ask for photographic evidence.

"He hadn't manifested as the Buddha Maitreya yet, and he was just going by his regular American name," she confided, as if having a name were evidence of humble roots, and therefore authenticity. "I mean, let's be real. He has a name, right?"

Erik or Eirik, Thorvaldsson or Raude, Erik the Red, expert navigator, leader of five hundred settlers around the Cape and up the coast. What else do you do, when you're in so many feuds, on a tiny island nation?

"Everyone just called him Ron then, Ron Spence," she revealed, in the let's-just-be-reasonable tone that some Christians use when they admit that, yes, if Jesus was a man, he must have taken a dump at some point. "They were saying, it's just a cult, whatever. But I've *met* him." She broke into her own story excitedly, as if it were too much for her to repeat aspersions without contradicting them. "I've met the mother of his children. So I *know* him." This was her proof, then: his ability to sucker a woman into raising his kids.

Erik the Red, son of a killer.

"I know now that he really is for real. But that night—" She shook her head. Something in me leapt in wild irrational hope. I felt the way I did when I read *Maria Stuart* and thought for a moment that the Catholic queen might just escape; that Elizabeth might spare her noble cousin. *Stupid*, I thought. *You know how this story ends.*

The settlers who remained in Greenland vanished without leaving a trace.

"I listened to the forces of darkness that had their hold on me," she admitted softly. "I left before he even finished speaking." She twisted her napkin. "It wasn't until months later, when I went to Wells and heard him speak again, that something just clicked. I think it was a realignment of energy. I thought, whoa, this makes really good sense. It was like he was speaking directly to me, you know? So I said, all right. I'll give this a try. It's not like I could possibly be any more miserable. Isobel," she said to me, more gently than anyone has ever said my name. "I was in a really bad way. I don't even want to go into it right now. But he saved my life. He really did." She gazed off across the valley and into the hills, where not one undistinguished ruin broke up the monotony of deep-rooted oaks and withered blonde grass.

"I went to one of the centers for a week." She sounded relieved, like a reprobate who's finally gotten to the part of the story where she turns her life around. This wasn't a confession. This was a tale of redemption. "They gave us good food. I felt so much better. I got deeply involved. I always just dive in, when I get into something. It's all or nothing, for me." It sounded very much bragging, like she would defy any weak-willed person to accuse her of doing things halfway. "Ron—His Holiness, he saw how committed I was, and he came to me one day, and said, I'd like you to manage a house for me. In Tibet." She paused. Something in her went palpably quiet, as she seemed to experience, once again, the importance of that honor. "I went to Tibet," she said slowly, enunciating each word, the way people do when they do not expect you to believe them. I thought she might be daring me to contradict her, as if going to Tibet were a matter of opinion or interpretation. I began to wonder how I'd tell the story about staying on the mountain, in the weeks that Alizarin and Morpheus were gone.

"I lived in a house with seventeen people," she remembered. Something about the number seventeen (its precision? Its oddness? Its primeness?) made me sure that she had, indeed, lived in a house with seventeen people. "So I know how to live in groups. It was up to me to manage these projects His Holiness was running. I got really good at scheduling and working really hard and making sure everyone was up on time. *We worked really hard,*" she repeated, with stubborn non-unionized pride. "We were fixing up houses for monks and nuns in Tibet and selling them so they could buy food and clothes. In Tibet, the nuns aren't recognized, you know. They have to support themselves, and it's really hard for them to get anything done. Ron said, this isn't right. We've got to do something about this. But after a while, I had to quit."

I thought she had rushed to the ending. Maybe I was witnessing a previously unexamined episode of disillusionment. This woman who was capable of acknowledging that she'd been fucked up and angry would eventually see that she'd also been tricked. Hadn't she just referred to His Holiness as *Ron*, without correcting herself?

"Why did you quit?" I asked in a low voice. I haven't done a good job of conveying this, but I cared about Fiona. I cared about her the way my heart might break for a smelly old three-legged dog I had no intention of saving.

She turned her pulsing eyes on me. "I got to the point where I was relying on my will all the time. I was pushing, pushing, pushing, and only developing my will."

I was deeply impressed, and a little afraid.

"Also." She paused as a lone crow winged across the cloudless sky. "I injured my back. I didn't pick up some enormous thing or have a building fall on me or anything. It was just the constant stress and not enough sleep and moving around from place to place all the time." She sounded exactly like someone who is capable of analyzing facts. "Sometimes, we'd set off across the mountains with a truck full of materials and it would take us all night. We didn't know the terrain, and a lot of times, the guides weren't much better. There aren't a lot of accurate maps in Tibet." She sniffed, like an old-fashioned British explorer who lives to be disdainful of inept native cartography. "We'd get there just a few hours before dawn, and we still had to set up and be ready because we had a crew coming. The nuns were waiting for us."

I was waiting, too. I, who never questioned her once, was waiting for her to slap her napkin on the table and declare that finally, she came to her senses and left him. Instead, like a woman yearning for a lover she spurned in her hot-headed youth, she said, "I'd like to go back. But the openings don't come up that often, and with my injury, there's not a lot I could do. It's nothing personal. I'm just not that useful anymore. He lets me make healing tools. There's not a lot of people who are allowed to make tools. But with the trust he has in me . . . Sometimes, I heal myself with the tools. It's working, I think, but the Lord doesn't always do what we tell him to do."

Mariana began to scream wildly. "Verdelein!" she screamed, like her one remaining child was trapped in the rubble of a burning building. "Verdelein! Verdelein! Verdelein!" She sounded as if she would scream this way for the rest of her life. Fiona smiled.

"I'll take care of that," she said, with the quiet authority of a nun who has wandered the mountains of Tibet, in service of her sister nuns.

MY MOTHER HAD gone semi-digital. There is no virtue in this, so her work was very good. She offered a detailed explanation of how she did it, with mirrors or lenses or maybe sex magic, but I wasn't paying attention.

That well-traveled envelope contained, not photos, plural, but one single printout from her digital camera. It was a dual image of her one and only child (as far as I know, she'd always add, with a graceful writhe and a smirk. My mother was an unexpected hit with the PTA and the Ladies' Auxiliary). I remembered her taking that picture, shortly after I'd left The John. I was wearing black, which, even in the rosiest bloom of my tow-headed youth, has always made me look worn out with sorrow or intestinal parasites.

I was standing in front of a heart's-blood velvet curtain in my mother's stage-set chambers, leaning my head against a wardrobe that was alleged to be part of my grandmother's trousseau. "That's a family heirloom," my mother told me. "Granny Franny bought it new with her very first paycheck." It occurred to me that the teenaged Francine Swift could stretch a paycheck like no one before her or since.

"What about the gun cabinet, Mom?" I asked. I was in a pretty good mood. My e-ticket to Frankfurt was waiting for me at San Francisco International Airport, Gate Number Nine. Every time I thought about it, I started humming, *Love Potion Number Nine*, and snapping my fingers softly. I was drinking heavily. I was also smoking so much, every breath felt like a revelation. "I thought she bought the gun cabinet with her very first paycheck," I teased my mother lovingly. "And a pair of real leather pink go-go boots, like Nancy Sinatra."

"Just try to look pensive, honey," my mother directed. "This is our new beginnings shot. One door opens, another door closes."

"It's the other way around," I told her, feeling unaccountably mild. "One door *closes*, another door *opens*. I can't believe we're arguing about clichés," I added, as if I'd never even heard of a mother and daughter who didn't dote on one another.

"They're cultural axioms," she responded, bringing some academic standing to the argument. Somewhere during this exchange of penetrating insights, my mother took the picture she would send me years later, in the valley of the mountains at Mariana's Hof. *New*

Beginnings, she'd written on the back, with the simplicity and affection that filled her letters.

I said it was a dual shot. I'm sure it was a simple procedure, involving one or two clicks of the mouse on my mother's antique desktop. But you would have thought she was Lady Lovelace (Ada, not Linda), by the way she crowed about how she'd doubled my image. Francine's wardrobe had vanished as thoroughly as that first paycheck, so many years ago. Instead, one picture of me pressed its left temple against the right temple of its mirror image. I looked like a set of identical twins, caught in a moment with the exact same expression on two versions of one face.

There was one minor discrepancy. Neither of these women looked anything like me. They were alert and melancholy. The two identical versions of their mouth slanted away from one another, like a cutting word, gone unsaid. Because of my black clothing and the deep internal red of my mother's curtains, my faces looked like plaster casts, my necklines smooth as bowling pins. My eyes were so dark they had no pupils, just a few highlights glimmering weakly, like the sun on a day with an air quality advisory.

If I hadn't just spent a whole semester posing nude, I would say there could not possibly be a less flattering picture of me in existence. Every asymmetry of my features was repeated, from my uneven eyebrows to the crumpled arches of my badly broken nose. My battered skin was stretched and tender from the wind and the sun.

By now, I was scrutinizing the double image with the same dispassionate care I'd had for Enid, my old garden friend from Alizarin's studio. I saw how the shadow on the bulb of the nose made a fanciful flourish as it deepened into the nostrils; how softly that thick purple ribbon of shade caressed the crooked lines of my injury. And then, slowly, seeping from the shadows, a sense of something cradling this damaged face emerged. The outside lines of cheek and chin were echoed in the living thumb that held the photograph. My thumb. The tendons of the neck agreed with the wrist—my wrist, where I saw the pulse behind the bones. There was an awkward softness here. I saw it, flickering among the pixelated freckles of an ugly woman's photograph.

I began to draw.

"MAY I SEE what you are working on?" There was something terrifying about how indestructible the old lady was. It would be a lot more reassuring if we were all just a little more fragile.

I showed her my drawing. I had delved into pixels and patches and spots of poor resolution and discovered there were glorious streaks of purple in the shadows of the nose and mouth. I'd found a mixture of warm orangey greens and cool brown pinks in the unshaded plains of the forehead and cheeks. Something about the unreality of all this color made me feel like I was really made of flesh. I could feel the grit of the pigments in the creases of my hands. If someone had taken my fingerprints just then, I would have been identified in hazy smudges of ambiguous color. As I worked, I could hear Mariana's labored breathing through the open door of the sewing room. I could feel my own heartbeat, as I blended and smeared and re-adjusted millimeters of first one nose, then the other; as I mapped the terrain of a country that was no longer a face, let alone a possession of mine.

I showed the dying woman my drawing. Wasn't that a dying request? Everything now, from extra ice cubes in her glass to midnight phone calls, could very easily be a last wish.

"Who is he?" she demanded. I could tell she was alert by how rushed and peremptory she was, like she knew the interval would be brief and wanted to get as much out of it as possible.

"He's a boxer," I told her. "See his nose?"

She examined me closely. Then she looked at the drawing again, more carefully this time. Photorealism isn't what I strive for, but I didn't say that out loud, because it's the kind of thing you only say if you're a pretentious jerk who can't draw.

"A boxer," she said thoughtfully. "With very small ears."

She was right. The ears were tiny pink deformities, like lumps of scar tissue on people who have been horribly burned or partially devoured. It takes so little to make a human face grotesque. Sometimes, you can do it with the stroke of a pastel.

"It's not done yet," I said lamely.

"No, of course not." She was still examining the drawing. "Lots of colors," she murmured. Then she fixed me with a look I will not refer to as respectful. It was, rather, a re-evaluation. "It's very bold," she said, and watched me.

I began to feel mildly horrified, like I'd opened the fridge and realized I was staring into a pair of highly intelligent eggs: smooth, impassive, full of secret thoughts. "Oh, well, you know," I murmured, or something very much like it.

She was watching me steadily. "I would not have expected you to make something like that." She sounded like she had taken it for granted that I was utterly without insight and now, without wasting too much thought on the matter, had changed her assessment and was indulging in a few moments of casual astonishment.

It always makes me feel a little oppressed, when people let me know they've been paying attention to me. I don't even like it when waiters remember my regular order. But this: being closely noticed by a woman who occupied my entire field of vision—this was a form of surveillance I had never experienced.

Had she been aware of me, all those times I'd rolled her back and forth and rummaged in her secret parts? She always stared off into space when I changed her diapers, her eyes as blank as egg yolks. It was comforting to believe that she had no idea what was happening. If that sounds unlikely, please allow a few moments for a brief anecdote: once, I spent close to an hour with a truly traumatizing quantity of semi-liquid shit. When I pulled back the blankets, the bed looked like the inside of a microwave where the world's most unappealing entrée has exploded. The shit had stiffened into a shell on her skin, halfway to her shoulder blades in one direction and almost to her knees in the other. The knowledge of how much shit a human body can produce has had a permanent effect on my concept of what it means to be human. Remember that Mariana was enormous. There were times when I felt like I was rummaging around in the cushions of a couch, for one more shred of shit-soaked diaper, one more ineffective mattress guard, one more corner of a soiled nightgown. It was undignified and strenuous in the extreme.

Hours later, she began to look around in alarm, as if she'd misplaced something personal and was afraid it might turn up somewhere embarrassing. "It came out of me like lava," she reported, with what sounded very much like satisfaction. "And now it's gone."

In Mariana's house, everything was neatly labelled. She had a complete set of Allen wrenches, and knew exactly where they were. Her VHS films were filed alphabetically by director. This was not a woman who lost track of her shit. Until she did. But then, in the latest switchback of her own decline, she turned her gaze on me and said, "I would not have expected you to make something like that."

She was watching me. She knew who I was. But what did that signify? It wasn't like those searching eyes would slash my furniture, throw my dishes on the floor, or smash the glass terrarium, where a pair of gentle young iguanas spent their days immobile as the statues of a pair of sitting gurus. No. This was not my father's house.

Then, as suddenly as if someone had hit a breaker switch inside her, the moment of examination passed. The light in her eyes went off. The refrigerator was still humming, but the eggs within were no longer watching. They were just a pair of sloshing things, contained by a shell as durable and fragile as the force of life itself.

AND THEN THE dying began. Heaven defend me from a death of old age. If I ever find religion, I will fall down on my knees and beg to be spared. There were convulsions, for one thing; and for another, there was Fiona.

I should mention the death kit at this point, since we've come to the dying already and I've failed to produce it. When someone dies at home, surrounded by loved ones or random strangers off of craigslist, the local hospice provides an assortment of painkillers, anti-anxiety medications, and anal suppositories. The expectation appears to be that a peaceful home death will be characterized by agony both physical and mental; and the inability to take an unassisted shit.

I remember a sense of motion; but that can't possibly be accurate. Mariana often woke up screaming about how her bed was careening across the floor, carrying her fast into the darkness. Did I mention that the metaphors of death are not subtle?

Because Mariana was terrified of the dark, Fiona hung a red paper lantern over the bed. This is how it happened that the scarred old veteran lay dying in a soft red glow, as warm as a womb in July of that year.

The night it began, the shadows huddled at a respectful distance, not entirely dispelled by soft red lamps or the golden glow of obsolete light bulbs. I remember the sensation of something crashing. If there is to be motion where nothing is moving, let there be a great cacophony where there is only a whisper.

I still don't know how someone who can barely move can do so with such force. How does a person who is mostly paralyzed convulse in a way that creates an impression of crashing and shattering, on a peaceful summer evening full of crickets singing songs?

All she could do was slowly flail her arms. She made no sound. Her face was a series of roundnesses: round, terrified eyes and a round black mouth full of silent screams. She looked like a mountain covered with trees, the movements of their limbs implying gently that the mountain is about to explode.

Fiona was in a half-crouch at the head of the woman whose death was no longer pending; whose dying, at this precise moment, in this light that would never be exactly the same again, had become an active thing.

I always thought the name Fiona had a graceful, catlike sound. And Fiona did have a certain cut-throat delicacy. Her manners were brutal and finicky. She had a devastated nervous system and a way of slinking that made her look skillful and sly. But now, in her bony half-crouch at the head of the bed, she had the stark angularity of a shadow puppet. That she was suffering I have no doubt. But the shape of it was unaffecting, like the passionate surrender of one who is utterly undesirable. It wasn't artificial—or at least it wasn't faked. But it was *made*, and held up to the light, where it led a most examined life.

"Isobel." She wasn't crying. Her eyes had gone so dark and deep there was no possibility of light at the ends of them. "Isobel." It was unmistakably an order; but there was something else there, too. It was a plea. *Please obey me*, it said. *If you have the least compassion, you will allow me to command you.* "We need your help." She turned to Mariana. "We need to give her these, Isobel." She held a pair of blank white pills in the palm of her quivering hand. "Reuben said I could, if it came to that. It's really urgent. *Isobel!* We need to do this *now!*"

She was talking to me the way people talk to someone who is standing open-mouthed in a moment where swift decisive action is required. And I will tell you that I felt the call to action, stirring in the darkest, tangled parts of who I am. But at the same time, I saw something sloping away in that darkness; something awkward and stubborn and difficult to visit with. I lunged for it.

"Is this going to finish it?" I blurted. "Because I am not okay with that." It is humiliating to remember that my moment of greatest moral fortitude involved my decision not to murder a helpless old woman who would be dead in a matter of days. It is also humiliating to recall that as I made my stand, I was acutely aware of the fact that I was being annoying.

I saw that Fiona would never forgive me for interrupting her this way. She was swept along on the most powerful current of her life, and here I was, quibbling over details.

"Reuben has given me permission," she reiterated. She was a lonely crewman on a storm-tossed sea, repeating orders the absent captain had given at dinner, before crockery smashed and provisions heaved into the sea; before the world began to churn with certain death and there was no longer any way to tell the ocean from the sky.

"I want to know what it is," I insisted. I knew I sounded like a lesser crewman with imaginary food allergies, examining labels as the last of our non-vegan edibles were swallowed by the waves.

"It's . . . I don't remember the name of it right now, Isobel." Fiona snatched at the death kit and flung it at me. I caught it clumsily against my chest and fumbled with the zipper.

"I'm sorry, Fiona. I have to know what it is." I was a bureaucrat on the lost continent, combing through visas as the shoreline sank out of sight.

"It's an anti-anxiety medication," she finally admitted, tearing her attention away from Mariana. "It's in that little bottle."

I found it. Lorazepam, I read. Administer as needed for the treatment of anxiety.

It must have been obvious by now. It would have been obvious, to anyone even mildly attentive to other human beings. I literally took a pill out of the bottle and compared it to the ones she held in her hand. I thought Fiona Jones was incompetent. I thought she was insane, and possibly homicidal.

"I'll help you," I said. The storm began to subside.

DEATH IS A voyage. I know because I read the entire hospice brochure. Hospice literature is illustrated with somber drawings in bright colors, like the ones that catch your eye before you realize you're looking at a cheesy religious publication. The brochure features a ship sailing over a horizon, against the backdrop of a setting sun. It's classic death imagery, though it omits the flames and regalia and the terrified sacrificial slaves a proper Viking funeral calls for. Clearly, it is not a requirement to have a Viking warrior funeral, every time you have a corpse and a boat in the same reference.

What the brochure is trying to convey is that death, like birth, can be beautiful and terrifying, with lots of water imagery. There are people in the world who call themselves "death midwives," because of the resemblance they see between the two great journeys. If you are one those people, I would like to let you know right now that I would rather not so much as have a cup of coffee with you. Ever.

To my mind, the part about death that most closely resembles travel is the interminable waiting around for the train that is never on time, the flight that's been cancelled, the donkey with a twisted gut, and finally, the room that hasn't been cleaned because the staff have all got dysentery. Death is all the headaches and a few of the soul-searing epiphanies of travel in an unmarked land. And, like all trips, the most important part of this one is choosing your companions wisely.

I know I made it sound like Fiona and I were adrift on the dark sea of death, our leaky dinghy provisioned with nothing more than heavy-duty palliatives and a few buttplugs. Well, we were. But we could also call a twenty-four hour hospice hotline and talk to a nurse who was endlessly patient and sometimes even kind.

After speaking with this nurse at great length, Fiona began to administer morphine. She kept immaculate records. Her handwriting was large, looping, and unmistakably feminine. It was slightly out of date. It was a little foreign, exactly what you might expect from someone half a generation older than you are, from a country very much like yours but just a little different, in every way.

Fiona called the nurse when Mariana seemed frightened or restless. She called when Mariana's breathing changed. She called when Mariana's breathing had not changed following the first change;

and she called when Mariana broke out in a sweat and when her hands and feet showed a shady purple dappling, which is normal for a dying person. And natural. Which reassurances have never, in the history of all reassurances, had a single measurable effect on anyone's sense of well-being.

When you call the twenty-four hour hospice hotline, you tell the operator who you are, what your patient's name is, and what you wish to discuss with the nurse. After a while, a nurse calls you back. It is not always the same nurse, but they all know everything about your patient, which is either an indication of good record-keeping, or an insight into how interchangeable we all are in our final hours. A hospice death is a grueling lesson in accepting what you cannot change, so there is no sense of emergency. Sometimes, the nurse doesn't call back for over an hour.

While we waited, Fiona paced. Mariana had been dying with a sense of purpose for two days now. Reuben and his family had appeared for part of an afternoon, spoken of snakes, and departed. I do not remember exactly what they said about snakes. I seem to recall that Hunter was morbidly allergic to peanuts, which led somehow to the inevitability of his being bitten by a rattlesnake and dying horribly. I got the distinct impression that Reuben and Colleen felt they were providing their son with advantages that they themselves had not enjoyed.

"I just don't believe it's enough," Fiona insisted.

She had never come out of the crouch she'd gone into the night the convulsions began. Her back was in such agony, she could no longer carry a basin of water to Mariana's bedside. She could not reach the towels on the upper shelves, which was just as well, because she could not bend to pick them up when they fell from her nerveless hands.

"I'm going to go meditate. I've got to focus on this." She scrabbled for the door, crouching like a gnome in one of those fairytales with deep Freudian implications.

I leaned against the counter by the telephone and thought about a patch of green on the curve of a cheekbone in the photograph from my mother. I was working on a painting now, from the same reference. In the painting, I had rendered this cheekbone in striations that were nearly chartreuse. They were interspersed with reds and pinks I'd mixed myself, following an intuitive recipe I'd never be able to duplicate. It occurred to me that this part of the painting looked like exposed musculature. I was just thinking about how someday, I would get an anatomy book and study the muscles of the face, when the phone rang. I picked it up.

"Is this Fiona?" The voice sounded compassionate but wary. Someone who knows Fiona, I realized at once. The voice identified itself as Agnes the hospice nurse, returning a call from Fiona Jones about Mrs. Blanchefleur. "Is Ms. Jones there?"

I made a few enabling excuses before introducing myself. "I'm living here, too. I'm one of the caregivers. I'm taking care of Mariana." I hoped I didn't sound resentful about being excluded from something distasteful and sad.

Agnes hesitated. "Fiona is concerned. Fiona feels that Mariana is in pain."

"I'm not a nurse," I replied. This was pot country. I knew when I was being invited to say something incriminating.

"What is your thinking on that?" she asked, as if I hadn't said a thing—which I hadn't. Not really.

"I'm not a medical professional. Mariana isn't speaking, so she can't exactly tell us how she's feeling." A surge of adrenaline did a few laps around my chest. "Hold on a second," I heard myself say. I felt my body propel itself into the bathroom and lock the door. I turned on the water and sat down on the edge of the tub. "I had that tub built specially for me," Mariana used to sigh, "and now I am the only one who cannot use it."

"She looks to me like she's in a coma," I said. I felt like a teenager, gossiping about the mean girls with that one cool old person who understands. It was exciting, to fly in the face of an authority that isn't quite legitimate, but is still very real. Agnes was silent. "I mean, I've never seen anybody who's actually in a coma." *Don't take me seriously,* I begged silently. *I'm just a nobody. I'm just a buttwiper.* "But, ah, she's not really moving. I mean, she's breathing . . ."

"Can you check on her for me?" Agnes was suddenly alert.

I hesitated. Because of Fiona's policy about the doors, I was trapped in the kitchen and bathroom until Fiona emerged from her room.

You remember that the living room, where Mariana lay, was not to be used as a thoroughfare. However, both of us could use the outside door on the master bedroom, where Fiona slept—as long as Fiona's need to rest and meditate in privacy could also be respected. Because Fiona was meditating right now, I could not approach Mariana from the sliding glass doors, which, for reasons that were never quite clear to me, was the only acceptable direction. How did Fiona enforce this policy? By being fragile and in pain.

"I would be happy to," I replied, feeling bold and almost brutal.

I do not remember how it felt, to move across the hardwood floor as I made my forbidden approach. I stopped beside the bed and looked down at Mariana. Her mouth was open. Her eyes were closed.

"She looks like she's sleeping," I said.

It felt almost crude, to state the fact so bluntly. To be sleeping, rather than dying, implies the indignity of snoring and farting and shifting around with no great purpose; of regenerating the vulgar body so it can go on living like there's no such thing as death.

"Any agitation?" Agnes wanted to know. Clinical language like this is also disrespectful. I could tell that Agnes would fail to account for the presence of spirits, changes in energy currents, or the implications of past lives when she made her assessment of Mrs. Blanchefleur's condition. I reported briskly that the patient did not appear to be agitated.

"She's probably not in pain," Agnes told me. Then, with the air of a lady gathering her skirts before setting off across a muddy field, she asked a question that sounded very much like she was trying to establish culpability. "Who is administering pain medication?"

I admitted that I hadn't concerned myself with such complicated matters. I was experiencing a severe adrenaline comedown. "Fiona can't really do much of anything else," I began, and trailed off lamely. I sounded exactly like an incompetent criminal's lazy, dumb accomplice.

Agnes made a sound that might have been sympathetic but probably wasn't. "Is Fiona keeping records?" she inquired pleasantly.

"Yes!" I exclaimed, jubilantly casting aside a lifetime of indoctrination regarding the qualities of those who snitch. "Fiona keeps records. Right here . . ." I began to scrabble through the binder.

Trained criminals are the best cooperating witnesses, because they know exactly which information is important.

"How often is Ms. Fiona Jones administering morphine?" Agnes asked.

She could have been filling out a form to replace a lost drivers' license. People don't sound that methodical when something is terribly wrong, do they?

I focused on the large, looping handwriting. "Today is the Fourth of July." Today is the Fourth of July, Agnes agreed. I think she would have agreed in the same soothing, neutral tone if I had said I had a dog named Spot.

"Okay. Today. Starting at six a.m." I scanned the columns of doses and times. It was one o' clock in the afternoon. "She's been giving her half a c.c. every . . . every half hour." I owed Fiona absolutely nothing. Snitching is a breach of trust. Without trust, there is no betrayal, and therefore no snitching. I kept a careful eye on the doors.

"I have a note here from Marissa," Agnes said clearly. Marissa? What was I supposed to know about Marissa? "From five o' clock this morning. Marissa, who is a highly competent, licensed professional, advised Ms. Jones to administer half a c.c every two hours. *Every two hours*, Ms. . . . what did you say your name was?" I whispered my name into the phone. "That's approximately . . . let's do the math here, shall we? Four times the amount of morphine she was advised to administer? Where did you say she was?"

"I think she's praying," I said, through lips that were clumsy and numb. I don't know why I spoke of prayer instead of meditation. I must have thought it sounded saner, though I don't know why. "I'll talk to her."

"Yes. I think that would be a good idea." It sounded like an accusation.

Fiona was walking almost straight when she finally came out of her room. She closed the door behind her with solemn churchly silence. She had sanctified the area with prayer and meditation, clogging it with fetishistic ritual. It takes a recklessness that borders on vandalism to overcome the power of such carefully constructed discomfort. But something about the simple variety of someone else's voice had taken the charge out of Fiona's proclamations. I handed her a steaming mug of Kava De-Stress tea. It was one of Caitlin's favorites.

"The hospice nurse called back," I told her, in my most casual conversational tone.

She nodded. She didn't seem to care.

"I had a look at the patient. So I could describe, you know, what I saw. To the nurse. She asked me to," I added, establishing culpability. It was as good as telling her I'd entered the room from an unauthorized direction.

"Oh. Good." She took a sip of her mud-colored tea. "Very sweet." She was languid and distracted.

"Agnes," I continued.

"Oh, yes. I've spoken to *Agnes.*" Her lips twitched meaningfully as she nipped at her kava again.

"Agnes seems to think that maybe Mariana might not need quite as much morphine as . . . we've been giving her."

"Yes. Well." Fiona set her mug aside with a little sigh, as if she couldn't imagine why she'd expected better from the likes of me. "I've been talking with my friend Stacey, too, Isobel. I don't know if you know it, but I'm not doing this on my own. I've been consulting with Stacey, who lives at the Center. She used to run a hospice in Arizona. She's a registered nurse, so she's a great deal more qualified than you or I. I told her what's been going on, and frankly, she's horrified. She says this happens all the time, you know. She says a lot of people are quite stingy with painkillers near the end because they're highly addictive. Well, they're also quite spendy, aren't they? Think about that, if you would." She accompanied this invitation with a frantic, unfocused glare. She wasn't really talking to me. She was giving a speech. "But her attitude is, who cares? Who cares if she gets addicted? She's *dying*, Isobel. Jesus god, don't you *get* it? I've been sitting with her for hours on end just watching her face and I tell you I see things—"

The skin of her face was blotchy and rough. I noticed that one of her eyelids drooped a little. She had a slightly receding chin. A wave of disgusted pity surged through me, following the same path the adrenaline had taken earlier. It made me feel like I'd taken a bath in dirty water.

"You've been working so hard," I soothed. I placed a hand on her shoulder and understood immediately why she was not the hugging kind. The bones jutted out of her with no rhythm or softness, thrumming through skin so hot it was itchy to touch. *Is that what it feels like to be her?* I wondered. I forced my poor hand to make a few feeble circles on the unhappy bones of her suffering back.

"Why don't you let me handle the night shift," I ventured, feeling my way firmly along an unseen path. Yes: I was still heading downhill. And yes: I felt the wind in my face, from going down fast. But now the breath was steady in my smokeless lungs, which made the lies come out so much more easily. "It's really unfair, that everything's been up to you for so long. It's not right, that you should have to do everything all by yourself. I said I'd be here for you, Fiona," I reminded her, which may have been true. If I hadn't said it outright, I'd implied the hell out of it. "Well, I'm here now." We were confederates in a matter of life and death, whispering secrets in ill-lit rooms.

I watched myself take shape in Fiona's private thoughts as the answer to her half-formed prayers. All I had to do now was close that blue-veined hand inside my calloused palm. I looked down and there it was, the outer knuckle of the thumb barely wider than the rawboned wrist. It was a hand for slipping handcuffs, a hand for palming keys. It was a hand for forgeries and fakes and fleeing her homeland for the salvation of her immortal soul. I left that hand alone, at the end of its ungraceful wrist.

But she was already nodding her auburn-haired head. "It's too much," she whispered. "You know, this is so stupid." She choked, and a wave of mucus receded into her throat and thickened the rest of her words. "I just wish—I wish Reuben were here, dammit. I mean, it's his mum. If it were my mum—" She sucked a few swallows of snot back into her sinuses. "It would just be so great, wouldn't it," she murmured, with a weepy little hiccup. "I mean, if we had a man here. I told you it was stupid," she reiterated, with a squelched unhappy wail.

"Oh. Well." I gave her shoulder a few ineffectual feminine pats. "We'll make do. I think women are so much more sensible about these things, don't you?"

"You know—" Fiona lifted her head and aimed her unfocussed eyes at the space I happened to be occupying. "I know this sounds crazy— there are more things in heaven and earth, right? But I know for a fact that she's in agony. I can't just stand by—" She paused for a moment. It looked like a technique of self-discipline, a strategy of war. "I know I've told you this before. About the connection. I've been here for so many months, and sometimes she speaks and sometimes she doesn't and then sometimes when she does she means something else entirely. But we understand each other. It's a telepathic connection," she said, all in a rush. "There it is. I know a lot of people don't believe in that sort of thing, but, well, I know better. I've learned so much from her. She's my friend, Isobel." She succumbed to another dainty torrent of hicuppy sobs.

I heard a hard little Agnes-like voice inside my mind. *She's not your friend, you little twerp,* it said. *Mariana Blanchefleur would have eaten you alive. Even in her seventies, when she was getting DUI's from rookie cops.*

"We won't let her be in agony. We'll take care of her." As soon as I said it, I thought of all those hard-faced men in Mariana's collection of neatly labeled film noir tapes. I remembered what it means, in black and white, to take care of someone whose existence has become an intractable problem.

I CALLED IN reinforcements later that day. "I hate to ask someone to brave the holiday traffic," I said brightly. In the slight echo on the phone line, I could hear the subtext plainly: *please accept this demonstration of concern for others as evidence of my sanity. Please . . .* I winced. I was crouching next the bathtub with water going full blast in the middle of summer, just in case Fiona suddenly got interested in what I was doing. In just a few months, Californians would begin to understand that a drought of possibly millennial proportions had settled on the land.

"Have you ever been around someone who was dying before?" the nurse inquired.

Her neutrality was so complete, it sounded like a rebuke. "Kind of," I hedged. Who hasn't?

"How much longer do you think she has?" the nurse asked next, ramping up the neutrality. We were emphatically discouraged from making predictions, so this nurse, with this question, made me feel a little like I was compromising myself—on the phone, no less.

I hesitated. "Two . . . or three days," I heard myself say. I knew it was true, as soon as I said it.

"I could send someone out . . ." she offered, clearly hoping I would remember how reluctant I was to have someone do such a thing.

"Yes, please," I said. I heard no echo on the line.

Hospice favors a sturdy, matter-of-fact approach to death and dying, well-seasoned with an ecumenical belief or non-belief in God or the Creator and the workings of the soul. There is a strange, hard-assed compassion to the hospice way of doing things. It's as if the Buddha were to interrupt himself during a lecture on the impermanence of all matter to say, yeah. Whatever. Just get over it, would you?

I met the nurse in the driveway. Her name was Barbara. She was a tiny, pigeon-chested woman with a strong, straight back. She took me in with a glance and gave me a firm, warning smile.

"Let me see the patient first," she ordered. She moved swiftly through the front door and brushed past Fiona, who was glaring like she'd caught me masturbating in the sacristy.

Barbara introduced herself in a way that made it very clear she was not offering her friendship. "I just thought I'd drop by to see if anybody had any questions," she announced, as if it were possible to "drop by" a place that was purposely out of the way.

The only thing further down the road from us was Bible camp, where smiling pastors told a tale of fire and brimstone rarely heard this far north of the Mason-Dixon Line. The road itself was darkened all day long by the shadow of very tall wooden fences.

"Any questions?" Barbara asked, drawing out her stethoscope. She did not put on gloves.

Fiona clutched her binder to her chest like she was clinging to an alibi.

"We were wondering . . . about the morphine," I piped up weakly.

"Ah, yes. The morphine." Barbara seized a dying eyelid and snapped it up, like a woman throwing open the blinds in full expectation of discovering squalor.

We all caught a glimpse of the still-gleaming white, slippery as an egg in butter.

"She's not there," Barbara declared, allowing the eyelid to ease back down. "Would *you* let someone yank on your eyelid like that? Without so much as a twitch?"

She faced Fiona squarely. She might have been sizing her up for a few friendly rounds in a boxing ring. But Fiona was standing before us all with her eyes closed, like a true believer ready to burn.

"Mariana!" Barbara shouted.

Fiona flinched.

With a flourish, the straight-backed little nurse whipped the blankets away from the patient. "She's not in pain. Trust me. I've seen pain." She sounded almost eager. "*But.* She has too many blankets. She can have a sheet," she compromised, and turned to the door.

"I'll walk you to your car," I offered. "Some of the dogs in the neighborhood. They know me."

Barbara gave a crisp little nod, like it wasn't even worth the trouble to tell me what she'd seen of dogs.

"So," she said, opening the driver's side door. She stood behind it like she was accustomed to using it as a shield. "She's not taking it well, is she?"

I smiled pleasantly, to indicate that I, in contrast to my colleague, had fully grasped the fact that death is natural; that we who live with it are tranquil and serene; that we do not, under any circumstances, freak out. At the very most, we might allow the natural progression of our feelings to express themselves, in clearly-defined steps as explained to us by our spiritual care advisors and the brochure that comes with the death kit. It is acceptable to grieve, normally and sometimes deeply. We do not freak out.

"It's freaking me out," I admitted, instantly sacrificing any credibility I may have had. "She's in this crazy cult—"

"What is your definition of a cult?" Barbara interrupted. She would have been a stern professor.

"She's a follower of this guy over in Lake County named Ron Spence who calls himself Buddha Maitreya." I felt myself washed in the double pleasure of presenting a well-researched fact and sharing secret gossip. "You can look him up on Guruphiliac," I continued, savoring my betrayal. "She seriously believes that he is simultaneously the reincarnation of Jesus Christ and Buddha. Which is one hell of a split personality disorder, if you ask me." I had been dying to say this out loud, but my timing must have been off. She didn't even look like she was trying not to laugh. "She calls him His Holiness in casual conversation. Like it's a term of endearment or something. She says she's cleansing Mariana's karma when she meditates—which I think is what she calls it when she gets high, and she thinks she's receiving telepathic messages from her about how she's in agony and needs four times more morphine than she's supposed to be getting."

I stopped for breath. There is a reason cult members discourage communication with outsiders. Outsiders are dangerous, because they don't give a shit about the carefully constructed context of a miniature society where everyone is tormented by poorly synchronized wavelengths. The outsider restores order, something that's difficult to do when you live where you work and your employment is contingent upon the trust of a nutjob stoner. The relief of standing bareheaded in the sun as I shared this dangerous information was so intense, I began to see tiny orange and yellow explosions, every time I blinked.

Barbara was watching me carefully. "And you are—? A neighbor? A relative? Friend of the family?"

"I'm a paid caregiver," I explained. "I live here, too."

Barbara nodded, like a woman whose policy about a bullshit story is to let it pass, unremarked upon but keenly noted. "Fiona Jones is the only caregiver we have on record." She showed me her teeth in what I eventually realized was a smile. "From the family, you understand. Mariana's son has given her permission to take whatever measures she feels are necessary. He trusts her." She watched me intently, scanning for symptoms of taking the hint. "He feels his mother is transitioning peacefully with Fiona at the helm. And she is." She shifted, so the sun shone off her hard-working holiday nurse's glasses. She looked like she was examining me from behind a pair of white goggles.

"People go crazy," she told me with weary kindness, like she was tired of breaking the news that everyone dies. "It's usually religion."

She had a long drive ahead of her, and possibly a lot more death and dying before she could go home and enjoy a few cold leftovers and maybe a lukewarm beer. Would she struggle to hear a final heartbeat over the sound of celebratory explosions? She told me an anecdote. I tasted the dust in my mouth. Wasn't there something about dust on the way out of Paradise? I wondered, as I hauled myself into the house.

Fiona was in a hot-eyed fury when I came back inside. I am embarrassed to say that it did not occur to me, until that moment, that she might have been skimming meds from the death kit. *It can't be the Lorazepam*, I reasoned, remembering how swiftly and utterly the drug had stilled the dying woman's convulsions. *And it's probably not the buttplugs.*

"Isobel." Her face was ravaged. What the hell right do you have to be ravaged? I wondered wearily. "I need to talk to you." She spun, hitching and crabbing and reaching for counters as she hobble-stepped through her room and onto the deck. The wisteria was blooming. Mariana had told us she planned to come back as a flower.

"Listen. I'm very upset." Fiona took a deep breath, to show how hard she was working to control herself. "I know for a fact that I told you to be sure no one came in through that door. Mariana is working very hard to make this transition and she simply cannot have people slamming in and out of here. It is entirely too much stress for her to handle right now."

I noticed she was wearing a vaguely Asian-looking housecoat with wide sleeves and a sash. My mind lingered on the broad blue hems before I comprehended the fact that one of her freckled blue-veined breasts was entirely exposed. It was just lounging there, looking calm and relaxed, nestled up against her slatted breastbone.

"I know I have very specific requirements," she was saying, "and that's hard for some people to take. But I know what I'm doing here. And if you can't respect my requirements, well. Reuben has told me to do whatever I think is best for his mother at this time." She fixed me with an accusing stare, as if she'd caught me rummaging through her jewelry box and couldn't believe she was thinking about giving me a second chance.

"It was the nurse—" I protested. I still catch my breath at how quick I was to blame Barbara. I needn't have bothered, though. Fiona did not intend to be distracted by irrelevancies.

"Yes. I've spoken with *the nurse*." She could have been a well-schooled heretic, dismissing an illiterate peasant's orthodoxy. "I've also been speaking with my friend Stacey, at the Center. You *know* she ran a hospice in Arizona. I think she's a little more qualified than these country nurses out here." She sounded pre-emptively satisfied, as if she'd put her money on a sure thing and now all she had to do was sit back and watch the horses run. "She tells me it's always the least qualified people who sign up for the holidays. After all, who else is going to work while everyone else is having a good time?" She gave me a peevish, triumphant look as she waited for the inexorable logic of this to sink in.

We're working, I failed to point out, because it was just as plain as a naked breast, as plain as the fact that we're all going to die.

MARIANA "PASSED," AS we call it when we are sick to death of brutal honesty, at 9:27 a.m. on July 6th. It was a Wednesday. Fiona was at her side, cleansing her karma with an etheric weaver. You can purchase sets of etheric weavers on eBay, or you can go directly to the Buddha Maitreya's website, where you can be sure it has been blessed by a healing infusion of Monadic soul-filled light by Buddha Maitreya Himself, the Christ returned.

Fiona looked radiant. She wearing an Ascending Pyramid Headgear from Shambhala Healing Tools and swinging her little pendulum over the great mountain of flesh that had been Nicki Daniels, Mariana Blanchefleur, or Fraulein von Bingen. No one would ever know, now, who she really was. It had never been any of our business.

I walked across the floor and turned the AC on high. Then I turned on the ceiling fan.

"Smells a bit like dying old lady in here, doesn't it?" Fiona remarked.

It was the most reasonable thing I had ever heard her say. I had the sense that something crucial had gone all wrong and we could never apologize for it.

The Ascending Pyramid Headgear, incidentally, is exactly what it sounds like: a glistening, crystal-encrusted pyramid, with a chin strap and a frame of heavy copper wire. There are reasons for all of these things: the crystals, the copper, the shape of the headgear. I am not in the mood to explore any of them right now.

I sat down beside Fiona Jones, too broken for Ronald Spence's nunnery, and looked at the remains of the woman we called Mariana. The mouth was sunken into the face, as black and unmysterious as a pothole in the road. *Thank God she's dead,* I thought. *And now she's safe.*

"Do you have any plans?" Fiona inquired. I thought I heard a wistful note, like she was already nostalgic for the time we'd had together.

"A friend of mine asked me if I'd help her in the garden," I said vaguely. "While she's in Israel."

Fiona nodded. "Well, if she's got something going along those lines in a couple of months. Maybe you could put in a good word for me."

"You smoke?" I asked.

She nodded again. "It's a meditation tool, really," she explained, bouncing the etheric weaver like a yo-yo. "I do it to help myself meditate," she clarified, in case I didn't know what a meditation tool might be used for. "But if you could keep it under your hat," she suggested, looking at me quite seriously from underneath the Ascending Pyramid Headgear. "I don't want people to think . . ."

I wondered if she knew how much pot Mariana's tenants were growing.

"What about you?" I asked. "Got any plans?"

"Reuben's going to let me stay here for a while. It's really quite good of him. It's not like he paid me shit." Her accent made this sound like a lady's condemnation of a gentleman's etiquette. "Listen. Maybe if you could bear witness to something for me." My suitcase was packed. My mattress was bare. "Do you remember. What she said. About her wishes."

I smiled. "She wanted to come back as a flower."

"No, no. For the house. How she wanted to have like-minded people here. Well, the kitchen isn't very big, but I've lived in a lot smaller places with quite a few people." Seventeen. I remembered. "And I feel like Mariana would be a kind of guardian spirit," she concluded, as if this were the best part of her argument. "She was quite spiritual, you know. Behind all that bluster."

I tried to recall if I had ever seen Madame Blanchefleur blustering, and could not come up with a single instance of it.

"I thought you and I worked quite well together," she said suddenly, looking into my eyes with an open, appealing expression I had never seen her use before. It took a few heartbeats for me to realize that I had something she wanted. "I'd like to talk to you more sometime. I think people like us, people who don't have a lot of material possessions and kind of *drift*, if you know what I mean. People who are sensitive. Well. I think you *do* know what I mean." This was a spiritual grope, I realized. She was trying to turn me on by telling me how good I was.

"Why don't you give me Reuben's phone number," I said carefully. It would be a difficult story to tell. "I'll be sure to give him a call."

THE VALLEY OF death is deep, remember, deep as the cold and deeper than heat. We had assembled there, at the appointed hour of our great catharsis. Tension had mounted. There had been madness and death and slowly dawning horror. The truth had gradually revealed itself. The main character of any proper drama would have seized that stupid pyramid hat and beaten her antagonist even more senseless than she already was. She would have forced a confession. She would have denounced the bitch and told her the sheriff was on his way.

Instead, I called an exasperated nurse and let a dying woman die.

I parked my truck by the side of the road and walked toward the forest. The angle of the sun changed. A silly Englishwoman said, smells a bit like dying old lady in here, doesn't it? I felt as though the forces of a long-awaited battle had gathered in secret, waited 'til dawn . . . and then wandered off to see if they could get cell phone reception somewhere else. I sat down on a rock.

The angle of the sun changed again. There are, supposedly, cartels that grow vast quantities of pot on public land in Mendocino County. They do not adhere to the principles of organic farming. They feed themselves nightly on cheap beer and pregnant wildlife, caught in the beams of illegal spotlights. I was not at all concerned about whatever savage thing it is that happens to women who sit on rocks in cartel country all night long, waiting for the transformative effects of their experiences to overtake them.

When I started taking psychedelic drugs, my father told me never to forget that the physical laws of the universe are always the same, no matter what exotic compounds are coursing through your system. Physics are unaffected by a twelve-year-old girl who has just swallowed a handful of dried fungus. "You cannot fly," he catechized me patiently. "You cannot breathe underwater." There were times when I felt like an amnesiac, reading letters to myself; when the facts about the world refused to play their part convincingly. Phosphorescent nights became fluorescent days, where gravity and oxygen were as alien as items on an android's packing list.

It turned out that taking lots of drugs with acronyms as unwieldy as the compounds they signified was excellent preparation for what was happening right now. I don't mean *preparation,* in the sense that I was prepared to handle adversity. I just mean that I recognized the landmarks, and the sequence of events. The thing that had been happening so fervently had simply stopped, with no regard for rhythm or order or the need for proper endings. It was over, like a drug trip or a dream. Like a brief infatuation or a lifetime of faith in a counterfeit god.

Also, as far as the physical laws of the universe went, I was well and truly fucked. I had no job. I had no money. I had no place to live. I got up and walked back to my truck.

I STAYED IN a converted barn for the long, still days of summer in the season that Fiona Jones and I committed murder. *Yes,* you say, *but she wanted to die.* You ask me how much longer she would have lived without the morphine. You comment complacently on the quality of life she would have had, if we had medicated her more stringently. And you who know me well say, *Isobel.* I wait, because I know what's coming. But you are relentless. You know the answer, and you ask it anyway.

Isobel, you say. *What if it were you?* Yes, well. I still say we killed her, and a murder is a murder. Grant me a cold-blooded killer, when

I am old and helpless, wearing diapers in the presence of outcasts. I know now why killers confess.

For weeks, I sat in front of my easel, painting very slowly. I was so tired.

My own mortality went around and around in my mind like rocks in a tumbler, the motor so weak and so slow that only the eons would wear down the edges. *I must die, I must die, I must die.* Around and around it went, but the charge of my life was so low, I could not get to the shine or the meaning of that cold tough gray exterior. I knew there was a nest of shining crystals in the hollow of the stone, but all I could do was watch as it took another lazy turn around the inside of my mind. *I must die*, but never penetrate the mystery.

Therefore, I must paint. There was no hurry. But it was more urgent than anything I'd ever done. Because someday, I would die. And if I died in the presence of ineptitude and madness, I wanted to know I'd painted long and well, that each stroke had been made in full awareness of mortality, and the fact that I was not yet dead.

Somehow, when I was only able to think, *I must die*, and gauge where I was in the progress of a single brushstroke, I became more fully alive than I had ever been before. I was more alive than when I pounded through the Stockton tunnel and exploded into the heart of downtown San Francisco at five o'clock on Friday afternoon. I was more alive than when I sat in the back of that cop car in the shadow of the mountain, calling on the shade of every preacher, con man, fugitive, and whore who ever passed through my bloodline. There, in the aftermath of death, my life became a textured thing. It was real, and it was mine, and all I knew about it was that someday, I would die.

ALIZARIN WAS NOT in Israel. I made that up for the sole purpose of creating an air of second-hand religious legitimacy with a crazy person wearing an Ascending Pyramid Headgear.

We met at the end of the long, treacherous driveway that wound all the way up to the purple door. The orange house looked grubby and sun-worn, like a life preserver that hasn't been properly stowed.

The irises had gone feral, lurking in among the weeds with unkempt leaves gone dry.

"I thought you were mad at me," she said immediately. "I'm so glad you came."

Alizarin has always had a serious deception deficit. I've seen her talk about growing pot like it was time for all of us felons to come out of the closet and start wearing pride beads. As if growing pot were a civil right.

"I thought you were mad at me," she said frankly; and waited for the truth. It would take a long time to readjust to the world that was not Mariana's Hof, where every word had been a counter-strategy.

"I was," I replied, walking away from the mountain of lies I'd been telling for weeks. I'd told those lies for the rest of someone else's life. Maybe Fiona had needed honesty, too, like a successful suicide who wanted nothing more than to be told, with great authority, that she is not to take her own life.

"That car had a known mechanical problem," I went on. I detected the falsehood almost immediately. I knew as well as anyone else about the slave and master cylinders. I took a deep breath. I'd composed so many angry screeds. "I think you were jealous about Morpheus. I think you should know: I never had a thing with him." It was easier than anything, to just say it. Easy and graceless and uninspired, like taking a survey about the human psyche's most monumental motives.

Alizarin looked like a woman who already knew what she was going to say. "Well, dearie," she began; and for some reason, I did not bristle at the endearment. I did not assume that it preceded a belittling reminder of hard-won superior knowledge. "I think it was pretty obvious that Morpheus had a swooning crush on you." Her honesty, today, was devoid of all brutality. "But I never thought you were actually *doing* anything. Or even *planning* it. I just think he could have been a little bit less of an asshole about it. Always going on about how you were a shining example of whatever it was. I mean, *please*. He's gone."

"You put him out of your misery?" I suggested, in a tasteful attempt at womanly sympathy.

She did not appear to notice. "He moved into that little rental we have in town. He said he thought it was more *convenient.*" She made it sound as contemptible as if he'd relocated to the shade of a manna tree, so he could lie around all day waiting for meals to fall into his mouth.

"I guess everyone is better off," I observed. Honesty develops a momentum all its own, once it gets started.

She looked aghast. "*I'm* not better off! He just made a unilateral decision about *our* marriage, based on *his* convenience, and took off." She was furious. Alizarin was going to be fine.

"And speaking of men. Just in case . . . you know." I did not. "Just to clear things up . . ." She waved an unclarifying hand. It's soothing when other people are confused and inarticulate. It makes them seem so harmless.

"When I started sleeping with your father. You know he'd been with Eileen, right? On and off, for three or four years?" Would I ever acquire the last piece of information about what sluts my parents were? "Well, he *told* me. That your mom, you know. So I thought, as long as no one *else* knew." She looked at me expectantly, as if she had just said something eminently reasonable and now it was my turn.

I remembered Eileen. Eileen had a weak chin and a flat ass and she lived in a vault with no windows and movie posters all over the walls. She had a fuck-all tawdriness to her, a promise of secret competencies. She reminded me of Janis Joplin. My mother once described her as "the living embodiment of the death drive"; which, for some reason, didn't seem particularly funny at the time. I don't think Caitlin had the sense to feel threatened by Eileen; or maybe she knew Eileen had sense enough not to set up housekeeping with a man like Gustave Reinhardt.

"As long as it was discreet," Alizarin elaborated at last. "I thought it was fine. He *said* it was fine. *And. Way* before anything happened. I used to *say* to her (to your mom, I mean): why don't you let Izzy and Jezzie have a slumber party at my house? They could play dress-up. They'd have a great time. You two go out, have fun. But she was like, no. I don't *think* so. We *don't* go out." She imitated my mother's cold, malicious, tight-lipped little smile, the one that makes her look like she is refraining from baring her teeth.

"You know the first thing she said to me when your dad and I moved in together," she said next, as if anyone ever would have told me that. "She accused me of trying to steal you." It always feels like a partial confession, to repeat what's been said about things you have done. "She said I was trying to take you away from her, and that I should just have more kids of my own." We stood there for a long time, thinking about sexual competition and reproductive success. "Which is really funny, because, of course, I don't know how long it's been since you talked to your mother, and, well, here you are." She grinned. "You should call your mother," she decided further, as breezily as if we were just a couple of old friends, gossiping in the driveway.

"And now," she declared, "I am sick to death of standing around outside. Come in and meet the woofer."

WWOOFer, I learned, is a grammatical invention that is sure to form the cornerstone of the next post-millennial theory on how languages evolve. It is a term that could be classified as a verbish noun with an acronym root, because a WWOOFer is someone who WWOOFs as part of a program called World Wide Opportunities for Organic Farmers. In yet another instance of flagrant disregard for the fact that cultivating marijuana is a felony, Alizarin had signed up with an organization that connects organic farmers with those who aspire to a life of thankless drudgery at the same. WWOOFers will perform almost any agricultural labor in exchange for room, board, and the chance to take part in the food revolution. They do not even object to being called WWOOFers, in spite of the fact that the term sounds like rural hipster slang for some kind of pot-specific infestation or sexual fetish.

Alizarin's WWOOFer was in the kitchen, grinding meat the color of cartoon carnage: somewhere in between a bloody fluorescent orange and a bloodier neon pink. Little chunks of this alarming matter kept falling onto the floor with a delicate slapping sound, whereupon several dogs darted for it with speed and precision. Every time they did this, the girl would produce a series of musical trills that might have indicated distress. Her name was something or other, and she had eyes like Ingres' *Odalisque*, the one whose image always shows up in literature about how women are objectified in Western art. The rest of her face was so stunningly lovely, her shabby clothes and jagged haircut seemed to exist solely as an apology for any hard feelings her beauty might cause. She glowed like an Old Master's oil painting, tossed into the corner of a grower's dingy kitchen.

There was no plunger to push the cartoon-colored meat into the grinder, so the Odalisque was pressing it in with one long-fingered hand, the tiny bones articulating as they met resistance from the still-resilient dead flesh. The grinder sporadically puked the meat back out the top, so she kept feeding it back in with quick little jabs, like she thought the machine would be less likely to notice she was taunting it that way.

"Um," I suggested. "Maybe there's a pushy-downy thing? So you don't have to use your hand for that?"

"Oh, that's okay," she assured me, and smiled as if she'd never dream of inconveniencing anyone with such a high-maintenance request. "I washed my hands," she added, still with a beatific smile that I'm sure the original Odalisque never would have offered for free, least of all to another woman.

"It has more to do with this not quite pro-cannibal stance I have," I explained, a little bewildered by her loveliness. *What a fucking idiot*, I berated myself. *I should have just said anti-cannibal. Or maybe, hey: left the cannibals out of it altogether. How hard is it* not *to make a fucking cannibal reference?* Everyone pretended I hadn't said anything.

"Did you see the remains of Daphne outside?" Alizarin inquired, changing the subject with masterful ease. In northern California, the topic of dietary morality is fraught with a level of tension normally reserved for general elections, the afterlife, and your co-workers' take-home pay.

"Who is Daphne?" I asked. My vision blurred, ever so briefly.

"Oh, she's not a *child* or anything," Alizarin explained. "She's not anybody's *child*, or *grandmother* or something. I guess Lance didn't get the memo about *sheep*dogs: you know, *wolf*hounds are supposed to hunt wolves, and *rat* terriers keep the rats off ships, so I guess it makes sense, linguistically speaking, har, har. He's just a dog. They're not *smart* but he's *such* a sweetie, poor guy. This the *second* time he's done this—did I *tell* you he got that lamb? I thought maybe he just wanted to play with it but I guess not. Maybe I brushed him too much when he was a little guy you're supposed to just completely *ignore* them but

I felt so *bad* for him . . . well, now he's done it. He only ate part of her back leg."

For some reason, I always forget that waiting for a period at the end of a sentence by Alizarin is like waiting for a German to get to the verb. I am always precisely as disoriented by it as if I've never encountered it before, with the result that I have no coping strategy.

"She's out there on the table. Would you like to see?" she offered, like she'd just put in a bed of marigolds and there was some chance of a reasonable person wanting to look at it.

Of course I wanted to see. I'd had so little honest blood and guts lately, so much ponderous cerebral back and forth. Maybe a little down-home nastiness was just what I needed to exorcise the fastidious, psychotic spinster spirit of Miss Fiona Jones. I approached the table calmly, like I really did think I'd earned the right not to be horrified by anything, ever again.

Immediately, as if they had sprung into existence that very moment, a cleaver and a large rusty knife appeared before my eyes. The blades were encrusted with blackening blood so dark and rich, it was almost voluptuous. The angles of the negative spaces between them were graceful and compelling. Alizarin spoke with great passion about the importance of home butchering stations. This, she explained, was a significant step toward total independence from the food monopolies, which were compromising the health of the planet with various barbaric practices. I began to think I must be incapable of all human feeling, standing there unmoved and dubious. There was something familiar about that old uncertainty. I tried to place it.

"We have a bucket here, for dog food," Alizarin told me, exactly like a person who has every reason to be proud of her facilities. Slabs of thick, creamy fat with streaks of bright red meat jiggled, as if they were excited to be examined by us. "That over there is just crap," she went on, indicating a second bucket containing slices of offal. She eyeballed it sternly, as if thinking hard about possible uses for such worthless material.

In the dead center of the previously white table was a twenty-five-gallon green plastic trash can. It was uncovered, like it wanted all the world to know it had nothing to be ashamed of.

The carcass rose from the can, emitting a thick stench of bodily interiors. It was headless and skinned and bathed in hazy late-afternoon summer sun. It was the kind of light that looks transparent, because so much of it was absorbed by particles of dust and smoke from distant fires. A finer painter than I will ever be would convey it with glazes and invisible brushwork. There were no slabs of meaty light here. This was meatless broth illumination, utterly indifferent to savagery and carnage and the qualities of friendship.

I wondered what stage of medical starvation I would have to be in to be grateful for a taste of dog-gnawed sheep. I had no doubt there was some condition of extreme distress where I, too, would confiscate a carcass from a scavenger and devour it with perfect contentment. After all, that's what hunting dogs are for, right?

Again, I began to identify something very familiar. I was struggling to find some plausible excuse to agree with a premise that was completely insane. With diligence, each successive scenario that involved eating this thing would seem more and more reasonable. Eventually, diligence and reason would add up to context. Dining on Daphne would become an oddball adventure, maybe even an exercise in overcoming fusty old social inhibitions that prevented all of us from fully inhabiting our destinies. Once I had achieved that level of context, I would open my napkin, place it on my lap, and proceed to eat a filthy reeking carcass named for a nymph so lovely, the god of reason went mad with desire for her flesh. At that moment, Alizarin would cease to be my friend. I would turn her into an oppressor, and submit to her.

Instead, something shifted. I wasn't ready, not yet, to tell her that sanitation ordinances exist for the sole purpose of protecting the populace from people like her. But I was not about to eat an animal that had been a chew toy for a dog.

"Look," I said. "I've got to get going. I need to get an alignment."

My father used to say you can't con the honest; but I maintain that honest people are easy to lie to, because they are not on the lookout for deception.

"I thought you already did that," Alizarin protested, in a tone that indicated she had so much more to show me.

"Oh. Yeah. Sure. No. That was just my truck. I actually need a separate alignment right now." I gave her a quick hug and fled. There was only one person I could tell about this.

SHE WAS NOT home when I let myself in. But there were clean sheets in the guest room, on a mattress so fresh it could not possibly have ever been whored on. I folded myself up beneath the blankets and fell asleep to the unaccustomed sounds of the city I grew up in. Sometime near dawn, I heard boot heels clicking on the pavement, and dreamed that men in swirling black capes had come to remove my remains. *At last*, I said; but they wore masks, so I couldn't tell if I was rebuking or welcoming them.

My mother lives near a set of steps built into the side of a hill. There are many of these in San Francisco. Hers is built on the side that gets the finest morning light, as if Caitlin Swift were a woman who revels in birdsong and the freshness of lettuce with the dew still clinging to its leaves. She has a giant tin sculpture of a giraffe in her front yard. It is rusting in the damp air, bravely draped with Christmas lights all year round. It made me think of Mariana, wearing all her gaudy brooches as she waited for the end.

It is a minor miracle, when lights come on and water runs in a house where no one is home. I always find myself in a state of pleasant anticipation when I am turning on the lights and faucets in someone else's house. I know I'm waiting for the part of the story with crimes and enchantment and love.

I helped myself to my mother's rice cakes. I ate some of her yogurt. In Germany, it is the height of rudeness to make yourself at home in someone else's kitchen. I'm pretty sure it's not especially courteous here, either. But it's so hard to strategize in your own culture, where you know the quality of light so well you can't always see where you're going.

I washed my mother's dishes with the environmentally ethical soap she buys from a large emporium that used to be a dingy little shop on the corner of 14th and Mission, redolent with the odor of things sold in bulk. I sat down at the clean round table she had stripped and finished herself. The enamel in her sink was chipped, and the fixtures were large and soft-edged, the way things were in the year I was born. Like no one was embarrassed about the shape of hands, or the fact that hands would touch things, and want to find them soft.

I had a piece of paper with Reuben's number written on it in a looping female scrawl. This was the writing that spelled out volumes of instructions and set flocks of yellow memos in flight. Fiona's notes had been an ever-present monologue of afterthoughts. This one included a second number, and the words *Let's Talk!!!* in big, excited letters. She really thought I was going to bear witness for her. She trusted me. She was very stupid.

I remembered her saying, "that information isn't really useful to me." I remembered her habit of interrupting me by telling me, "you know, I think most of what people say is just commentary"; as if I were required to produce original insights, every time I opened my mouth.

I told Reuben everything. I felt hyper-obedient doing it, like a loyal family servant with no class consciousness.

By now, it was most emphatically Saturday. The clacking boots were still. The dew was off the lettuce. I had no home, but I had more than doubled my worldly goods with painting supplies. I had a fine old wooden easel and a giant picnic basket full of pigments from Gamblin and Grumbacher. I had Langnickel brushes and a roll of linen canvas. I had been rich on several occasions in the past two years, and the signs of poverty and sudden wealth were all over me, like I'd been redeemed by magic or inheritance.

There is a fairytale quality to untraceable wealth. If Rumpelstiltskin were with us today, he'd be turning weed to gold in brightly lighted secret chambers, hidden in the woods. It is a shining secret to emerge from a trim shack with its fug of smoke and resin. The cold late autumn rain is a revelation. It is bright and clear, partly because you're stoned; but mostly because you can finally replace the tires on that piece of shit truck you've been driving around. You can buy art supplies your talents don't deserve. You didn't have to smirk and bat your lashes. You didn't have to prove yourself. Sooner or later, though, someone guesses your name, and there you are: trapped in the valley of death.

I went back into the guest room and set up my easel with the double portrait. I sat down on the unstained mattress. I was having trouble with the background. There was a shape between the edges of the two faces, like the space between the little fingers when you bring the palms of your hands together loosely and allow the fingertips to touch. In the photograph my mother took, that space was a uterine darkness.

"It looks like a birth," Caitlin said. "The negative space."

She was standing in the doorway with her yoga pants and ponytail, looking fresh and trim and unafraid, the way people do when their documents are in order and the kids have turned out fine.

"Did you do that on purpose?" she asked next, exactly as if I were not committing a home invasion in the company of a large oil painting.

She moved closer, peering at it through a pair of red-framed bifocals. My mother, painted lady of the darkest hours, was a spinster wearing librarian glasses.

"I could show you pictures from your own birth, if you like," she offered kindly. Maybe she was, after all, kind. She offered a bright smile. "You look wiped out. Let's have something caffeinated."

So I had a heart-to-heart talk with my mother over steaming mugs of seven spice organic chai, like ladies in the exposition scene of a feel-good summer hit. I talked about painting. I talked about light. I asked her if she knew what WWOOFers were. I fell silent when I realized she was watching my mouth, a sure sign that all she wanted me to do was stop moving it.

Still, she took her time before stepping into the conversation, like a lady who flags down a cab with every appearance of urgency and pauses to check her makeup before getting in.

"One of the things I like about Alizarin," she began, and paused again. Clearly, the mechanism for liking things about Alizarin was of the vintage diesel variety, the kind where you have to wait for the glow plug to come on before you turn the key. "The best thing about Alizarin," she tried again, and this time the thing sputtered to life, "is that she doesn't try to make her students turn out bad imitations of her own work. She can have a classroom with twenty people in it, and they're all doing something completely different. Alizarin can tell people how to paint without drowning out their voices." She smiled like was talking about an old friend. "You don't expect that from someone who never shuts her fucking mouth."

"Mom?" I felt like I was knocking on the door to a room I hadn't even known existed. How had I not known about this room? This studio with sunshine pouring in at all the windows, crackling through Caitlin's then-unstraightened hair, as if to illustrate the intensity of the action beneath. "How do you know that?"

She grimaced. When I was growing up, any time I asked my mother a naive question about sex, she would signal the onset of a sarcastic reply with a grimace just like that.

"Well, dear," she'd begin drily. "When a man and a woman love each other very much . . ." She favored detailed descriptions of sadomasochistic rituals, which were more effective at maintaining my youthful virtue than any abstinence-only program ever could be.

I thought she was about to do something similar right now; that she considered the answer so obvious, the question deserved the most derisive treatment possible. But the heart-to-heart mood, with the herbal tea and mellow morning light, was firmly in place.

"I did a little painting in my hippie days," she acknowledged slowly, like she'd come to terms with the indiscretions of her youth and even looked upon them with some amused fondness.

"With Alizarin?" I prompted.

She nodded, still projecting a soft-lit sense of gentle nostalgia.

"What about . . . ?" I eyed her warily.

"Of course." She was as serene as if her whole life had been so unimpeachable, it was impossible for her to incriminate herself with such an admission. "Most female artists with anything going for them in the looks department do," she informed me, unable to have a conversation that was entirely free of pedantic insights. "Alizarin supported herself and Jezzie for years, modeling in classes at Fort Mason. Of course, the models' guild is highly respectable." She sighed in a way that made it impossible to determine whether she found this to be a drawback or a selling point. "You know your father posed for Alizarin too," she told me, which I hadn't guessed but should have. "Poor artists. It used to be so hard for them to find naked men to look at. Especially muscly little circus performers. Your dad was built like a pocket-sized Greek godling," she noted with some relish. "Classical proportions, portable dimensions." She spent several moments savoring her memories of my father as a stripling youth. "Everyone slept around back then. It was almost rude not to." She grinned. "We all know I've done *my* share of poaching."

And then she looked startled, like she'd come to a point she'd been trying to avoid. She spun her mug in her fine-boned hands, and hot creamy fluid poured onto her fingers. She tried to make a joke about jism and stumbled like an undergrad who hasn't done the reading. I wished she would either say what she had to say, or go outside and run around the block a few times. Skinny little nervous women are not a joy to behold.

"Which brings me to the question that's been burning a hole in my whoozit for I don't know how long." She was so jaunty and nonsensical that if I were a cop, I would have searched her then and there on reasonable grounds. "I never asked, and you never said anything, so I thought, well, you know how I feel about hangups . . ." *You never would have bought a house in San Francisco without them*, I thought; but I knew how to look at my mother quietly now. It is the key to treachery; and a certain kind of serenity, too.

Now that she had my attention, she looked out the window for several long moments. I watched her do a thing I'd seen so many times, it had never occurred to me to be properly impressed by it. She did it without any perceptible movements of her face; but when she looked back at me, she was wearing a mask. The eyes were simultaneously sharp and languorous, alluding to the fact that a woman can be vigorous and satisfied at the same time. There was a curve in the corners of her mobile mouth, hinting at precision work in mockery and understanding. And her skin seemed tighter, which made her look inquisitive, but also like she already knew everything, so what was there to ask?

"Are you mad at me about, ah . . . ?" She cocked a perfectly shaped eyebrow, and a corner of her plump-lipped mouth came up a little higher. Was that Botox, or collagen? It was suddenly obvious that my mother, always young and eternally beautiful, had had a facelift. Maybe two. *Phlebotomist, my ass*, I thought. *I'm looking at a damned good ageing whore. This one isn't going down without a fight. Or a price,*

I added, because that's how my mother would finish the line. My mother the liar, true to herself.

"The John?" I supplied.

"Well. Yes." She paused, which I think is her way of impersonating someone with delicate sensibilities. "You know, I didn't *encourage* anyone," she rushed on, very much like someone overcome by remorse. "That was *strictly unauthorized—*"

"Mom." I put my hand on her shoulder. "You did me a favor. Or that girl did. Dim Sum. Karen. Whatever. That guy was bullshit." Was this really the most soaring oratory I could come up with right now? Wasn't this supposed to be the serendipitous moment? The one where the discordant notes of our epiphanies found each other's harmonies and sang?

"Total bullshit," I assured her, and rubbed her shoulder briskly, like I was trying to get the warmth to return.

EPILOGUE

MANY YEARS AFTER I returned to California, I took a right turn at a Deodar tree. I was meeting a man whose name I didn't ask, because I still knew him by the one he'd been using when he gave me my own.

"Turn right at the Deodar tree," my grandmother said, and settled back into whatever silent train of thought was wending its way through her brain.

"What does a Deodar tree look like?" I ventured.

"It's native to India," she replied. "I'm sure you've seen it in films set in India."

There was a time when you were ignorant if you did not know the proper names of plants and animals; could not draw the chambers of a flower and the angles of its leaves with a drawing master's instinct for the beauty of a line. There is a whiff of that age about my father's mother, seductress of the cloth. Lisette Saulé, who wears sunglasses indoors like a blind musician or a movie star. Like a woman with secrets, and letters to burn.

We had a visitor that day, a visitor whose letters—though of course there have never been letters—we would have burned immediately. Had there been letters, one would have been filled with diagrams of knots used in the rigging of ships; the next with a detailed account of the behavior of insects, dotted with long Latin puns. In person, his conversational style was highly narrative, accompanied by bodily movements of riveting eccentricity and precision. His physicality was that of a man who has undergone a great deal of esoteric training and is no longer capable of moving like an ordinary human being. He made a series of urgent, repetitive motions with his hands that made my grandmother think he'd either developed Huntingon's or suffered a severe head injury.

It was neither of those things. He was fascinated by the shapes of the energy around him, he said. He was caressing unseen juggler's balls that formed in the curves of his palms; that played beguiling tricks with space and rounded the parabola of time in patterns that sharpened and shone.

He was only about two and a half decades younger than my grandmother, and he was an old man now. His hair was white and clean. He held himself erect, because of the terrible pain of growing old. "It's so bad," he said gravely, "that it's terrible." He could have been a high-ranking analyst, delivering the results of an important study to the chairman of the board. "You know where that's from, right?" Like many people in my family, he was unwilling to drop an unexplained cultural reference into a conversation. "It's Andy Kaufman, Foreign Man," he revealed. Then he made a brief appearance as Foreign Man. "Take my wife!" he cried in an unidentifiable accent. He began to flap his hands hysterically. "Her cooking eez is so bad!" he shrieked. "That eet's terrible! Thank you! Thank you!" He concluded with a body-shaking show of laughter, as if he were doing a wholehearted but not entirely accurate impression of an earthling in the throes of delight.

Then, because humans look at memorabilia in addition to conducting laughter-making rituals, Lisette Saulé unearthed a photo of her son as a smiling young man, the summer before I was born. He had a sharp-collared shirt and curly brown hair. His head was tilted toward the sky, his throat exposed like a sacrifice.

She brought out a drawing. "He did this under the influence of LSD," she remarked, as soberly as an art historian, delivering a discourse on the Green Muse. "He said that LSD made him very creative." She smiled politely at the drawing. Remember, she was born at a time when natural philosophers were drawing plants in pen and ink, labeling them in Latin. "He may have overestimated its effectiveness."

"Oh, I was on acid *and* speed when I drew that," our visitor clarified. He gave a light nostalgic chuckle as he rummaged around for a different pair of eyeglasses. He was holding the drawing like a man who is fascinated by the shapes of the energy in his hands; but also like someone whose eyes are going bad, so he has to look at things askance.

"Look! It's a little birdie. Eating spaghetti." His face was a mass of gentle laugh lines as he pointed at the tangle of pen strokes. "The quality of the line seemed a lot more solid when I did it," he conceded, as if he had been raised by a woman who spoke like a museum docent when examining any work of art. I thought of how young he used to be, how stoned, living in corners on the edge of the world with his visions of birdies, pulling up worms. He was the sweetest, most innocent felon I ever did know.

By this time, my grandmother was tired, so we walked outside in broad daylight. Cars roared past us. People made deliveries. A meter maid wrote parking tickets. Dozens and possibly hundreds of people saw us. We could have been any old man and much younger woman, meeting one more time after so many years.

I left him in the parking lot of a drugstore while I went inside to print some pictures of myself and some of the things I had done in the last twenty years. I imagined the pictures existing in a place I'd never been, mystifying the officials who would go through his belongings after he died, alone and unclaimed. They would begin to get an inkling that he wasn't who he'd always said he was, when he appeared on their shores so many years ago. I wanted him to be proud of me, too. I wanted our final reunion to be an experience that soared with emotional authenticity and a kind of formality, with paperwork and declarations and maybe a few epiphanies.

When I came out, he was watching a giant green balloon in the shape of a popular cartoon character. The balloon was gyrating wildly, desperate to draw attention to a once-in-a-lifetime opportunity to buy a used car. It straddled a fan the size of a Volkswagen, which filled it 'til the great balloon flung its arms into the air, aiming eyes the size of hubcaps at the blue impassive sky.

"I've always wished I could do that," he admired. "Just flail around bonelessly."

The balloon was terrifying a small dog and making babies cry.

I handed him the photographs. There I was, smiling and wearing lipstick, standing next to a painting at my show in a small gallery. I grinned on a beach with a nice young man. I picnicked in the Odenwald with people I knew in the miscellaneous way that people are friends when no one is staying for long.

He kept murmuring wordlessly. *Ah,* he murmured. *Ah.* "It's so much more than I expected," he said at last. He pressed the photographs against his chest in a disorganized way, as if he couldn't figure out how to hold them.

"Here. You can put them in this." I made an unnecessarily efficient production out of tidying them into the folder the drugstore had provided. He watched like I was showing him how to do a magic trick.

He was always like that: struck dumb with wonder by the simplest things, spurred into action by others that shatter more practical souls. While he was transfixed by a giant green advertising balloon, an entire graduating class of business majors moved into the workforce with a sense of purpose. While they were holding conference calls on the importance of thinking outside the box, he was dodging dangers none of them had ever heard of. He was on a wire, poised to leap into his destiny as they pondered the nuances of casual Friday. He was exactly who he always was and who he always would be. There would be no final bow, no encore, no cheerful farewell strains of music played by clowns as families trailed out of the tent and into the sunshine. He would be a wire-walker, all the days of his life, and his eyesight would dim as he watched the horizon move further and further away.

HE TOLD ME about his search for an identity. People of his generation were always looking for themselves. He gave me names and dates and details that would make a true crime writer go into paroxysms of ecstasy. They washed over me like figures in a NASDAQ report.

I do recall that he went to a graveyard where an infant boy was buried, in the days when my grandmother's children were young. He found the boy's gravestone and determined that the child had died on the day that he, like a reincarnation of himself, was born. "He was Catholic," he said, "so I looked up all nine relevant diocese in the area. And then I called them, and the Monseigneur or whatever gave me all the information I needed. Catholics love records," he added, like a man remarking on a very good meal.

Because he had become a kind of grave robber, collecting the names of the dead, he also found a boy with spina bifida and club feet. This child had drowned in the days before people were born with

Social Security numbers, which is key for a fugitive of a certain age, trying to acquire a set of identity documents. It's better if you can get the proper agencies to give you real papers for someone who's been dead a long time, since forgeries are fairly easy to spot. Plus, there is that inviolable law about creating something from nothing.

"*Congenital talipes equivarus,*" he enunciated. He was fully prepared for a quiz on the conditions he was supposed to have. If anyone ever asked, he explained, "I could always say I had *spina bifida occulta,* and that it was asymptomatic. And if they noticed that I have normal feet, I could say, oh, I had night strapping. And a heel tendon pull." They sounded like the kinds of things that could only be done at a crossroads on a full moon.

He told me about Wesley, who turned him in; Wesley with seashells braided into his hair, beautiful and amoral as the spirit of betrayal itself. "I thought he was really my friend," he remembered, like he was outlining the plot of a story that had moved him deeply in his youth. "I had a very warm feeling for Wesley." He shook his head. "That was such a crazy scene. Cah-ray-zee." He laughed, and his old teeth flashed, showing straight and strong and just a little yellowed. It was the earthling laugh again. "I miss it so much."

And then, I think because he knew we'd never meet again, he told me the story of my birth. He said the attending nurse cut my mother. "What's that called," he said, cutting the air with his small showman's hand. Episiotomy, said I, not knowing how or why that word should be my own. "When the doctor came back, he told me it was a completely unnecessary procedure," he said, like the time had come to tell great secrets. "I never told your mom," he finished, watching me steadily with pale blue eyes.

When he was gone, I noticed that I was influenced by him. Sometimes, I hear his inflections in my words. I feel the balance of his spine in the way I walk. I see myself acting out stories like a latter-day vaudevillian, like him. And why not, after all? The love is so plain, the crime so insignificant.

Sarah Reith was born into a circus family in San Francisco, and ran away to join the army as soon as she turned eighteen. She was a parachute rigger at the jump school on Fort Benning, Georgia, where one of her incidental duties was "wind dummy," or jumping out of an airplane ahead of a class of airborne students so the instructors could check the wind conditions. After concluding that life as a dummy lacked intellectual stimulation, she used her GI Bill to earn a BA in creative writing at Mills College for women. She worked as a bike messenger and a barista for some years before going back to school in Germany. She studied for her MA in German literature in the shadow of a medieval castle, burying her nose in little yellow volumes with very dense print and lots of umlauts. She is currently a reporter in Mendocino County, working on her second novel.